SAVAGE
NIGHTS

ALSO BY MIA GABRIEL

Lord Savage

SAVAGE
NIGHTS

MIA GABRIEL

St. Martin's Paperbacks

This is a work of fiction. All of the characters, organizations, and events portrayed in this novel are either products of the author's imagination or are used fictitiously.

SAVAGE NIGHTS

Copyright © 2016 by Mia Gabrel.

All rights reserved.

For information address St. Martin's Press, 175 Fifth Avenue, New York, NY 10010.

ISBN: 978-1-250-07681-6

Printed in the United States of America

St. Martin's Paperbacks edition / February 2016

St. Martin's Paperbacks are published by St. Martin's Press, 175 Fifth Avenue, New York, NY 10010.

10 9 8 7 6 5 4 3 2 1

1.

"You're not frightened, are you?" The seventh Earl of Savage leaned closer, curling his long arm around the back of my shoulders in a gesture that could have been protective, or something else entirely. "If you've any regrets—"

"None," I said swiftly, determined to show no hesitation, no doubts. "And if I shiver, it's from excitement, not fear."

He smiled slowly, and if I hadn't shivered before I did then. Desire did that to me, and I'd never desired a man more than I did Savage. Wild, reckless, burning desire, desire that I'd never dreamed possible or ever wished to end: that was what I felt for Savage.

We sat in the curving back bench of his Rolls-Royce, racing through the inky darkness of the Hampshire countryside, towards London and away from the house party at Wrenton Manor. There was no moon, no stars, and the only light came from the car's headlights and silver carriage lanterns. Sitting on the other side of the curtained glass, Savage's driver clearly had orders to carry us to London as fast as was possible. Savage and I traveled at a breakneck pace, heedless of anything save each other in our luxurious haven.

"You shiver from excitement," Savage said. He eased aside the front edge of my sable coat to find the red silk of my evening gown. Following the rules of the house we'd just left, I'd daringly worn nothing beneath it—no petticoats, no chemise, no corset—and as he laid his hand upon my thigh I felt at once the heat of his palm and his fingers through the slide of light silk.

He heard the little catch in my breathing, and his smile widened. A flash of reflected light briefly lit his face in the darkness, a glimpse that was exactly long enough to remind me of how seductively, impossibly handsome he was. In that flash his face was all planes and shadows, hard in all the ways that a man should be, and framed by hair as black as his evening clothes. Yet his mouth was sensuously full, and his pale gray-blue eyes could glow with a white-hot intensity that weakened my knees whenever he looked at me, the way he was studying me now.

"You *are* excited, Mrs. Hart," he said. "You're almost feverish. It's rather obvious, isn't it?"

"To you it is," I breathed. "Because of you."

"How very scandalous," he said with mock severity. "Are all the widows of New York society as eager as you?"

"The past doesn't matter." I didn't need to be reminded of my loveless, stultifying life as Mrs. Arthur Hart that I'd left behind, or of the overbearing husband who'd been impossible to mourn. In my head I'd already begun to divide my life into the time before I'd met Savage and the time since I'd become his. Impatiently I shrugged my shoulders free of my fur coat, too heated now for either its warmth or its ostentation. "The past doesn't matter at all, not for either of us."

"Seven days together in London," Savage said, his voice

low. He pushed up the hem of my gown and slid his hand beneath it, roaming higher across my silk stockings and above my jeweled garters to the heated skin of my thigh. "That's all I offer."

"That's all I want," I said. "You, for seven more days, and seven more nights."

"There will be talk, you know." He pulled me onto his lap, where at once I felt the hard, blunt thrust of his cock through his trousers pushing against my bottom. "It means nothing to me, but for a woman—"

"Let them talk," I said, full of bravado. I meant it, too. Considering the dramatic exit we'd just made together from a house party that had included some of England's best-bred society, I would be surprised if there weren't gossip. I ran my palm across his chest, over the immaculate white linen of his shirt and the hard muscles beneath. "They will say what they will regardless."

"A brave declaration," he said as if he didn't believe me. He hooked one finger into the deep neckline of my gown, slowly pulling it down to bare my breasts. I arched towards him, relishing the feel of the silk sliding over my skin. Framed by the red gown and the dark fur, my skin was as pale and luminous as the moonlight, and even in the shadows he must have seen how my nipples were already tight and hard, aching for his touch. "Words may not be the only risk."

"I told you before," I said quickly, perhaps a little too quickly to be convincing. "I'm not afraid."

"You never are, are you?" He was tracing the full underside of one breast with the pad of his thumb and purposefully ignoring my aroused nipple. "Not even when you should be."

"Savage, if you are trying to—"

"Hush," he said, pressing his fingertip to my lips. "All

I ask is that you do not forget the obvious: that whatever happens between us cannot be undone."

"I'd never wish for that." Restlessly I parted my legs with a whisper of silk, feeling the smooth wool of his evening trousers against my bare thigh. I was offering myself to him, wanting him to take me there in the car. The speed, the darkness, even the driver on the other side of the glass only served to heighten my desire. With Savage I was shameless; he'd made me like that.

"But you wish for many other things," he said, glancing down.

"It's been hours, Savage," I said breathlessly. "That dinner was interminable, sitting there beside you and not being able to touch you. I want you now, here. I *need* you."

His hand stilled on my breast. "You're being forward, Eve. Bold, even brazen. That's not how an Innocent should behave with her Master."

A guilty flush spread over my face, and I was thankful for the half-light in the car that hid it. He was right, of course. Just because we had left the house where he'd introduced me to the Game (a clever house-party conceit with Masters and Innocents, rules and forfeits, that we'd played at all the time we'd been guests at Wrenton) did not mean our roles had been abandoned, too. How soon I'd forgotten what he'd spent this last week teaching me!

"No, Master," I murmured, instantly obedient as he expected me to be, and as I'd come to expect of myself as well. "I forgot, Master."

"You forgot." He sighed, cupping my breast in the palm of his head and running his thumb lightly over my nipple. "You should be punished for being so forgetful."

"Yes, Master." I held my breath, not daring to show

how much his torturous little caress was affecting me. "I deserve to be punished."

"The most obvious punishment, of course, would be to deny you what you most crave." He shoved the hem of my dress over my hips to bare me below the waist. He slipped his fingers through my dark curls to find the opening of my sex and pushed one thick finger inside. The moisture of my blatant arousal made it easy for him to thrust deep, finding the place inside me that was most sensitive. I gasped, unable not to, and arched my back to take him deeper.

"There," he said, his voice growing rougher. "That's what you crave, isn't it?"

"Yes, Master," I said, the two words breaking along with my self-control.

"Yes," he repeated, adding a second finger to stretch and stroke my swollen, greedy passage. "Yet if I were to deny you this, then I would also be punishing myself."

"Yes, Master," I said, my sex tightening around his fingers. "That is, no, Master, you do not deserve the same punishment as I."

"What a perceptive Innocent you are, Eve," he said, his own breathing growing ragged. "You've redeemed your earlier impulsiveness."

"Thank . . . thank you, Master," I whispered, my body trembling taut and straining for the release that he was building within me. From experience I knew he could keep me poised here on the torturous edge of release as long as he wanted to, and I knew, too, that he'd do exactly that if I couldn't prove myself worthy.

He smiled, a devil's smile in the half-light. "What would you like as a reward, Eve?"

My fevered quim begged for him to finish what he'd

begun and set me free. But that wasn't the answer he sought, and if I begged he'd only deny me more.

"Your reward?" he asked again. "Surely there's something you would like, something that would please us both."

"Your . . . your cock," I managed to say. "I would like your cock, Master."

"Exactly." His smile widened as he drew his fingers from my sex, and I shuddered at the sudden emptiness. "It's yours to take."

Quickly I turned on his lap, sitting with my knees on either side of his thighs. With shaking fingers I undid the row of black buttons on his trousers and at last freed his cock: hard and ruddy and as eager for me as I was for it. I pulled my gown over my head, leaving nothing between us except the long strand of pearls he'd given me yesterday. I loved that he was still clothed with such formality while I was not, the same way it had been the night he'd first fucked me.

With a kind of reverence I took his cock in my hands, heavy and hot and hard as granite in my palms, and he groaned at my touch. Bracing one hand on his shoulder against the swaying motion of the car, I poised to lower myself onto his cock, rubbing the honey-sweet moisture of my quim on its head and prolonging this last delicious moment of anticipation for us both.

"Now, Eve," he ordered harshly. *"Now."*

And with a shuddering sigh I sank down and took him as deep as I could.

Bliss.

2.

"It's later than I thought," Savage said, pushing aside the motorcar's silk curtain a fraction to glance from the window. "The night is nearly done, and so is our journey."

"I wish it weren't so." I tried, and failed, to keep the regret from my voice. Savage and I had been nearly inseparable since the first night at Wrenton Manor, and our time together had been intoxicating, and yet it had only left me with an insatiable thirst for more. I couldn't contain the ache of longing that marked the end of the last seven days . . . and nights. "I wish it could've gone on forever."

"There were some moments I'd rather not relive," he said drily. "In life, I find it is generally best to look forward, rather than back to the past."

I understood. I'd no wish to repeat the unwanted attentions of Baron Blackledge or Savage's violent reaction to them, either. At least that was what I hoped he meant, and not something I'd said or done. Seeking reassurance, I slipped my hand beneath his evening coat to rest it lightly on his thigh. I was once again dressed, of course, as was he, both of us ready for town and no longer for each other's desires.

From the moment we'd reached the edges of London, trading starry midnight skies for the harsh glow of the streetlights, things had begun to change subtly between us, and it seemed that with every passing hour the magic that had bound us together was fading as surely as those stars overhead. I felt the propriety of the city outside the motorcar's windows pressing down upon us, as surely as a leaden weight.

Yet all of that made little difference to the desire I felt for Savage. It still excited me to feel the hard, lean muscle of his thigh beneath the soft black wool of his trousers, and even more to realize that the slight tensing of those muscles came in response to my touch.

"I cannot wait for the future," I said, running my fingers lightly across his thigh. "As long as you will be there to share it with me."

His hand covered mine and held it still. "You don't know what you're saying, Eve."

"I do," I insisted. "I know that with you I'm happier than I have ever been in my life."

The hint of a humorless smile flickered across his face. "You shouldn't look for happiness from me."

"What if I have found it?"

"Then you are mistaken." He turned my hand into his so our fingers were linked. "I can offer you pleasure— great pleasure—and diversion for the next seven days, and nights, but nothing else. Expect more and you will only be disappointed."

I didn't believe him but knew better than to challenge further. He'd his share of dark places in his soul, as I'd mine, and I'd respect his unwillingness to share them.

Instead I leaned closer and curled my fingers more tightly into his.

"You never disappoint me, Savage," I said softly. "Never."

He made a noncommittal little grunt, but he did not pull away. "When you look at me like this, Eve, I'm almost tempted to believe you."

I smiled and let my hand slip from his to slide down the inside of his thigh. "I tell only the truth to you, Master."

"Wicked creature," he said, and in the slanting light from the streetlamps I saw that his smile had widened. "I mean to test that truth tonight with your first trial here in the city."

My breathing quickened with anticipation; oh, he'd trained me so well in this last week!

"Whatever you wish, Master," I said. "Once we arrive at your house—"

"We're not going to my house," he said. "Rather, *you* are not. You will be returning to your hotel."

"Back to the Savoy?" I asked, my disappointment keen. "Without you?"

"Exactly," he said. "We shall consider it your first trial here in London."

"But not alone," I said, already bereft. "Not without you."

"It is decided," he said, clipping the last word so there'd be no doubt of his intentions. "This is the way things must be. We're in London now. I have other matters that beg for my time."

I retreated from him and sank a little lower against the motorcar's silk cushions, hugging my arms around myself in misery. I understood all too well. Every other man I'd known in my life had had matters that he'd placed ahead of me, too: business, finance, politics. I'd thought Savage was different, but perhaps he wasn't.

He had parted the motorcar's curtain and was no longer looking at me. Instead he was staring through the glass, his profile sharp and angular in the half-light of this last hour before dawn.

It was an hour when respectable people were still sleeping in their beds, and yet the darkness was already losing its potency and the city was beginning to come alive for the day. Rumbling lorries and wagons were starting their first deliveries by the light of the streetlamps, and the lower kind of laborer trudged through the shadows to employment that no one else wanted. The pavements were glistening and wet with damp, and even through the motorcar's sealed windows came the dank smell of the streets, the sewers, and the river.

In defense I drew my sable coat more closely around me for protection. London was a harsh, modern world coming to life, a reality that held no place for the rare, magical kind of passion Savage and I had shared at Wrenton. I couldn't deny it, and I wondered if Savage felt it as well.

All of which was reason enough for us not to part now.

"You promised me another seven days with you," I said softly. "You said my education wasn't done."

"The fact that you dare complain to me now proves that," he said evenly. "Petulance is a most unattractive quality, and one I should think unworthy of you."

"I'm not being petulant," I said wistfully. I wasn't, either. I was disappointed and already beginning to miss him; that was all. "Rather, I do not wish to be apart from you."

With a sigh he turned back towards me, the slanting streetlight casting sharp shadows across his cheekbones and the starched linen of his shirt. Yet despite the chill of so much black and white, his eyes still burned when he gazed at me, as smoldering hot as coals.

"The Game as we played it at Wrenton has no place in London," he said with more patience. "You must understand that, Eve. Here we'll play by different rules, with different tests and trials for you to prove yourself. It can be no other way. The only thing that will not change is the prize you will earn for yourself if you do as I say."

He leaned closer, taking my chin in his hand so I could not look away; nor did I wish to. I'd learned it was always in my own interest to pay attention to him, and my pulse quickened at his touch.

"I promise you, dear Eve," he continued in that deep, resonant voice that could make me shiver with delight, "that if you do prove yourself, then the rewards from these challenges will be beyond your imagining. All you must do is trust me, and obey."

"Yes, Master," I said, my gaze locked with his. "I will trust you, and I will obey."

A hint of a smile crossed his lips. "In all things, Eve."

"In all things, Master," I repeated in a whisper, and his smile widened a fraction.

"Very good," he said. "Be sure not to forget."

Without releasing my jaw he kissed me, his lips relentless until mine parted, and his tongue worked deep into my mouth to mark his possession.

I trembled, fighting the desire to break free of his hand and rub my body against his. It didn't matter that I'd spent most of the journey from Wrenton riding his cock. All I wanted now was to open my coat and part my thighs and once again shamelessly offer myself to him the way I knew he—and I—liked best.

Yet I didn't. This was not the time to forget my training

as an Innocent. I'd learned that the pleasure to be found in the challenges could well outweigh even the rewards and that everything—the trust and the waiting and the obedience—served to make that pleasure even more intense.

Finally he broke away, still holding my jaw steady so that our faces remained close. He was not nearly as impassive as he was pretending to be: although his eyes were hooded, his pupils were dark with excitement, and the vein at his temple pulsed with it.

"Your challenge tonight will be a simple one," he said in a rough whisper. "You must walk through the lobby of the Savoy, address the clerk at the desk for messages, and then proceed to your room. You must do these things alone, as you have done them countless times before."

I couldn't keep the little catch from my breath. Of course I'd done all those things before in many grand hotels, including the Savoy, and done them without a thought. If that were all, then this first challenge would be no challenge at all.

But I'd never done them at this hour of the night, when no respectable lady would be returning unattended by a husband, friends, or servants. Because of all that Savage and I had done in the motorcar my hair was missing pins and falling down, and without a comb or brush there was no possibility of repairing it myself. I still wore the red silk Poiret gown with the glittering black beads that had been perfectly appropriate for the final dinner at Wrenton, but I wore it without a corset, petticoats, camisole, or drawers. I was completely without the layers of lace-trimmed armor that protected a lady's decency, and the thin silk clung provocatively to my hips and belly. I might as well have been naked, for that would have been less seductive than this lascivious second skin of scarlet silk.

As I realized exactly how exposed I would be my glance dropped down to my breasts, barely covered by the dress's panel of black lace. Pebbled with desire, my nipples thrust lewdly against the lace, with the long strand of pearls he'd given me spilling over it. Instead of feeling shame, my heart quickened at the brazen sight and I felt my breasts become more sensitive still as the lace teased my nipples.

Savage followed my glance and smiled.

"Ah, so you understand the challenge, Eve," he said. "Consider well what you must do. Dressed as you are, you must walk across that long marble floor, past the inquisitive eyes of the doormen, the footmen, the bellmen, and the men at the desk. All those men, all watching you, and seeing your dishevelment at this hour, and realizing how aroused you still must be. They'll see the flush of your cheeks, how bruised your lips are from my kisses, the languid sway of your walk, and the fullness of your breasts. They'll see you for what you are, a woman who has been fucked, and fucked well. No matter how high you hold your head, they'll be unable to look away, and every one of them will be wishing he had been in my place."

"I can wear my coat, can't I?" I asked with an odd mix of desperation and desire. While I could imagine all too easily the leering men he was describing—what attractive woman has not endured a similar scene while walking past a group of men?—the fact that I would appear so wanton, so alluring, was unsettling and yet strangely arousing as well.

I had always kept my feelings private, even secret. Could strange men, in fact, tell so much from my face alone? Would they see what I'd done—what I'd do again—with Savage? Was I that vulnerable?

If so, then this challenge that Savage proposed would, in

fact, be far more difficult than I'd first thought. Instinctively I reached for my fur, pulling it around me for protection.

He realized what I was doing and chuckled.

"I should make you enter wearing only your gown," he said. "It would give you a more complete notion of the power of your effect upon men. But for this week you belong to me, not to them. As you may recall, I do not like to share."

He was smiling, but I remembered all too well how he'd violently beaten another gentleman who'd dared to touch me at Wrenton. To say Savage did not like to share was a laughable understatement. Yet I didn't feel trapped by his possessiveness. Instead it made me feel cherished, treasured, as if by keeping me safe from other men he'd set me free.

"You may keep your coat," he said softly. "Let them guess, and only guess, what is hidden inside it. The challenge is for you, not them."

Relieved, I drew the coat more closely around my shoulders. "Thank you, Master."

He raised a single brow. "You thank me without knowing the complete challenge?"

"You said I am to walk through the lobby to the desk, then to the lift to my rooms," I said. "Wasn't that the challenge?"

"In part," he said, lowering his voice as he slipped his hand inside my coat. Instinctively he found my breast, shoving aside the pearls to fill his palm with my tender flesh. A slash of light from the streetlamp illuminated his hand cupping my lace-covered breast, my nipple pressing through between his fingers, and I shuddered as much from the erotic picture as from the sensation he was drawing from my body.

"I want you to do all those things, yes," he continued, "but at the same time I want you to be thinking of how your breasts ache for my hand and for my mouth."

He bent his head and sucked hard on my nipple. The wet pressure of his tongue and mouth through the fine web of the lace made me shudder and clutch at the black silk of his hair. He gave my nipple one final swipe with his tongue, then grazed his cheek against the side of my throat, the stubble of his beard rough on my chin.

"I want you to think of that," he whispered into my ear, his hand closing over my breast again. "And I want you to remember the feel of my cock when it's buried deep inside you. I want you to remember how thick it is, how it fills you, and the heat of passion that burns you from inside. I want you to remember the pleasure of it, how wet you become as you writhe around my cock, and how I fill you with my seed until our juices run together, until you come so hard you cry out with the force of it. *That* is what I want you to remember as you walk through the halls of the Savoy, and that is what I expect you to describe to me tomorrow."

How could I think of anything else after I'd heard that? I was close to coming again now, my breath ragged and my body arching against his. But as I turned to offer my mouth again to him more light spilled through the windows on us and I realized that the motorcar had come to a halt.

"Ah, we have arrived," Savage said, easing away from me. He smoothed his dark hair back from his forehead as he composed himself, once again the reserved, slightly bored English lord. "Here is the Savoy now."

I hadn't the same ease (or perhaps it was experience) with restoring myself. I scrambled to pull down my skirts and gather my coat together, my fingers clutching deep into the plush sable just as the doorman unlatched the door and swung it open.

"Good evening, Mrs. Hart," the liveried doorman said as he held the door for me, recognizing me as a guest of the hotel.

I looked down, avoiding his eyes as I thought of everything Savage had said earlier. I was flushing furiously, and I couldn't help but look back at Savage, sitting in the shadows.

"Good night, Mrs. Hart," he said. There was so many notes to his voice, the benign pleasantly underscored with challenge, and command, expectation, and perhaps a hint of amusement as well. "It was my . . . *pleasure* to be of service to you this evening."

"Thank you, my lord," I murmured, striving to respond in the same manner. "It was entirely my pleasure, and my honor."

I stepped from the motorcar, ignoring the doorman's offered hand—partly because I wished to be aloof and distant but also because I wanted to use both my hands to keep my coat as tightly closed as I could to hide my revealing gown.

After I had sat so long in the darkened motorcar, the electric lights illuminating the Savoy's entrance and lobby were so bright that I had to pause, wincing as my eyes grew accustomed to the brilliance.

"Do you require assistance, Mrs. Hart?" asked the doorman with practiced concern. "Might I summon—"

"Thank you, no," I said, drawing myself up. If I was to survive Savage's challenge, I would need every scrap of the hauteur that my position in New York society had required. The subservient role I'd been playing this last week as Savage's Innocent would not do now, and with my chin high I collected myself for the long walk across the plush red carpet, up the steps, and into the hotel.

Behind me I heard the doorman close the door to the motorcar, and I imagined Savage watching me begin his test, waiting for me to falter or not do as he'd bidden. Or perhaps he wasn't watching at all and had instead already put me from his thoughts. He'd said he'd other business to attend to, the way that men inevitably did. Perhaps he was considering that business now instead of me, resting his head back against the cushions with his eyes closed, and—

No. In my heart I knew he was watching me. I could sense it, feel it, as surely as if his hands were still upon me. He might pretend otherwise and speak of other obligations, but I knew that we'd become so closely twined this last week that he could not help watching me, even if he wished to.

The thought gave me confidence, and I began walking. I did not walk briskly, as was my usual custom, but slowly, even languidly, for his benefit.

I kept my shoulders relaxed and let my uncorseted hips sway within the cocoon of my fur coat. Even if no one else could see it, I felt the red silk slither over my body, sliding over my skin in a private, sensuous caress. The long strand of pearls that Savage had given me hung heavy over my breasts, each luminous bead already warmed from contact with my body. With each step as my thighs whispered together I felt his seed as a lubricious reminder of how often he'd fucked me tonight.

It was all enough to make me forget my New York hauteur. Instead, for him, I walked like a goddess, proud and without shame.

I wanted that to be Savage's last glimpse of me and his

last memory of me before we met again. If the goal of his challenge for me was for me to feel the power of being temptation incarnate, then this was how I must walk—the way I'd learned while I'd been not only Savage's Innocent but his lover as well.

I walked up the carpeted steps, my footfalls muffled by the luxuriant plush, and past the two doormen who held open the shining black doors with their polished brasses. I glanced at the tall mahogany clock: a quarter past four in the morning, roughly what I'd guessed.

At this hour, there were no other guests in the usually crowded lobby. I was the only one. The neat rows of leather-covered armchairs were unoccupied, the palm trees in their huge Chinese pots nodded with no one beneath their fronds, the signboards with the day's menus for the tearoom, the supper room, and the dining room went unread, and even the white sand in the ashtrays was raked and pristine.

But while all the other guests might be in their rooms, the lobby wasn't empty. Far from it. Just as Savage had predicted, the men employed by the hotel were in attendance exactly as if it had been the middle of the day: bell-boys, porters, and doormen in livery uniforms, the desk clerks and managers in morning coats, and assorted other men engaged in sweeping and cleaning and polishing.

Every one of them had stopped what he was doing to watch me.

I pretended to take no notice, my eyes straight ahead and my chin high, yet I couldn't keep the blush from my cheeks. It wasn't there from guilt, but from the sheer force of their combined attention.

Again, Savage had been right. These men could guess what I'd done with him, and more, I sensed that they admired me for it, wishing they'd been in his place. I couldn't say exactly how I knew this, but I did, and it was a kind of admiration I'd never felt before.

Even in my disheveled state—or perhaps because of it—I felt not only beautiful but also desired. It had nothing to do with my name or my family or my costly clothes or jewels. For the first time in my life, I was being noticed not as a lady, distant and remote and meant to be admired but not touched, but as a *woman*, primal and erotic, and I reveled in it.

Finally I reached the elaborate main desk, and I stopped as I always did after returning.

"Good evening," I said, although it was much closer to morning. "Have there been any messages for me while I was away?"

"Good evening, Mrs. Hart," the desk clerk said, clearly struggling to maintain his professional demeanor with me. "Yes, there have been many messages and letters, but your lady's maid has collected them each morning for you. I expect she'll have them waiting for you in your rooms."

"I am sure she will," I said. I was still clutching my coat together, but as I stood before him I lessened my grasp and let the front slip open, giving him a glimpse of red silk and black lace and my own pearly skin, and my obviously uncorseted breasts and belly.

He glanced down, unable not to, and cleared his throat. A mottled flush rose from his stiff starched color through his neatly clipped beard to his cheeks, and all the training in the world could not stop his gaze from devouring the sensual sight that I was offering.

I smiled and shifted my shoulders so the coat opened further. I realized I was toying with him, tempting him with pleasures he could never possess, and I realized, too, how exciting it was to be so unabashedly brazen.

He cleared his throat again, struggling to regain his

composure. "Shall I, ah, summon a porter to carry your cases to your room for you, Mrs. Hart?"

Now I was the disconcerted one. In my haste to flee Wrenton with Savage I'd left all the belongings I'd brought there earlier—all my clothes, my jewels, my trunks. I hadn't given them any thought at all. I assumed that all my things would be sent after me later today by Lady Carleigh, Wrenton's mistress and our hostess, and the nearest thing I had to a friend in London, or in New York, for that matter.

Yet to arrive at my hotel without so much as the keys to my own rooms was more awkward. I should be mortified. Doubtless this, too, was part of Savage's challenge, another lesson I must learn.

But I would triumph. My smile widened for the clerk. He might blush, but I did not.

"Thank you, no, but I'll need no further . . . assistance," I said, turning to walk to the lift. Again, I could feel a score of male eyes watching me, but I didn't care. My coat floated around me now, alternately concealing and revealing my red silk gown and my body beneath it. I wanted them to look, and I wanted them to desire me, exactly as Savage had directed.

But I belonged exclusively to him. That was my armor. If this was another of Savage's variations of the Game, then I'd played and I'd won, and I couldn't wait to tell him what I'd done.

I rode in silence in the lift to my floor, and I refused the operator's offer to accompany me to my door. It was just as well. At least he didn't witness the spectacle of me rapping on the door of my own suite as I tried to wake my servants. Surely one of them must hear me; I'd brought a small staff with me from New York, the ones who'd claimed to be most devoted to my welfare.

Finally one of my footmen opened the door a crack, his face groggy yet startled to see me. Behind him stood my lady's maid, Hamlin, in her nightgown and wrapper, her round face surrounded by a halo of curling papers. I pushed the door open and swept inside.

"Why did you keep me waiting?" Now that the excitement of my return was done, I was suddenly exhausted and drained, and all I wished for was my own bed. "It's preposterous that I must be kept waiting outside my own door."

"How were we to know you'd return at such an hour, ma'am?" Hamlin said indignantly. She had been with me since I was a girl, and she'd earned the right to be more outspoken than most servants ever dared. "You should've sent word to expect you, ma'am. What lady travels like a thief in the night, I ask you?"

"I am no thief, Hamlin," I said wearily. "You know that. I returned to London by motorcar with another member of the party. Now I am very tired, and wish to go to bed immediately."

"Of course you do, ma'am," Hamlin said, becoming reassuringly protective. "Poor lamb! Here, let me take that heavy coat from you, and I'll lay out a fresh nightdress."

I gladly let the heavy fur drop from my shoulders into her waiting hands. I rubbed my hands up and down over my bare arms, my skin prickling and overly sensitized. My walk through the lobby had left me uncomfortably aroused, with no way to ease my longing. I already missed Savage more than I'd thought possible, and if I'd known where he lived I think I would have gone after him.

Behind me, Hamlin was sputtering with alarm.

"Look at you, ma'am; just look at you!" she exclaimed, shocked. "How could you go about without your corset or petticoats, ma'am? Didn't you have a proper lady's maid looking after you?"

"Of course I did," I said defensively. "It was my choice to leave off my underthings. I preferred how the dress looked without them."

"More like you've left your sense, ma'am," Hamlin said grimly, attacking the hooks on the back of my dress with indignant fervor. "What lady goes about without a corset or petticoats? And look at you! You've lost flesh, you have, else you never could've worn this dress without lacing. Didn't that Lady Carleigh feed her guests? Oh, I knew that Wrenton Manor was a wicked place, ma'am, and full of wicked persons, too, I'm sure."

"Hush, Hamlin; it wasn't like that at all." I shrugged free of the dress, standing in my shoes and nothing else. With Savage I'd grown comfortable with my body and with being naked. "The company was largely charming and well-bred, with a great many titles. You would have approved."

Hamlin sniffed, her ultimate sign of contempt. I might be at ease with my nudity, but she was not and quickly slipped a lace-trimmed nightgown over my head. As she began to tie the ribbons in the front she paused and sniffed again, as if she smelled something of a suspicious nature.

Which, in fact, she had.

"Them pearls, ma'am," she said slowly. "Those don't look to be the ones given you by Mr. Hart."

I twisted away from her, placing my hand protectively over the long strand around my throat that Savage had given me.

"No, Hamlin, they are not," I said. "They are a good deal finer than the ones that Mr. Hart gave me, and given as a mark of true regard, which was never the case with my husband. And that is all you need know of them."

Hamlin's face pinched with stern disapproval.

"Yes, ma'am," she said. "But allow me to say, ma'am, that your poor dear husband must be spinning in his grave at the very thought of you wearing *them* pearls instead of the ones what he gave you, and—"

"That will be all, Hamlin," I said curtly. "You may return to your bed."

"But, ma'am, your hair—"

"I can manage myself," I said, turning away to prove the conversation truly was done. I knew Hamlin, just as she knew me, and if I'd given her any encouragement she would have begun scolding me in earnest, servant or not. There couldn't be a more potent reminder of my old life in New York than Hamlin's disapproval, nor could the juxtaposition between my past and the new life I'd begun as Savage's lover have been more jarring. "Now leave me, please."

"Very well, ma'am," she said, adding an extra sniff for emphasis. "Good night, ma'am."

I heard the door click shut behind her and let out a long sigh of weary relief. I kicked off my shoes and drew the last pins from my hair without bothering to brush or braid it. I washed and turned down the lights; it was true these were little tasks that I seldom did for myself, but tonight I found peace in them, Finally I climbed into the large bed, made up with my own lace-edged sheets, and settled back against the small mountain of pillows. Given the hour and all I had done, I should have fallen asleep at once.

I couldn't.

As exhausted as I was, I still felt too unsettled, too on edge, to give myself over to sleep. With the heavy drapes over the windows the hotel room felt as airless and muffled as a tomb, and I longed for the always-open windows of the tower room I'd shared with Savage at Wrenton.

But what I longed for far more was Savage himself.

Before I'd become his Innocent and he my Master I'd always slept by myself. One week with him had changed me forever, and now my bed seemed intolerably lonely without him in it.

I missed the heat of his male body lying close against mine, the scent of his skin, the rhythm of his breathing, the weight of his arm curled protectively around my waist and his cock pressed against the small of my back.

I missed the unpredictability of his presence, when at any moment I might be drawn from my sleep and into his world of pleasure, his fingers lightly teasing my cunt awake before the rest of me realized it.

I missed waking to see him watching me, the little flicker of connection in his pale-blue eyes when our gazes met again. I missed the security of having him there and knowing that he'd never let any harm come to me while I was with him.

Most of all, I missed the focus he'd given my life. I hadn't realized how lost I'd become, moving like a ghost without a soul through my days and nights, until he had appeared to lead me. I'd called him Master as part of the Game, but that was exactly what he had become to me, and that was exactly what I'd wanted and needed.

Without Savage with me I was lost again, and in that oversized bed I felt like a rudderless boat drifting farther and farther from the safe shore that he'd become for me. I twisted his pearls around my fingers as my thoughts raced ahead.

That walk through the lobby—he'd called it a challenge to test my confidence, but what if instead it had been his way of casting me off? What if he'd tired of me already? Lady Carleigh had told me that his intrigues were famously brief. What if he no longer needed me while I needed him more than ever?

In desperation I pushed aside my nightgown and spread my thighs and bent my knees. I had never touched myself before I'd met Savage, but he had encouraged me to learn how to please myself as he'd watched.

I pretended he was watching me again now. I slid my hand over my slit, parting my slick, puffy lips and gliding my fingers back and forth. Savage had told me I had a beautiful cunt, and I wanted to believe him. Certainly the swirling currents of excitement were beautiful. Savage had kept me in a near-constant state of arousal, and I was still swollen and my flesh sticky wet, so that when I stroked harder I couldn't keep back the shuddering gasp of pleasure.

I closed my eyes and tried to imagine it was Savage touching me. With my other hand I crushed my breast in my hand and squeezed the tip. I remembered how he'd tugged on my ruddy-red nipple through the black lace of my gown, how his teeth had grazed the tip just short of pain.

I slid lower, one finger into my passage, then two and three, as I kept the pad of my thumb circling lightly around my pearl. The little nub of sensation sprang to life, sending fiery tremors through my body. My fingers could never replace Savage's cock—what could?—but they helped me remember, and I rocked my hips upward, straining towards my release.

Briefly I touched my fingertips to my tongue. I loved the musky, salty essences of lovemaking, and I thought I could still taste Savage as well as myself.

I pictured his thick cock grinding into me, tormenting me as he withdrew almost completely before thrusting and filling me completely. I remembered how taut his face became as he concentrated on fucking me, how every muscle of his body strained and slickened with sweat and his black hair fell forward like a raven's wing over his forehead. He'd push my thighs more widely apart with his palms and slide his hands beneath my bottom, lifting me up to meet his cock while I clutched at his shoulders, gasping for breath and for him, for him.

I came in a fevered, jerking rush of bliss, falling back against the pillows. Blindly I rubbed at my slit as I tried to make the moment last, but still the last waves of pleasure and fantasy faded away and my heartbeat slowed back to normal.

Yet still there was no Savage, and to my sorrow I was still alone.

3.

"Good day to you, ma'am," Hamlin said briskly as she pulled open the window curtains. "You left no word on when you wished to be awakened, but you have a visitor waiting for you downstairs."

"A visitor?" Immediately I sat upright, certain the visitor must be Savage. "Hurry, hurry; I must dress and go down at once."

"The footman said Her Ladyship would wait for you, ma'am," Hamlin said, holding my robe up for me. "He said you could find her in the tearoom downstairs."

I paused, disappointment sweeping over me. "Her Ladyship?"

"Yes, ma'am, yes, Her Ladyship the Viscountess of Carleigh," Hamlin said importantly. If ordinary Americans were impressed by noble English titles, then American servants were doubly so, as eager to bow down before a peer or peeress as if the Revolution had never been fought. "Come now; you mustn't keep Her Ladyship waiting overlong."

No, Lady Carleigh wasn't Savage, but because they

were friends she might have word from him for me. I dressed as quickly as Hamlin could manage, once again in the full accoutrements of a fashionable lady.

My body chafed beneath the confiding layers of lace and linen, buckram and steel boning. As much as I would have preferred to keep to the simple Innocent's dress that I'd worn (or, rather, not worn; it had been so insubstantial a garment that I might as well have been naked) as part of the Game at Wrenton, I knew that I couldn't appear in the Savoy's tearoom in anything less than a gown by Worth.

I chose a suitable confection of yellow silk gauze and lace embroidered with white lilies and draped my pearls—Savage's pearls—around my throat. Just as Hamlin was making the last adjustment in the curve of the plumes on my broad-brimmed hat there came an impatient knock on my suite door.

"At last, my dear Mrs. Hart, at last!" exclaimed Lady Carleigh as she swallowed me in a well-perfumed embrace, with a kiss on either cheek. "I was *so* perishing of impatience that I couldn't bear to wait another moment to see you. You departed in such haste last night."

"I'm very happy to see you, too, my lady," I said, and I was. "Forgive me for keeping you waiting so long."

Since I'd come to London I'd grown quite fond of Lady Carleigh. With her red-gold hair, lush figure, and exuberant personality, she was considered one of the leaders of the "fast" set led by the king, and there were whispers that Her Ladyship herself had been one of the titled beauties who had shared the royal bed.

After what I'd witnessed at her country house, I'd come to believe that those whispers were likely true. She and Lord Carleigh appeared to have a forgiving marriage based more on amusement than on fidelity, and since I had come to London to escape the stultifying, puritanical morality of New York society I found her hedonism fresh and a welcome change.

Besides, she'd been the one to introduce me to Savage. What more could I wish from a friend?

"You are well, then?" she asked, studying my face so closely that I felt my cheeks warm. She and Lord Carleigh had invented the Game to entertain their houseguests, but when Savage and I had played our roles with more intensity that anyone else she'd feared things had gone too far between us. "No ill effects from a surfeit of, ah, country air?"

With Hamlin and my footman within hearing she was clearly being discreet about Savage. I appreciated her reticence. I'd never before had a lover, and I'd much to learn about how to manage it. At twenty-five I should have been past the age of inexperience and innocence, but the only other man I'd ever lain with had been my much-older husband in our loveless, passionless marriage of convenience.

"Not at all," I said. "I found the country air enjoyable and, ah, invigorating."

She turned her head slightly, considering me seriously from beneath the curving brim of her hat. "You are certain of this, my dear?"

"I am," I said firmly. "My only regret was that I hadn't time to take more of it."

At last she laughed, reassured. "Then we shall see if we can arrange that for you. I do wish my friends to be happy." She glanced curiously around my suite. "You must be happy enough here. What charming quarters you have for yourself!"

"They suffice," I said. "Should I send for tea for us?"

"Gracious, no," she said blithely. "I mean to sweep you downstairs where all the world can admire you and that splendid gown. One never knows who one might meet in the tearoom."

She winked slyly, and my heart quickened. Surely she must mean Savage. Who else could it be?

"Then by all means we should go to the tearoom," I said, eagerly taking up my purse.

"In a moment," Lady Carleigh said. "Have you looked through your mail and cards since you've returned from the country? While we were away from town the Lord Chamberlain has extended invitations to next week's evening Drawing Room."

"Truly?" The evening Drawing Room was held by the king and queen at Buckingham Palace, and it was the only way that a woman could be presented at Court. Without that presentation there would be no invitations to any of the balls and other social engagements at the Palace, and so that first invitation to a royal Drawing Room was crucial.

Such invitations did not come easily to Americans, either. Like all my fellows from across the Atlantic, I had to rely on the American ambassador for assistance. He had found me a suitably unimpeachable sponsor—a dowager marchioness whose gambling habits had made her welcome my "gift" in return for her support. The ambassador had then sponsored my application, duly vouching for my character and reptuation, but there were also endless investigations of my past and worthiness conducted by the Lord Chamberlain's office. No explanations for rejection was ever forthcoming; one simply wasn't invited.

I didn't ask for a servant to bring the tray with my mail but hurried to it myself, my heart racing with anticipation. After a week, the large silver salver was near to overflowing with invitations, notes, calling cards, and letters from New York.

One envelope stood out, its heavy cream-colored stock setting it apart. I quickly opened it, and there was the desired invitation: *The Lord Chamberlain is Commanded by Their Majesties to invite Mrs. Arthur Hart . . .*

I didn't need to read further but held the card up in triumph so Lady Carleigh could read it for herself.

"Oh, well done!" Lady Carleigh said, clapping her gloved hands together. "Come now; we must celebrate properly."

She linked her arm through mine, asking about my presentation dress and other nonsense until we were seated at a small table in a window alcove in the tearoom. The room was crowded with ladies and a few gentlemen, as was always the case with tearooms. To my disappointment, there was no sign of Savage, nor, really, could I imagine him in such an environment.

"I asked specifically for this table," Her Ladyship said as we settled ourselves in our chairs, sweeping our skirts gracefully around our legs. "It's the choicest one in the entire room. The light will show us to best advantage, and we will be seen by everyone who enters, but we shall see them first. Best of all, we can speak in complete confidence, with no one able to overhear us."

The waiter brought us a large silver pot of tea, as well as plates of scones and dishes of clotted cream and berry jam. I still had not accustomed myself to the English notion of a cream tea (as this was), for to me scones and jam were properly eaten at breakfast, not in the middle of the afternoon. But because the countess had ordered it for me I would eat it and marvel at how we would likely speak of the most decadent things while our mouths were filled with clotted cream.

"You do not know how fortunate you are to have received that invitation to the Drawing Room, my dear,"

Lady Carleigh said as she ladled sugar into her tea. "I feared you wouldn't, you know."

I nodded sagely. "Because I'm an American."

"Not at all," she said. "In the time of the old queen—may God rest her soul!—any lady who had a less than impeccable history was not welcome. Her Majesty would cancel a Drawing Room entirely rather than have a merry lady presented to her, no matter what her rank."

"But my history *is* impeccable!" I exclaimed. "That is, until—"

"Until Savage entered your life." She pursed her lips over the teacup. "Now you know that my own—what shall I call it?—my own experiences have been far from impeccable, but I had scarcely returned to London myself today when I heard of your extravagant return here to the Savoy this morning. You must have cut quite a pretty figure, traipsing through the lobby like a lost Aphrodite."

I gasped with dismay. "How could you hear of it?"

"Servants," she said succinctly. "Though the reference to the ancient goddess is mine, not theirs. Surely it must be the same in New York. I'm certain my footmen must have friends among the waiters and porters here, and in their circles scandal travels with alacrity—nearly as fast as in Society."

I was horrified, and despite Lady Carleigh's assurances of the privacy of our table, I leaned closer to her and lowered my voice in urgency.

"Savage proposed it, my lady," I said. "He said it was another challenge, another trial, for me as his Innocent. He told me to walk through the lobby wearing the same clothes I'd worn to my last dinner at Wrenton. I was supposed to act as if nothing were out of the ordinary. He wanted me to feel no shame, either. Rather, he wanted me to glory in my role—which I did, my lady."

"Please, call me Laura," Lady Carleigh said, then laid her hand over mine on the table. "If I in turn may call you by your given name."

"Oh, yes, please do," I said, flattered she'd grant me that familiarity. "It's Evelyn. Thank you, Laura."

I'd nearly said "Eve," the variant of my name that Savage preferred. No one else had ever called me that, but I loved the sound of it on his tongue and in his voice, and the meaning he'd added to it, too. Evelyn was the woman I'd been and Eve the woman I'd become with him—but of course no one else, not even Laura, could know that.

"Evelyn, then." She smiled, but it was a smile tight with concern for me. "This is what I feared would happen to you. I'd hoped you would have been able to enjoy his company, yet also resist if his, ah, 'challenges,' as he calls them, became a hazard to you."

"His challenges have never been a hazard to me," I insisted. I couldn't explain to her what Savage's challenges did mean to me, because I hadn't the words. They simply weren't yet in my everyday vocabulary. How could they be, when I'd been raised to consider sex as a distasteful obligation for procreation and nothing more?

"They have been exciting, daring, surprising, and . . . and many other things besides," I said carefully. "Most of all they have been pleasurable, but not hazardous. It's never that with Savage."

"But they will be, Evelyn, if Savage insists on such public challenges," Laura said. "The Game is meant to be exactly that: an amusing sport to pass the time among friends in the country. It doesn't belong here in London, where things can be misunderstood. Savage himself should know better. Society will turn a blind eye to all manner of indiscretions, so long as a reasonable attempt is made to mask them."

"You preach hypocrisy, then?" I asked, testy from her accusations.

"I preach common sense," she said severely, "and there was nothing sensible about how you returned to town last night. I'll grant that most of it was Savage's fault. Turning you out of his car at the door of the Savoy just before dawn was not a gentlemanly thing to do. It was rash and reckless and selfish, and I do not wish for you to suffer because of it."

In some way I understood what she was saying. The lady was always the one who suffered in the judgment of Society. If I hadn't been swept away by my role as Savage's Innocent, I would never have made such a public display of myself as I had this morning. Still, I had come to London for adventure, and this was part of it. Besides, I didn't believe that Savage himself would cause me any harm or that he'd ever wish to. There was no denying that he was a strong man. He could be firm and decisive, but he wasn't cruel.

At least not to me.

"Savage would never hurt me," I said. "You know him, and what kind of gentleman he is."

Laura frowned, considering her words.

"I know that I have never seen him like this," she said slowly. "The way he behaved at Wrenton—withdrawing from everyone else, keeping you to himself, coming to blows with poor Mr. Henery—that is not the Savage I know. Your maid at Wrenton told me he'd left bruises on you."

I flushed, not from shame, but from excitement, remembering how I'd come by those bruises, how the silk cords he'd tied to the bedpost had cut into my skin only enough to bind me and no more. He'd known exactly how tightly to tie them, how far to push me towards pleasure.

"They were marks of passion," I explained slowly, "not pain. It was all part of the Game for me, and an enjoyable part, too. You needn't have worried. If he'd truly injured me, I would have left him."

"Perhaps," Laura said, clearly skeptical. "He can be very persuasive, and like most gentlemen, he is accustomed to having whatever he wants. When we first met, I assumed you were more . . . more worldly than you are. More experienced. You Americans are usually so forthright."

"In most matters we are," I said, thinking of my own puritanical upbringing as well as my sham of a marriage. "But in matters of carnal pleasure, we remain as tight-lipped and priggish as Oliver Cromwell himself."

"A handicap you seem to have overcome," she said wryly. "But you can understand why I thought you would be a good match for an experienced gentleman like Savage. Who would have guessed that he would become such a different man with you, Evelyn?"

"Has he?" I asked, surprised. I knew he'd had many lovers before me, and I couldn't believe that I was so unique, being such an unpracticed novice in carnal amusements.

"Indeed he has," Laura said. "And I must say, neither I nor Lord Carleigh knows what to make of it."

I could not help but smile. It was oddly flattering to hear that I could have influenced Savage in any way. I thought I was the one who'd been changed by our intimacy, not the other way around.

"Since Savage and I were not acquainted before last week, I have no basis for comparison," I said. "All I know is that he pleases me, and I please him, and that is what matters most to me."

She looked down at her tea, tapping her fingers lightly

against the sides of the cup. "I do not wish to frighten you, my dear, but there were questions surrounding the death of his wife that were never properly answered or addressed. To be sure, it was many years ago now, but still, one wonders."

"He spoke to me himself about his wife, and how she died," I said, eager to defend Savage. "It did not seem suspicious to me."

It hadn't been easy for Savage to confide in me, especially when the story of his marriage was so sad. His wife had been a childhood sweetheart who had gradually lost her wits, and despite having the best medical care that could be procured, she had finally killed herself by jumping from a window as he'd watched in horror. To spare his poor wife's memory, he had kept both her illness and her suicide to himself, with the result that the world had wrongly suspected him in connection to her death.

Because I wasn't sure how much of this unhappy truth was widely known, even among friends like Laura, I didn't now want to volunteer more.

"It was tragic, yes," I said carefully, "but he was not at fault for her death, or to blame. He did what he could to save her."

"So the inquest determined." Laura sighed again and shook her head, the little feathers on her hat trembling. "All I advise is that you take care, Evelyn, and guard yourself."

I bristled at what she was implying. "Forgive me, Laura, but I do not see how—"

"Don't become testy, I beg you," she said, and smiled to take the sharpness from her words. "Pleasure is an excellent thing, but it shouldn't overrule common sense. Sometimes the most exciting gentlemen can also be the most dangerous to a lady, and if—Good heavens, I cannot believe he has come *here*!"

"Savage? Here?" Eagerly I twisted about to see the tearoom's entrance.

"Yes, yes, but you needn't look his way, unless you want him to believe you are suffering from a schoolgirl infatuation," Laura whispered. "It's never wise to let a gentleman believe he is the center of your universe."

She'd meant it as a jest, a way to lighten the somber mood of our conversation, and her sly little wink proved it.

But she'd no way of realizing that in less than a fortnight Savage had, in fact, become the center of my universe.

"I suppose your servants must have told him you were here with me," she continued, unaware of my confusion, "and he came to seek you out. Well, it cannot be helped now. All I ask is that you remember what I have said to you, Evelyn, remember every word. Do not make me regret having introduced him to you."

My heart was beating so rapidly with anticipation that I scarcely heard her warning, and before I could compose myself he was there, standing before our table. He first bowed to Laura, as was proper because of her rank, and then turned towards me.

We had been apart only a matter of hours, but I felt as if I were meeting him for the first time. In a way it was a second beginning, a retreat to a more formal and proper meeting with us both, for a change, fully clothed.

He was dressed in a dark morning suit with a pale-gray vest, and all impeccably tailored to his broad shoulders and tall, lean frame. Swept back from his forehead, his black hair gleamed in the sunlight from the window, and not even that afternoon sun could soften the sharp planes of his face. Only his mouth was soft, full, and sensual in dramatic contrast to the rest of his face.

It took all my willpower not to glance down at the front of his trousers and look for the telltale bulge of the cock that not even the most masterful tailoring in Savile Row could entirely mask.

No, I didn't look. But still my nipples tightened into tight, hard buds of longing simply from having him stand here before me, and I was grateful for the many layers of clothing and corset that would hide my obvious response from the rest of the room.

From the other ladies, yes, but not from him. From the way he slowly smiled at me, he knew. He always did.

How could I dare to pretend this afternoon would be any different? He was the kind of man whose mere presence made women turn in the street to stare as he passed by, and certainly many ladies in the tearoom were twisting about in their little gilded chairs to catch a glimpse at him as he stood at our table.

But I was the only one of them who knew how heavy his cock felt in my hand, how the velvety head would weep against my palm with eagerness.

Only I knew the taste of that salty drop, or how his cock would swell against my tongue and lips when I sucked it.

And only I knew the exquisite pleasure of feeling that cock in my cunt, surging forward to fill me completely with its glorious heat and power.

To have him here and not be able to touch, to taste, to take, was an almost unbearable torment. He lifted my hand lightly in his own and bowed over it, our gazes locked. I felt sure that his pale eyes—neither blue nor gray but some subtle, silvery blending of the two—could see all my secrets, and I felt my cheeks warm beneath their scrutiny as I imagined him reading my wicked thoughts.

"Good day, Mrs. Hart," he said, his resonant voice

making desire coil deep within my belly. "How fortunate I am to find you here."

"How lucky for Lady Carleigh and for me as well, my lord," I said, my voice breathless in response to his. "We are the most fortunate ladies in this entire room."

He was holding my hand longer, far longer, than etiquette required, and I felt the warmth of his touch through my gloves, a touch that was more than enough to remind me of how that same hand had learned my body so intimately.

"Will you join us, Savage?" Laura said, ever the hostess. "Perhaps the waiter can find you heartier fare than tea and scones."

"You are very kind, Lady Carleigh, as always," he said. He pointedly laid his hat and walking stick across one of the empty chairs—one of Society's little signs that he would be with us only briefly—and took the other chair beside mine. "Do not trouble yourself with a special order on my account. Tea is enough. You know I am not a demanding sort."

He smiled at me again as if this were some tremendous joke between us. Of course I understood what he meant. No matter how he behaved at the tea table, in bed he was, in fact, very demanding, very exacting. He was precise in what he wanted, and he'd taught me to be the same way, with thrilling results.

Unaware—or at least pretending to be so—Laura poured his tea herself.

"I am glad to see you are well, Savage," she said. "You left us so suddenly last night that we feared you were ill."

"Not at all," he said, taking the offered cup of tea. "I had simply come to the limit of my capacity for your kind hospitality."

The porcelain cup and saucer looked impossibly delicate

in his large, tanned hands. His shirt cuffs were stiffly starched around those hands, and on them were the cuff links that I'd come to associate with him, black onyx with an overlay of a gold serpent, a diamond in its open mouth: jewels that were unique and wickedly masculine, just like he was himself.

"Oh, your *limits*," scoffed Laura, sipping her own tea. "You have no limits, Savage. That is much of your problem."

"My problem, or my potential?" he asked, more playfully than I'd expected from him. "To be without limits means that one has limitless possibilities, and that one is ready to embrace and experience all the world has to offer."

Laura rolled her eyes and made a pretty moue of her lips. She might warn me to be careful with Savage, but she wasn't above flirting with him, too.

"A foolish bit of nonsense, that," she said. "You know perfectly well what I meant. It was ill-bred of you to depart so abruptly last night, especially since you stole this dear lady away from us as well."

Deliberately he set his cup down, and though he answered Laura, he looked directly at me.

"It was Mrs. Hart's choice to come with me, Lady Carleigh," he said. "I trust she was not disappointed in her decision."

"Oh, no, my lord," I said, wishing I could control the breathless longing in my voice. "Not at all."

I didn't agree with Laura's suggestion that it was unwise to appear too interested, but I didn't want to seem like that foolish schoolgirl, either. When I'd played Savage's Innocent he'd wanted me to be confident in my replies to him. I still wanted to please him in that way, even though we weren't playing the Game any longer.

Or were we?

"I am glad you have no regrets," he said, his quirk of a not-quite smile telling how much more than glad he was.

"I suppose it's just as well you brought Mrs. Hart back to town when you did, Savage," Laura said. "While she was away in the country she received an invitation to next week's Drawing Room, and she'll need as much time as possible to prepare. The curtseys alone require considerable practice, not to mention the agility of a wretched acrobat."

Beneath the heavy white tablecloth, Savage pressed his knee close against mine, an insistent, suggestive pressure that was all the more exciting because above the table he was continuing his conversation with Laura.

"Ah, a Court Drawing Room," he said. "Tedium by royal decree."

"Hush," scolded Laura mildly. "I know we have no choice and must go to the Palace as commanded. But for an American like Mrs. Hart, it's a great coup simply to receive an invitation."

He turned back to me. "Is that so, Mrs. Hart? This invitation to a crowded, overheated, and interminable ritual is something you covet?"

"It is, my lord," I said. "Because the invitations are so seldom granted to Americans, they become all the more desired."

He sipped his tea and pressed his knee more firmly against mine.

"That is the way with most things, Mrs. Hart, isn't it?" he asked. "Desire increases when the object of that desire is withheld?"

Of course I understood his double meaning, and to prove it I daringly slipped my foot free of my slipper and stroked it suggestively around his ankle. His expression didn't change, but amusement flickered through his eyes.

"I am serious, my lord," I said. "My acquaintances in New York believe that there is a price for everything in the world, and that with sufficient funds—which most of them possess—everything can be bought. When they visit England, they expect the same."

"True enough," Laura said. "Consider how many scions of noble trees have been snatched up by wealthy American fathers for their daughters just so they could claim a title."

"But they can't buy an invitation to a Drawing Room," I said. "I know, because I've heard them complain bitterly about it, and lament the dresses made for Court that were never worn."

Savage chuckled. "So that is why you want to endure a Drawing Room, Mrs. Hart? To be able to wave the invitation in the faces of your rivals in New York and humiliate them with it?"

"In part, my lord, yes," I admitted. I loved to hear him chuckle, a rare event, and to know I was the cause of it. "But I also believe that I must take every new opportunity that life offers me, and experience it to the fullest."

"An excellent sentiment," he said, "as well as the only way to survive such an unholy torment."

Our bantering was making him want me more. I could see it in his eyes, how they'd narrowed a fraction as he'd studied me. This intrigued me, for when we'd played at Master and Innocent I'd been forbidden to speak except to answer his questions.

There'd been none of this seductive give-and-take, and as much as I'd enjoyed being the obedient Innocent, I liked this, too. It also made me want him more, just as he wanted me, and lightly I stroked my stockinged food along the hard muscle of his calf.

"Nothing is an unholy torment in the right company,

my lord," I said, lowering my chin a fraction so that I looked up at him from beneath the curving brim of my hat. "But then, I need not say that to you."

"No," he said. "But we can maybe test both your theory and your endurance together next week at the Palace. And here when I asked for you to be invited I thought it only to keep from being bored myself!"

I gasped with surprise. "You did that for me, my lord?"

He shrugged carelessly. "I told you: it was done last week from purest selfishness. Since no excuses are accepted by His Majesty and I must attend myself, I wanted you there as well to keep me from falling asleep. It was an easy favor to ask."

"You asked Bertie himself, didn't you?" Laura asked, faintly accusing. Bertie was the disrespectfully affectionate nickname for His Majesty, and I'd heard it used several times last week among the guests at Wrenton. "No doubt you told him how . . . agreeable our Mrs. Hart was, and that was enough for him to summon the Lord Chamberlain posthaste. There is nothing the King likes better than a pretty new face."

"She is not 'our' Mrs. Hart, Laura," he said drily, again looking at me rather than at the countess. "Rather, at present she is mine, as His Majesty will learn for himself soon enough."

I heard Laura sharply draw in her breath, but I didn't look her way, either.

"That's bold of you, my lord," I said softly to Savage. It was the answer that I should say and not the one I wanted to say: that he'd been completely right and for now I *was* his and hearing him say so had made me ridiculously happy. "I'm afraid I cannot excuse it."

"Then don't," he said evenly. "Come riding with me in Hyde Park instead."

"She can't go now, Savage," Laura protested. "You shouldn't even ask her. You know what people will say. Why, it's nearly four thirty in the afternoon! No one goes riding at this hour."

"I do," he said, "and I expect Mrs. Hart does, too. Will you join me, ma'am?"

I didn't have a horse in London, but I did have a splendid new habit, and now I had Savage to ride with me. I put every word of caution that Laura had shared earlier from my head. Regardless of the hour, riding was a respectable pastime. For Savage and me, it was also one that could lead to many other activities that weren't, particularly so late in the day.

The lack of a horse seemed inconsequential. I smiled, and so did Savage.

"Yes, my lord," I said. "Yes."

4.

It's often said (primarily by gentlemen, of course) that a lady spends at least half her day in the ritual of dress.

In other words, she is expected to change from a dressing gown to a morning dress to one for luncheon, followed by another suitable for making calls, another fit for dinner, and then, finally, a dress for evening, whether the theatre, opera, or a ball, and then a nightgown and peignoir for bed: six changes in all, with the possibility of more if there are also specialized activities in her day-book such as sailing or hunting. Considering that a lady must also allow time for adjusting her hair, selecting the proper jewels, and shifting shoes, gloves, hats, and stockings to match the rest of her attire, that estimate of half a day spent in the dressing room with one's maid could well be accurate.

I explain all that for a purpose. First, to show the tedium of my ordinary day. And second, to prove how swiftly I managed to change from my tea dress and into my riding habit: a mere quarter hour passed from the time I parted with Laura and Savage in the tearoom until I was briskly crossing the hotel lobby in my full riding habit, with one of my footmen dutifully accompanying me to act as my groom.

In short, any lady can achieve miracles if she is properly motivated, and the thought of Savage waiting on horseback could have offered sufficient motivation for an entire legion of London ladies.

Nor was I disappointed. We'd arranged to meet at the park's main stables, where many Londoners kept their horses. I was earlier than we'd planned, but he was already there. He stood in the stable yard, speaking to one of the grooms, as he held the reins to a magnificent black gelding: clearly no hired nag, but his. The sight of Savage nearly stole my breath, as it always did. How could it not?

Unlike other gentlemen who had begun to wear less formal clothing for riding, tweed jackets and derby hats, he preferred to remain firmly in the older style. He wore a black frock coat that came to the middle of his thighs, snug buff trousers tucked into top boots, black gloves, and a snowy white shirt with a white silk neckcloth. On his head was a gleaming beaver hat with a high crown and a curved brim, also in black.

Everything was tailored exactly to accentuate his imposing frame, as his clothes always were. On another man so much black would be funeral, but it suited him with his dark hair and light eyes, making him stand out even more. He'd told me once that he felt misplaced in the modern world of electricity and motorcars and that he'd much rather have been born in the dashing, dangerous age of men like Wellington and Byron.

Yet that was the kind of man that Savage was, darkly elegant yet with a hint of animal wildness. It didn't matter if we were playing the Game or not: he was still my Master. No wonder I found him so intensely attractive.

"Good afternoon, my lord," I called to him, making as much of a curtsey as I could manage with the trailing skirt of my habit over one arm as I walked. As was the fashion, my habit was mannishly severe, with a row of tiny buttons up the tight, corseted bodice and sleeves over the draped skirt. My hat echoed Savage's in style, although I wore mine pinned at a flattering angle and the black silk netting of the trailing veil gave it a decidedly feminine touch.

I knew the habit was becoming to me, and yet from the way that Savage looked at me as I approached I might as well have been naked. His gaze swept over me with a familiar possessiveness that was slightly predatory, and I felt myself shiver as if he'd touched me already.

"Mrs. Hart," he said, touching the brim of his hat to me. "I'm glad you are here. I've heard that American women are veritable Amazons in the saddle. Are you?"

"I am reasonably accomplished, my lord," I said. "I won't lag behind you or hold you back, if that is what you fear."

He raised a single skeptical brow, taking that as a challenge. I hadn't intended it that way. I *was* a skilled rider, not that parading up and down in a park would be much of a test. But I'd do better to let Savage judge me himself; he would anyway.

A groom was already leading out a smart bay mare for me as well as a sturdy chestnut for my servant. Both were better than most hired horses, and I suspected Savage had taken care with the choice. I was glad that he wasn't objecting to having my servant ride behind us. The man would stay back behind us as we rode, out of our hearing, but his presence would give me an aura of respectability. I had heard Laura's warning, and I could see the wisdom of a certain degree of propriety. I wanted to be with Savage, yes, but I didn't want to become notorious because of it.

With that in mind I was relieved that Savage stood back as I used the mounting block to climb onto the lady's side-saddle and let my servant hand me my reins and adjust my stirrups. As I arranged the drape of my skirts over my legs I couldn't help but watch as Savage mounted his own horse in a single athletic motion. He swung his horse around to join mine, and together we rode through the arched gate of the stable yard and towards the wide avenue through the park inelegantly known as Rotten Row.

Despite its name, the sand-covered bridleway was a beautiful place to ride at this time of day. It was surprisingly peaceful, for all that we were in the middle of London. The sun was low on the horizon, casting long shadows through the trees that lined the avenue, and Savage set an easy pace, little more than a walk, so that we could converse.

"You didn't lie, Eve," he said. "You do ride well. But then, I should have guessed as much from our past . . . experience."

I looked up quickly through the haze of my veil and smiled, glad that we were alone so that he could call me by the name he'd invented for me, instead of my husband's surname.

"Thank you, Master," I said simply, happily falling back into the Game.

He grunted, pleased I'd done so. "I've missed you, Eve," he said with unexpected honesty. "I do not like sharing you with others."

"I missed you, too, Master," I said softly. "Lady Carleigh has become my friend, but I prefer to be alone with you."

"As it should be," he said. "Now tell me of your challenge last night."

"I did exactly as you bid me do, Master," I said quickly. "I walked through the lobby by myself, dressed as I was, spoke with the clerk at the desk, and then rode in the lift to my suite."

"That's not what I meant, Eve," he said, a slight irritation in his voice. "Anyone could have told me that."

"Forgive me, Master," I said, bewildered. "But I thought that—"

"Do not *think*, Eve," he ordered. "Only feel. Feel, and remember that this was to have been a challenge."

I nodded, and in confusion I looked before me as I strived to collect my thoughts. The crowds that usually thronged both the avenue and the adjacent walks had gone home to prepare for the evening. In addition to a few solitary gentlemen there were small groups of officers from the Household Cavalry in their scarlet tunics and plumed silver helmets, exercising their horses along the row.

I was the only lady in sight.

It had been the same way in the Savoy's lobby early this morning, when I'd walked past all the leering men. The only difference was that with Savage at my side the men we passed on horseback now might steal a glance in curiosity, but most only nodded at me in respect. None of them would dare appraise me as freely as the men had this morning.

But that was what Savage had wanted, wasn't it? Wasn't that the challenge he'd set for me? For me to experience what it was like to be ogled and desired by strangers?

"I thought I was accustomed to being a woman alone when I entered the hotel, Master," I began slowly. "I thought I knew what to expect from the challenge. But it wasn't like anything else I'd done before, ever."

"Go on," Savage said, his eyes hooded but bright with interest. "Tell me more."

"If it pleases you, Master." I swallowed and continued. "I knew that no one could tell what I wore beneath my coat. That coat is heavy, as furs can be, and no one else would know that I wasn't wearing a corset, let alone petticoats, or a camisole, or even drawers. No one could have known, and yet I was certain somehow that every man I passed did."

"Why did you think that?"

"From how they looked at me," I said. "It began with the doorman who tried to help me from your motorcar. He didn't say or do anything that was not respectful, and yet I could see the longing in his eyes."

"I warned you that men sense these things about a woman," Savage said. "They can tell when she has been fucked, and how much she relished it. In countless inexplicable ways, you displayed your satisfaction. Your eyes were heavy with pleasure, your mouth swollen from my kisses, your walk languid with satisfaction."

I nodded, remembering. "All of those things, Master. And yet it wasn't that I was shameless, but fearless. Because of you, I was proud of who I was."

I expected him to smile, but his mouth remained a solemn, implacable line. He took being my Master very seriously.

"Because in that moment," he said, "you were not a lady, but a woman. What was your response to this attention?"

I gave a little shake to my shoulders. "I told you, Master. I was proud of it, and I was—"

"No, Eve," he said patiently. "I wish to hear of how your body responded to being the center of so much male desire. Did it arouse you? Did you feel the heat in your quim?"

"Oh." I blushed behind my veil. I shouldn't have. With Savage I'd learned to speak with a frankness that would have stunned me a month ago. But somehow the combination of wearing a restrictive, formal riding habit along with being in the middle of Hyde Park with my groom riding behind me made that same frankness more difficult to repeat. I felt once again like Mrs. Hart, not the Innocent Eve.

"Do not be shy, Eve." Clearly Savage was aware of my misgivings, but instead of sympathy I heard an edge of irritation in his voice. "You've come too far for that now. I asked you to tell me if you were aroused by the challenge, and I expect you to answer me."

I nodded, though my thoughts were spinning. I didn't know why I was suddenly so modest. I didn't want to displease Savage. I never wanted to do that, not after he'd done so much for me.

In desperation I tried to recover my memories of this morning and find the words to describe what he'd requested of me. It was as if by wearing my usual, confining corset and clothes I'd lost all of my newfound freedom and returned to my old, restricted self. I felt an uneasy, unladylike sweat gathering beneath my habit and my chemise, trickling between my breasts, and I was acutely aware of the muffled, rhythmic sound of our horses' hooves on the sand-covered avenue, the rustle of the evening breeze through the leaves overhead, and the creak of my mare's leather saddle.

Yet most of all I sensed Savage's growing unhappiness beside me. He sighed, and my despair increased. What was wrong with me? How could I have survived the challenge itself, only to fail him in the telling of it?

"Eve, please," he said, and to my surprise his voice had softened in a way that made me long to please him all the more. "I simply want to share the challenge with you, that is all."

"I do not wish to disappoint you, Master," I confessed with frustration.

"You never do that, Eve," he said, soothing me. "Not you. Now remember last night. Remember how we left Wrenton in the middle of dinner. Remember the red silk dress with the black lace that you wore, with nothing beneath it. No corset, no drawers. That pleased me very much. You were wearing it still this morning at the Savoy."

"Beneath my fur," I continued with a little hitch of emotion in my voice. Hearing him describe what I'd worn made my task easier. "Last night I'd felt very daring wearing a dress like that. I knew it would make me more . . . more accessible to you."

"It did," he said. I heard the rawness in those two words, revealing perhaps more than he intended. "It pleased me, too. Very much."

I nodded, my memories returning along with my confidence.

"Wearing a dress like that, I didn't need a lady's maid," I said. "In the motorcar, I pulled it over my head. I sat across your legs and rode your cock as we drove, and you squeezed my breasts, and I rocked with the movement of the motorcar to make it better for us both. And because it was you and your cock filling my . . . my cunt, it was perfect."

"Perfect," he repeated. "Now go on, Eve. Tell me more."

I nodded and shifted in the saddle. This conversation about last night was arousing me now. I felt the familiar tension gathering low in my belly and the petaled lips of my cunt begin to swell. Surreptitiously I rubbed against the smooth, padded leather of the sidesaddle in the hope of easing some of that delicious tension.

But there was no relief, and instead the gliding pressure only made matters worse, a poor substitute for Savage himself. He was so close to me, and yet he might have been on the other side of the world for all that he would do to ease my suffering. My nipples were hard and aching from pressing against the boned prison of my corset, and I shifted once more against the saddle.

"Stop that, Eve," Savage warned, catching me. "You'll unsettle the horse, wriggling about like that."

"Forgive me, Master, but I cannot help it," I said miserably. "I want—"

"Your wanting has nothing to do with it," he said. "You do not have my permission."

"Yes, Master." Like a drunkard pushing away from the bottle, I turned my gaze away from him and towards the trees, hoping that would help me control myself.

"Look at me, Eve," he ordered, and reluctantly I did. Even after only a few moments, I was struck anew by the power his handsome face had for me. "If you finish your story to my satisfaction, then we can return to the stable, and you will be rewarded. Now continue."

"Yes, Master," I murmured miserably. "I will."

I had to tense my thighs to keep my seat in the saddle, which only magnified the sensations I was feeling in my quim. I twisted the reins more tightly in my hands, trying not to move but to focus on what I said and not the heat coiling inside me—even if what I was describing for Savage was exactly what I was feeling.

"As I walked across the lobby, Master," I began again, "I felt the silk of my dress slide over my skin, and the lace pull across my nipples. I felt your seed and my own juices slip from inside me to slide along my thighs. I let my coat fall open as if by accident, letting the men see more of my breasts beneath the red silk. It excited me to know they were admiring me and lusting for me, but the only one I wanted was you."

He grunted. "Is that the truth, Eve?"

"Oh, yes," I said, desire melting the words into a sigh of longing. "I felt strong and powerful and seductive, but all of it was wasted because you were not there with me. If you had not driven away, I would have run back to the motorcar to be with you. I wanted your cock, Master. I wanted you, just as I want you now."

"We shall turn here, Eve," he said, "and begin to make our way back to the stable. You have succeeded at the challenge. You will be rewarded."

"Thank you, Master," I said, my heart racing at the thought of what my reward might be. With Savage there were so many possibilities. . . .

The silence as we rode crackled like electricity between us, yet Savage refused to quicken the pace. Even as I sat still as I'd promised the motion of the horse beneath me was like a caress that could not be avoided. I glanced down at the front of his trousers to see if he, too, had become excited by our ride and conversation, but to my frustration his long riding coat hid any telltale signs. I hoped he shared my agitation and that those trousers were feeling abominably full and tight.

We passed another group of cavalrymen, cantering two by two back towards their barracks. I scarcely took notice of them, but Savage did.

"Did you see that, Eve?" he asked, incredulous. "Did you see how those men looked at you?"

"No, Master," I said. "I took no notice."

"Everywhere you go it happens," he said as if I hadn't spoken. "Men lust after you. It makes no difference what you wear. Even now, dressed as you are, they cannot help themselves."

"It's not my fault, Master," I protested. "I'm not doing anything willfully to . . . to entice them."

"That's true," he said. He was looking straight ahead and not at me, his profile severe. As was often the way with him, I couldn't tell if he was angry or only making an observation. "You need do nothing, and yet it will happen, again and again. First at Wrenton, then at the hotel, and now here."

I didn't want him to blame me. "It's not my fault, Savage. You must know that."

"I do know it, Eve," he said. "It's simply how you *are*. You have always been beautiful. Now that you have been awakened to pleasure, you are irresistible as well. Your mouth, your eyes, your body. There's a ripeness and a glow to you. Men cannot keep themselves from desiring you."

"It's never been like that for me before," I protested. "You've made me that way, Master."

"I won't deny it," he agreed. "Nor do I regret it, for I've benefited, too."

He fell quiet again, forcing me to ask the inevitable question.

"This . . . this change in me," I said carefully. "Are you happy with me as I am now?"

He frowned with obvious disbelief.

"Why wouldn't I be happy?" he asked. "You are as close to perfection as any Innocent I have ever encountered. With more education, you *will* be perfect."

"Thank you, Master," I said, unable to keep from smiling with joy behind my veil. "But I meant about the men who look and desire me."

"That is different." He shook his head, his jaw tightening briefly, and I thought uneasily of how quickly—and violently—his temper had flared at Wrenton when fueled with jealousy. "It doesn't please me, no. How can it? It's tempting to lock you away forever so that no other man could ever enjoy your beauty—someplace far from London where you'd belong only to me."

I hadn't expected that, and it shocked me. I thought of how he'd shut his wife away when her madness had grown uncontrollable, and I thought, too, of Laura's earlier warning. Most of all, I remembered my wretched childhood, surrounded by security men even as I struggled to free myself from the cocoon of my father's great wealth and paranoia.

"You couldn't do it," I blurted out. "I may be your Innocent, but I won't be your prisoner, no matter what the reason. When I was a girl my father shut me away from the rest of the world, and I vowed I'd never let it happen again."

He glared at me, as startled by me as I'd been by him, and unconsciously he tightened his hands around the reins in his hands, making his horse whinny in protest.

"I said I was tempted to do so, Eve, not that it was my actual intention," he said roughly. "Damnation, I want you with me by choice, Eve, not force."

"It's because of my father," I said, trying to explain. "I do not want to be trapped and smothered again."

"You are free to leave me whenever you wish," Savage said as if I hadn't spoken. "You are not my prisoner, and never will be. You need only say you want to leave, and then go. Do you understand me?"

I nodded slowly, unsure of what had just happened.

Did that constitute a quarrel?

And if so, had I won or lost?

"I will not leave you, Master," I said finally. "I don't wish for that, either."

He didn't answer, but his face relaxed, and I dared to continue.

"As your Innocent, I still require more training to

please you," I said. "Only you can do that. No other man could."

"No other man will have the opportunity," he said firmly. "None."

"That is what I wish as well, Master," I said. "Exactly as you promised."

He nodded, gathering his reins as we entered the large stable yard again. There were more people and a few carriages here now, and the grooms and stableboys were darting back and forth with fresh horses. Apparently we weren't the only ones who'd seen the appeal of a later afternoon ride.

I drew my mare beside the stable mount, and one of the stableboys hurried forward to hold her so I could climb down. To my surprise, Savage himself stepped forward to help me as I did, his hand on the small of my back for support. It was a small, gallant gesture, yet I felt the heat of his touch radiate from my back through my body.

"Send your man back to the Savoy," he said, leaning close so we wouldn't be overheard. "You're coming home with me now."

"Yes, Master," I murmured, breathless with anticipation. After last night, I'd feared he did not want me in his house. "Should I have him return later?"

"No," Savage said. "You can send for him in the morning."

In the morning. I nodded, my excitement building.

My servant had just climbed down from his own horse, and I called for him to join me.

"I no longer require you here, Robert," I said, attempting to use my customary brisk manner. "You may return to the hotel."

Robert frowned uneasily, unwilling to believe me. I

understood his reluctance. My servants considered me a fragile widow, in need of protection and looking after. They would be as unaccustomed to my new role as I was myself. Perhaps even more so.

"Are you certain, Mrs. Hart?" he asked. "It's no bother."

"I will be well enough, Robert," I said with more kindness. "You may go, and leave me."

"Do as your mistress bids you," Savage said curtly. "Leave us."

"Yes, my lord," Robert said, his expression fixed as he bowed and left.

"You needn't have been so sharp," I protested. "Robert meant well."

"He questioned your order," Savage said. "He failed to show you the respect you deserve as his mistress, and he had no right to distrust me so openly."

I'd thought only of myself, but now that Savage had explained it I realized that Robert was suspicious of him, much as my maid, Hamlin, had been earlier.

"Then I apologize for Robert's behavior towards you," I said. "I'll address it when I return."

"It's not simply a question of addressing his behavior," Savage insisted. "How can you trust your life to a man who—"

"Mrs. Hart!"

I recognized that booming voice at once and swiftly turned around. Baron Blackledge was also dressed for riding, his bull-like frame encased in a dark-green jacket, buff trousers, and gleaming dark boots with spurs. He wore a tweed homburg hat angled over his fleshy face, no doubt in homage to the king's taste for similar hats, but without His Majesty's aplomb. Beneath the hat, Black-ledge's ginger-colored hair was crisp with too much pomade, and his brows bristled so aggressively I wondered if he used the same pomade on them as well.

In fact, everything about the baron was aggressive. I'd learned that last week at Wrenton. First he had tried to win me in a mock slave auction that had been part of the Game, and when that had failed he had forcibly tried to take me as his own. He was an overbearing bully with a taste for inflicting pain upon others, and I'd no doubt that if he'd had the chance he would have raped me and used me most barbarously.

Only Savage had saved me then, and automatically I shrank closer to his side now as the baron came charging across the stable yard towards us.

"I did not expect that our paths would cross again so soon, Mrs. Hart," he said as he joined us. He stood with his legs planted wide apart, ignoring Savage completely, and lightly slapped his leather quirt against his thigh. "You left me last night before I'd time for a proper farewell."

"She wasn't with you, Blackledge," Savage said, his voice low and filled with warning. "There was no need for her to say so much as a word to you."

I glanced around nervously. All around us, other riders were coming and going with their horses, unaware of our small drama, and stableboys and grooms passed us without so much as a glance. No doubt they all believed this to be simply one more polite conversation between two well-dressed gentlemen and a lady.

I knew otherwise. The tension growing between the two men was as palpable as a rising thunderstorm, and I knew if I didn't speak the results would be every bit as dangerous.

"Please leave us at once, Baron," I said, striving to sound as stern as possible. "I have nothing further to say to you."

But Blackledge only laughed, showing too much of his teeth. I hated how he looked at me, as if I were a commodity to be purchased and used.

"Dear Mrs. Hart!" he said. "How you amuse me! Why would you squander your beautiful self on this bastard when you could be mine?"

"Because Mrs. Hart is a lady of taste and refinement, Blackledge," Savage said curtly. "She has no interest in a damnable parvenu like yourself."

I edged closer to Savage, making my allegiance clear. Without looking down I sensed his hands had clenched into fists at his sides, both from anger and in readiness. Blackledge was the larger man, but I'd witnessed the raw fury of Savage when his temper took control, and I prayed this confrontation wouldn't come to that.

Not that Blackledge cared. He raised his bristling brows, and his smile became a sneer.

"I'd say she has an interest in me," he said. "She's no better than any common strumpet in the arches of Covent Garden. She's hungry for what I can give her, Savage. I see it in her eyes."

"No," I said, my denial automatic. "I want nothing from you."

I slipped my hand into Savage's arm. His muscles were rigid beneath my fingers, ready—too ready—to attack. I did not want anything from Blackledge, but I also didn't want to inspire a common brawl in a stable yard.

"Come, my lord," I said, trying to coax Savage away. "If he will not leave us, then we shall leave him."

But Savage wasn't ready to leave. Instead he acted as if he hadn't heard me, all his energy focused on Blackledge. We'd finally drawn the attention of the others around us in the stable yard, with a loose circle of bystanders pausing to watch what might happen next.

"Apologize to Mrs. Hart, Blackledge," Savage demanded, his voice raised and sharp. "Take back what you said of her, and apologize now."

Blackledge didn't move. "Why should I take it back, when it's the truth? Look at her and how ready she is for me, and tell me she isn't."

He raised the quirt and lightly touched the braided leather lash to my breast in a suggestive caress. I gasped at his audacity and jerked backwards and away from him as if I'd been burned.

But as swiftly as I moved, Savage moved faster.

He tore the quirt from Blackledge's hand, snapped it in two, and threw it to the ground.

"Apologize," he ordered, his voice an ominous growl. His pale eyes were hard as flint and every bit as unyielding. "Apologize now."

"The devil I will," Blackledge said, taking a step towards Savage. He, too, had clenched his fists, his thick fingers like leather-covered sausages in his gloves. "She's not worth that—"

"Excuse me, m'lord," said the stable master, deftly stepping between the two men. "We don't need this kind of misunderstanding here in the yard. Any sort of ruckus upsets the horses, and I won't have it."

For a long moment, neither man flinched. It seemed as if every other person in the yard was holding his breath, unsure of how this would end.

"You, too, Baron," said the stable master. "Gentlemen or not, I can't have the pair o' you brawling in my stable yard."

And it was finally Blackledge who stepped back.

"For the sake of the beasts, then," he said, straightening his tie and scowling in retreat. "But mark what I say, Savage. This isn't done between us. Mrs. Hart *will* be mine, whether you like it or not."

He looked past Savage to find me, standing several steps away with my hands folded over my chest to mask my trembling hands and racing heart. He narrowed his eyes and stared at me pointedly, his gaze flicking over my body as if he was imagining me in some obscene position. Then with a muttered oath he turned on his booted heel and crossed the yard to where he'd left his horse.

In the circumstances I wished I'd been braver. I wished I'd behaved like a true heroine and been the one who'd stepped between the two men to stop them. I wished I'd spat with contempt at Blackledge and not cowered like some cowardly, weak-minded woman.

But the truth was that seeing Savage so near to battling with Blackledge again on my behalf had frightened me, frightened me badly. I'd feared for Savage's safety, and my own as well at the hands of Blackledge.

What had unsettled me even further, however, was that having these two men ready to fight over me had unleashed some sort of primal pleasure within me. Savage's games while we'd been riding had kept me in a state of excited arousal for the last hour, and to watch him defend me as he had only made my blood quicken more. He wanted me badly enough that he'd fight for me, and as shameful as such a confession might be for a modern woman, it still had made me in return want him all the more.

Now he stood with his back to me, his broad shoulders still tensed. The stable master had left us soon after Blackledge had, and the others in the yard had returned to their own affairs, perhaps a little disappointed that they hadn't witnessed anything more worthy of gossip. Grooms had taken our horses back to the stable.

Only Savage and I were left standing still in the bustling yard. It was an awkward stillness, too. I longed to reach out to touch him, to put my arms around his waist and press my face against those shoulders and breathe deeply of his scent. I wanted to thank him for what he'd done, and I wanted to reassure myself.

Yet despite how intimate we'd become, I hesitated. I was sure he wouldn't want so public a show of affection between us, nor—with Laura's warning still in my ears—would that be wise for me, either. To most of the world, Savage and I were no more than acquaintances, and for now it should remain that way.

But discretion wasn't the only reason I didn't join him. No matter how much I wished it otherwise, that well-tailored back turned towards me was like a wall that I didn't dare challenge. I knew better than that. In the week we'd been together he'd made it clear that there were times when he prized his solitude and did not want it to be interrupted. This, apparently, was one of those times.

Or so I'd thought.

Without warning he wheeled about and grabbed my arm.

"Come with me," he said, though from the way he was marching me across the yard I had little choice but to go with him. His expression was fixed and his jaw set, and as I hurried my steps to keep pace with his I couldn't begin to read his mood.

He was grasping my arm hard, almost to the point of pain, but not quite. I didn't protest; this was what I'd wanted, to be with him.

He led me into the stable and down the long row of stalls. Some held horses, snuffling and whinnying behind the gates as we passed, their scent mingling with the smell of hay and polished leather. I blinked, trying to accustom my eyes to the shadows. The lanterns had not been lit yet, and the sun of the fading day slanted through the windows and the door.

I tripped on the brick floor, but he held me up, still pulling me forward with him. The last stall was empty, and he drew me inside with him. He released my arm, shoved the gate shut, and shot the bolt to the latch. The gate would offer no degree of real privacy—most men of any height would be able to see over it—but I sensed that was not the true reason that Savage had latched the gate. He didn't wish to keep the stable workers out so much as he wanted to keep me locked in.

Locked in with *him*.

I took a single step towards him to prove I wasn't frightened. I wasn't. I was insanely aroused, my blood racing through my body with desire. Slowly I lifted the veil back from my face so he could see the longing that I was sure must be there. My eyes were heavy with it, my lips aching for his.

He took off his hat and threw it aside, then crossed the short distance between us. I'd never seen him quite like this, his face furious with unabashed lust. When he'd been face-to-face with Blackledge his pale eyes had been as cold as winter. Now, when he met my gaze, those same eyes seemed to burn with desire, the same wild desire that was now licking through my body.

He seized me by the waist to pull me close, but I'd already reached for his shoulders—ah, those shoulders!—and was digging my fingers deep into the superfine woolen-covered muscles. He caught me off-balance and then pushed me back against the rough wood of the stall. The wall shoved my hat forward, and impatiently he tore it from my hair, scattering the pins that Hamlin had so carefully used to secure it.

The hat didn't matter now. Nothing else did, except his mouth devouring me, claiming me, marking me. I could taste the possession of this kiss, the savageness that was a part of his name. I felt scorched, branded by it, and yet the more he pressed his body against mine, against the rough boards behind me, the more I wanted.

He held my jaw steady in his hand to make sure I wouldn't escape. His thumb pressed into my cheek, and the animal scent of his leather gloves somehow made his kiss more primal and demanding.

When he broke away I gasped, as if the very source of my life had been stolen away from me.

"You're mine, Eve," he said, his voice as rough and demanding as his kiss. "You don't belong to any other man but me. You are *mine*."

"I am, Master," I breathed. "Yours."

What other answer could there be?

5.

"Mine," Savage repeated, his breath warm on the skin beneath my ear. "Never forget it, either."

I closed my eyes, relishing the pressure of his body against mine.

"Let me prove it to you, Master," I whispered. I slipped one hand between us to find his cock. He was enormous in his trousers, straining against the confining fabric, and there was no mistaking the heat and power of his erection beneath my hand. Daring, I blindly found the first button on his fly and unfastened it.

"As soon as we reach your house, Master, I'll—"

"No." At once he seized my wrist, his grasp like a vise. He drew back just far enough to see my face, and for me to see his. The slightest of smiles played on his sensually full lips. His silvery-gray eyes were half-closed and unfathomable, and yet I could have gazed into them forever.

"You will prove it, Eve," he said. "But not later. Now."

"Now?" I repeated, breathless with both surprise and excitement. Each time one of the horses moved in the stalls around us, I imagined a groom or stableboy coming to find us. "Here?"

"Here," Savage said. Along the edge of the stall ran a small ledge where grooms could lay brushes or bits of tack, and without warning he grabbed me by my waist and lifted me up to set my bottom on the ledge. I felt like a piece of porcelain placed precariously on a shelf, and I flailed my hands to find my balance and keep from falling.

"Hold me," he ordered gruffly. "You're exactly where I want you, and I won't let you fall."

"But what if . . . if we are interrupted?" I asked, and even as I asked I realized that the idea of a witness excited me. "What if one of the grooms sees us?"

"What he will see is that you are with me," Savage said, his voice gruffly imperious. "That is all that matters."

I nodded, accepting. It was all that mattered. I looped my arms around his shoulders and felt instantly more steady. He'd become my rock that way, my anchor, and fresh desire replaced my first uneasiness. We were nearly eye to eye now, and I leaned forward to offer him my mouth again.

But he'd other ideas. He grabbed a fistful of my habit's skirts and swept them back over my legs. He grunted with purely male approval at what he'd discovered, and I smiled.

"It's not my Innocent's costume, Master," I said. That had been a wisp of a garment, a plain white shift that had been nearly transparent, worn with nothing beneath it.

"It's not what ladies wear for riding, either," he said, his gaze still focused on my legs in black silk stockings and laced riding boots with curving heels.

"It's what I wear for riding with you, Master," I said. "Does it please you?"

He grunted again, cupping one of my knees in his hand, his palm sliding across the slippery silk.

"It does please me," he said. "Very much."

Beneath my severe habit, my garters were red silk with silver clasps. Instead of my usual white linen undergarments I'd worn black silk drawers edged with wide bands of black lace at the knees and trimmed with red ribbon rosettes—the kind of drawers usually reserved for a ball gown or, more likely, for an evening that began and ended in the bedroom. While I'd shocked Hamlin by my choice, I cared only for Savage's opinion, not that of my maid. The long slit that separated the drawers' legs was meant for ordinary convenience, but I knew now it would be put to another purpose.

He hooked his hand beneath my thigh and wrapped my leg around his waist. I rocked back on the ledge and lifted my second leg myself, crossing my ankles around his back. With my thighs raised and parted, the open slit in my drawers separated, revealing the white skin of my belly and the dark hair below, and my quim rosy and weeping with arousal.

"That's how I like you, Eve," he rasped, tearing at the buttons on his trousers. "Always ready for me."

I whimpered as he ran the ridge of his finger between my nether lips and unerringly found my pearl. He dipped deeper into my cunt to gather more of my essence, gliding over the little nub in teasing small circles. I heard my lubricious wetness and the slippery sound of his fingers moving over me. I sucked in my breath and instinctively lifted my hips to meet his touch.

I felt the blunt heat of his erection bump against the bare skin of my upper thigh, and I held my breath in anticipation. I knew what was coming, and I wanted it as much as I'd ever wanted anything.

He pressed the engorged head of his cock to my opening and pushed. I felt my passage giving way for him, opening to accommodate his thickness. His dark hair slipped forward over his brow and his nostrils flared, and I glimpsed the same possessive fury that he'd shown towards the baron. It excited me, that fury. How could it not, when Savage wanted me that much?

He tightened his hold on my hips and bent his knees for a better angle, then thrust hard.

I gasped with both the force of him and the heat, my back bumping against the rough boards behind me. Because I was constricted by my corset I seemed to feel his cock filling me more snugly, more completely, as if my entire core had tightened around him.

He felt it, too, swearing under his breath and into my hair. I curled my legs higher over his back to take him deeper and ride him as if he were another horse beneath me. He drove into me with quick, powerful strokes, and I gasped each time, unable to keep quiet despite the risk of being discovered.

I didn't care, nor did he. He finished each stroke with an upward jab that dragged over my pearl, his balls slapping hard against my outer sex. The tension building within me was overwhelming, and my fingers dug into his shoulders and I crossed my ankles high across his back.

"That's what I want from you, Eve," he growled, nipping at the side of my neck like a stallion with a mare. "Fuck me, and give me what I want."

I was desperate to take every inch of him, just as he was desperate to possess me. I glanced down to where we were joined, fascinated. In sharp contrast to my white thighs, his cock was fiercely red, glistening with my juices as he drew out almost to the purplish head before pounding back into me.

The fire was burning inside me now, and I felt every muscle tense and beg for release. Helpless, I quivered on the edge and arched and twisted against him. His eyes were unfocused, his features tense as he drove us both harder, faster, hotter.

Abruptly he bowed his head and pressed his face against my shoulder and into my tousled hair. His breathing was harsh, his body jerking hard, and I knew he was as close as I was myself. I spread my legs wider, and he ground against my wet, open sex in a way that sent an extra spark of pressure against my pearl. That was enough to send me over the edge, spiraling into the flames of my climax along with him.

My head fell back against the stable wall, my breath still coming in gasps. My fingers loosed their grasp on his shoulders, and although I kept my thighs clasped tightly around his waist, my thighs felt heavy and my muscles trembled. Yet I was unwilling to break our joining or the magic of it a moment sooner than I must.

I closed my eyes, spent and limp. Savage often reduced me to this, an overwhelming sense of bliss and exhaustion.

"Eve." His lips brushed against my cheekbone, and I dragged my heavy eyes open. His own breathing was still ragged and sweat gleamed on his forehead. His pupils were round and black, making his pale eyes uncharacteristically dark and unfathomable.

Yet with his climax his face had altered subtly. His angular features hadn't exactly softened—I doubt there was any power that could make that happen—but there was something near to contentment, and the merest hint of vulnerability. It was the only time he ever let down his guard to show me this side of him, and I relished it, knowing how rare and fleeting it was.

"Master," I murmured softly, the only reply that was necessary and likely all I could sensibly make.

"*That* is why I will never share you with any other man," he said, his own voice rough and low and confidential. "You see how it is, Eve, how it must be. You are meant to be mine, and no one else's."

I smiled. Of course I was his. How could he ever doubt it? Happiness glowed within me and made me blush with contentment.

He kissed me again, a languid, leisurely kiss as he flexed his cock one last time within me, just enough to make me catch my breath and suck his tongue deeper against mine. My eyes fluttered shut again, the better to let my other senses savor him. I loved his taste and his scent, both so unabashedly male that I'd never tire of either. I was now aware of the distant voices of the grooms and stableboys in the yard and the soft snuffling and stamping of the horses in the neighboring stalls. I reached up to slide my fingers into Savage's hair, as black and sleek as a raven's wing, and frame his face with my palms as we kissed.

He slicked his tongue one last time over my lips and eased away. I opened my eyes in time to see his cock slide from me—turgid now but still impressive—before he tucked it into his trousers. I always hated this moment, when we ceased to be one and he again became separate from me—and became the distant Savage who kept his secrets locked tight within him.

I slipped from the ledge and smoothed my skirts over my petticoats. Joyless, sensible black wool smothered and covered me once again, even as Savage's seed remained in a sticky trickle between my thighs. This time he hadn't offered me his handkerchief, and while I could have employed my own, I chose not to. At least I'd that small part of him still.

My legs were unsteady beneath me, and I had to lean back against the ledge for support as I watched him briskly putting his own clothes to rights. I knew I should begin to do the same, yet all I did was watch him, my arms hanging empty at my sides.

How could I long so desperately for him while he . . . he did not long for me? It was as if I were no longer there or, even worse, I no longer mattered.

"Don't leave me, Savage," I pleaded softly. "Please."

He paused and looked at me with surprise.

"I've already asked you to return to my home with me," he said, all reason. "What would now make you believe I would abandon you here?"

I shook my head, unable to put my uneasiness into words that would not sound foolish. Perhaps it *was* foolish, and that was my real trouble. Hadn't I left New York for London to prove my independence?

Savage closed the space between us. He cradled my jaw in his hand and turned my face back up towards his. His fingers were warm and sure against my cheek, and I found even that small touch to be electric.

"Oh, Eve, Eve," he said softly. "What must I do to make you trust me?"

"That . . . that isn't so, Master," I whispered. Fearful of what he might see in my face, I wanted to look away from his hooded, silvery eyes, but the way he was holding my face made it impossible. "I do trust you, in all things. I *must* trust you."

"Exactly so." His mouth curved in the slightest of smiles, surprising me by its boyishness. "For this week, you are mine, and in return I promised to make that time . . . memorable. We agreed before we left Wrenton, yes?"

I nodded, not trusting my voice. A week together was

all he promised. Only a week, and the first day was already nearly done.

Only six days left.

His grip on my jaw had relaxed. I rubbed my cheek lightly against his palm, turning his touch into a caress.

He noticed and smiled again.

"I fully intend to keep my part of the bargain," he continued, "and I can only hope you will likewise keep yours. Of course, if you are unhappy, you may leave. I will not keep you against your will. Perhaps I flatter myself believing that you are here by choice, not by—"

"Nothing could make me leave you now, Master," I said fiercely. "Nothing."

He turned his head slightly, appraising me. "No other man?"

"There is no other man than you," I declared with breathy urgency. "There couldn't be."

"You are sure of this?" His hair was still tousled around his face, a bit of unruly imperfection in his usually impeccable appearance. "You are certain?"

My thoughts flew back to his earlier confrontation in the stable yard with Lord Blackledge. How a man like Savage could possibly feel threatened by a bully like the baron was beyond me. Like any woman with a breath of sanity, I would never involve myself with Blackledge.

Yet I couldn't tell if Savage was testing me now or if he truly feared he'd a rival.

He shouldn't, because he didn't.

"There could never be any other man but you, Master," I said firmly. "Not now, not forever."

He raised a single dark brow. "Forever is a very long time, Eve."

"It is," I agreed. "But it still would not begin to be enough for my time with you, Master."

Without shifting my gaze from his I turned my face into his hand and first kissed his palm, then nipped at it, my teeth finding the fleshy part of his open hand.

He didn't flinch, but fresh desire—and amusement—flashed in his eyes. He ran his other hand in a purposeful caress along my throat, over my breast and waist, and finally cupped his fingers over my sex. The gesture was muted by the layers of my habit, but it was still arousingly possessive, enough to make me catch my breath.

"And that, Eve," he said, his voice seductively low, "is precisely why you are so irresistible to me. Now come; it's time I took you to a setting more worthy of your beauty than a stable."

I repinned the tangle of my hair and retrieved my hat, my gloves, my crop. I pulled the black veil low over my face, shadowing whatever sin might show in my eyes. Sin, yes, and still-simmering excitement, but no shame. As I strolled across the stable yard beside Savage I kept my head high and shoulders back, chatting amicably with him about the pleasant weather.

To my relief, there was no sign of Blackledge, nor any of the cavalrymen who had fueled Savage's earlier jealousy. Or perhaps that, too, had only been part of the game that Savage was playing with me ever since we'd arrived in London. I couldn't always tell with him, nor, really, did I care.

Savage even paused to speak to the stable master about one of his horses. I waited beside him with my hand looped informally through the crook of his arm, for all the world as if the animal had been our true reason for visiting the stables. Likely any passersby would think we were a lady and gentleman who had just met over tea, instead of fucked each other mindless in a horse's stall.

It was easy for me to pretend, too. None of it felt real: not the other riders with their horses and carriages, not the stableboys and grooms, not the late-afternoon sun slanting through the trees and over the shingled roofs and chimney pots.

Savage alone had become my reality. *For a week,* I reminded myself. For *this* week, and I curled my fingers a little more tightly into his arm.

I expected his driver and the cream-colored Rolls-Royce to be waiting for us along the street outside the stable, but instead Savage led me to a dark-blue carriage drawn by a perfectly matched team of grays. As elegant as the carriage was, it was also slightly old-fashioned; I'd already given up my carriage in New York years ago in favor of a motorcar.

Yet I couldn't deny the pleasure of having the liveried footman open the carriage door and the little folding step for me, or the fact that that door itself was painted with Savage's family crest, picked out in gold and silver. His family had been part of the nobility for hundreds of years, and while my father's money had bought me every luxury, it couldn't begin to purchase the air of long-standing grandeur that the crest represented. I was impressed and more than a little awed as I slid across the leather cushion.

Savage joined me, and as soon as the door was closed after us he rested his gloved hand on my knee and let his fingers press along the inside of my thigh through my skirts. That was all: a simple mark of possession, and one that made my heart beat faster.

"I trust traveling by carriage is not too grave an affront to your modern American sensibilities," he said as the carriage rolled forward. "Motorcars are useful in the country, but I still prefer a carriage in town. As I have told you before, I am at heart an old soul, and I resist the harsher indignities that the twentieth century finds necessary."

I smiled, pleased that he'd continued his conversational manner now that we were once again alone together. It wasn't that I didn't wish to let him be my Master—far from it—but I was also fascinated by Savage as a man. I'd already learned that he was intensely private about his own affairs and that he volunteered next to nothing of himself. There had been only a few times when he'd relaxed enough to speak of his past and his interests, and I recognized the rare trust that such confidences displayed.

"London isn't New York," I said, turning back my veil over the brim of my hat. "New York has to have everything that's new because it doesn't have anything old, the way London does. My father always said that was the way America succeeded, by always looking forward and never back."

He turned on the seat to look at me more directly, his pale eyes filled with genuine interest. "Do you believe that as well, Eve?"

"I do," I said, my cheeks warming beneath his scrutiny. "My father was a clever man. He could look forward and anticipate what people would want. That was how he became a rich man, you see: providing things that people didn't realize they desperately wanted until he offered them to them."

"Like railroads?"

"Railroads, yes," I said. "But Father invested in all sorts of other things, like electrical iceboxes and ovens and new kinds of motors. I remember once seeing a new kind of waterproof shoe on his desk that he was considering as an investment."

"A waterproof shoe," Savage repeated, bemused. "So he shared such marvels with you?"

"Oh, no." I was unable to keep the old regrets from my voice. "I was only a girl. A disappointment. I learned of what he did from overhearing his conversations. If I'd been a son, I would have been taken into his confidence and into his business, but being a girl . . . no."

He frowned a little, as if I'd said something especially worth considering. "Yet you speak of your father far more than you do of your husband."

I shook my head, not exactly denying his statement but not quite agreeing, either.

"The only real reason I married my husband was because Father wanted me to." I smoothed the backs of my gloves, smoothing away my wretched marriage at the same time. "But both of them are gone now, so none of it matters any longer. I'm left as the dutiful daughter and widow."

I made a tight little smile, trying to make light of what I now recognized as the greatest mistake of my life. I'd been so young, and Mr. Hart—it had taken two years of marriage before I could bring myself to call him by his given name—had been kind enough, if utterly disinterested in being more than a perfunctory husband to his sixteen-year-old bride.

But if I hadn't married Arthur Hart, I would not now be his widow and, much more important, I would not be sitting in a carriage with the Earl of Savage, his hand on my thigh as I prattled on and on.

"That was no doubt much more than you wished to hear," I said ruefully. Here I'd thought I'd learn more about Savage, and instead I'd only run on about myself. "I'm sorry to be so tedious."

"You're far from tedious, Eve," he said softly. "I've told you that before. I wish to learn everything about you."

I twisted to face him. "But you see that is how I feel about you, too, and yet I—"

"Oh, I am not very interesting at all," he said with a careless shrug. "I am much the same as my father, and his father, and all his fathers before that. Your family may delight in change, but mine never has."

"You *are* interesting to me," I insisted. "That same family that you say is so boring must be fascinating. You're an English earl, a peer of the realm. How could that be dull? I am certain there were no waterproof boots in your father's desk."

He smiled. "Not once."

"Then tell me what was on his desk," I begged. "Tell me of what you did as a boy, and where you went to school and on holidays. I wish to know *everything*. Tell me about your parents, and if you've any brothers or sisters, and your own son, too."

Instantly his face shuttered against me and his smile vanished. Too late I realized I'd overstepped.

"I told you, Eve," he said brusquely. "My life is of no interest to anyone, especially not to you. We've arrived."

He turned away from me and towards the window as the carriage slowed. I was left to wonder how—and how badly—I'd misstepped. Once he'd confided to me the nightmarish details of his young wife's death. What I'd asked now hadn't seemed anywhere as personal as what he'd volunteered. Had I been too inquisitive? Had my questions about his family somehow offended him?

The carriage door opened, and he stepped out first and turned to hand me down. It was a courtly, old-fashioned gesture, one that had been lost with motorcars. It was also unexpectedly romantic, having him hold my hand like that as if I were a dainty, helpless creature instead of a modern American woman. I liked it.

"This is my house," he said, pausing for a moment to

let me consider the façade. Still holding his hand, I dutifully gazed upward.

By New York standards, the house would not have merited much notice and would, in fact, have been completely overlooked among the mansions that lined Fifth Avenue. But I had been in London long enough to understand that things were measured differently in England and that Savage's house here on St. James's Square was, in fact, very grand indeed.

The house was four stories tall and faced in pale stone, with three large, long windows on each floor. I knew enough of architectural fancies to see that the house was meant to have the air of an Italian villa, with an imposing front entrance and massive carved stonework around it. Each of the windows on the upper floors had its own balcony overlooking the Square. The final floor was more of an attic, with elaborately carved swags framing smaller windows, and a heavy overhanging cornice with brackets added a solemn finish to the house's façade.

As town houses went, it was much like Savage himself: tall, elegant, and aristocratic. It was also outwardly a little forbidding, like Savage was at this moment. How was it that I could physically so completely belong to him, as we'd been in the stable, and yet because I'd impulsively asked about his family he'd once again retreated into this icy, noble-bred gentleman?

It made no sense to me. He wanted me to trust him, yet he seemed incapable of trusting me. If I was going to spend this week with him as my master, I was determined to thaw that chill. He had not released my hand after helping me from the carriage, and I took advantage of that now, daring to curl my fingers into his.

Lightly I rubbed my thumb against his palm, mimicking how I'd licked and nipped at the same place earlier. I regretted that our gloves would mute the sensation, but in an odd way the soft leather seemed to enhance it, skin against skin. In public, on the pavement before his house with his servants all around us, that was all even I could risk, but I hoped he'd understand.

He did.

He glanced down at our joined hands, and his mouth curled in the merest hint of a smile.

"It would appear you wish to retreat indoors, Mrs. Hart," he said. "Is that so?"

"Yes, my lord," I murmured, looking up at him from beneath the brim of my hat. "If you wish it as well."

He grunted with amusement and together we climbed the short stone steps and entered the house past the bowing footman and butler. Apparently the servants had been told to expect me, for I was greeted by name, which also made me smile. Savage could be a most thoughtful man.

As he handed his hat and gloves to the footman I gazed around me, looking for more clues to Savage's tastes and interests. The front hall of the house was every bit as grand as the façade, two stories high with a floor patterned in a checkerboard of black and white marble, a sweeping staircase of white marble, and a life-size dark bronze statue of Mars on the newel. Portraits of Savage's ancestors hung in heavy gold frames in a somber parade along the walls and up the stairs. The only bright spot of color came from a large vase of bright yellow flowers in an equally bright Chinese porcelain vase, sitting in the arched alcove of the landing.

"We'll dine upstairs in the front parlor, Mrs. Hart,"

Savage said, playing the agreeable host. I liked how he used my formal name before others and only called me Eve, the diminutive he'd coined, when we were alone. It made it more private, more illicit. "No doubt you'll wish to change from your riding clothes first. I'll show you to your room myself."

He placed his hand on the back of my waist and guided me up the curving staircase.

I hadn't brought any other clothes with me, but I knew better than to mention it. No doubt he already had a special dress waiting for me, something like the Innocent's costume I'd worn at Wrenton, and I wondered how revealing it would be. The one thing I'd taken care to bring with me was the long, costly strand of pearls he'd given me, worn for safekeeping beneath my habit. No matter what he expected me to wear (or not wear), the pearls, as always, would be appropriate.

I'd removed my gloves now, too, and I trailed my fingers along the polished mahogany banister as we climbed the stairs. Then I stopped and stared, leaning a fraction over the banister.

I'd been too preoccupied with Savage himself until this moment to realize one of the most startling aspects of Savage's town house. While it appeared to have been modernized with the glass globes of gas fixtures, the hall was instead lit by candles in the wall sconces and in the chandelier that was now eye level with us on the stairs. At least two dozen little flames danced and bobbed on the wax tapers in the chandelier, their light sparkling through the crystal drops. I leaned forward over the rail, fascinated by the sight.

"I've told you before I don't like modern lighting," he explained, following my gaze. "My father had installed gaslight, but I refused to use it. There is electricity below stairs, of course. I won't make the servants follow my ways, particularly in the kitchen, but upstairs it's how I prefer it. Nothing flatters beauty like candlelight, or destroys it like a greenish gas jet or electrical bulb."

I nodded, remembering how he'd insisted that his rooms at Wrenton be lit only by candles, too. He had had candles placed all around his bedroom, and we'd cast all kinds of wanton, shameless shadows against the walls until, one by one, they'd guttered out and we'd finally fallen asleep, exhausted. He was right: while not as efficient, candlelight was far warmer and more seductive than any modern lamps, and I realized that I now associated it entirely with him.

He must have guessed my thoughts, too, from the suggestive smile playing over his lips. His hand circled around my waist and he held me tight so I was pressed tightly against his chest and his lips were beside my ear. Together we were leaning over the banister, the black-and-white marble floor far below.

"You like candlelight, too, don't you, Eve?" he whispered, his words warm against the side of my throat. "You're remembering what we did together by its glow, aren't you? How the flames of those candles around my bed were nothing compared to the fire I found in your sweet quim, a fire that only my cock could quell?"

"Yes, Master," I breathed, remembering exactly as he'd wanted me to. "Oh, yes."

His grip around my waist tightened, holding me fast as he leaned me a little farther over the banister. The black-and-white floor below combined with the bright flames was a dizzying sight—or perhaps it was simply his nearness that was making it all spin before me. I closed my eyes, focusing on him.

"If you obey me tonight, Eve," he continued, "then I will make certain you'll have even more to remember. Much more. Would you like that?"

"Y-y-yes," I stammered. "Yes, Master, I would."

"Then come with me now," he said, shifting away from the banister and from me. I straightened, intending to follow him, but my head was still spinning, and instead I swayed back towards the long staircase of marble steps. Terrified of falling, I gasped and flailed my arms, searching for the banister to support myself.

At once he caught me, drawing me back from the edge of the steps and the banister.

"There now, Eve, you're safe; you're safe," he said, his voice soothing as he folded his arms around me. "I'd never let any harm come to you."

I felt foolish now, certain I'd overreacted. Yet I made no effort to move away from him, resting my face against his chest.

"I'm fine," I lied, still shaking. "Truly. It has been a long day, and I—I suppose I am a bit weary, and felt dizzy, and—"

"You needn't explain," he said, carefully leading me up the last few steps to the landing. "Not to me. I'm sure you'll feel much better once you've dined and changed from your corset into something less confining."

I blushed at the mention of my corset. It made no sense, I know, to blush over him mentioning my unmentionables after all the other intimacies we'd shared, especially when he was likely right.

"I'm sorry," I said again, and he placed his fingers gently over my lips to silence me.

"We'll speak no more of it," he said firmly. "Here is a room where you may undress, and rest, if you wish."

"Where are your rooms?" I asked. That was much

more important to me. If I'd wanted my own company, I would have remained at the Savoy.

"Across the hall," he said. "Would you like me to send for one of the maids to—"

"I'll manage for myself," I said quickly. I could undress easily enough; it was dressing once again that was more of a challenge, but I would worry about that later. "Truly. I'm quite well now."

I eased myself away from him to prove it, though I rested my hand along the back of a nearby armchair just to be sure. This was clearly a bedroom for a special guest, with exquisite white furnishings trimmed with gold. A plush Aubusson carpet covered the floor, and the curtains at the window and on the bed were a deep-blue velvet, edged with more gold braid.

But there was no doubt that the room was meant for me. A short, filmy shift of white silk, much like the one I'd worn as an Innocent at Wrenton, had been laid across the bed, waiting. Beside it was a simple long robe of red silk satin, which I guessed was also intended for me.

"A glass of wine, then, to restore yourself." He went striding across the room to the sideboard, filled a glass halfway from the decanter, and brought it back to me. I was touched by the genuine concern in his eyes, his brows drawn together with uncharacteristic worry. "Drink it, and no excuses."

"Yes, my lord," I said, dutifully drinking what he'd offered me and setting the glass down on a nearby table. I felt the wine's effects almost instantly, warming and relaxing me from within, and I smiled at him. "You see I'm quite myself again."

He wasn't convinced. "You're pale."

"I'm supposed to be." I pulled the pins from my hat,

lifted it from my head, and tossed it onto the chair. "I'm a lady."

He didn't answer at first, and when he did speak he surprised me.

"You're a lady who has become important to me," he said gruffly. "I told you that before. I do not wish any harm to come to you."

I realized how difficult it must have been for him to say that. It was just as difficult for me to answer.

"I feel the same regard for you," I said softly.

"'Regard,'" he repeated, and smiled wryly—from amusement, chagrin, or because he'd expected another, more passionate word from me?

I blushed and looked down, confused. I was still new at these games that were so familiar to him, and there were times I said or did the wrong thing. "I'm sorry if I—"

"No, no, I'm the one who must apologize, Evelyn," he said. "What happened to you just now is entirely my fault, and regrettable. I understand that now. I expected too much of you this afternoon."

"But you didn't," I said swiftly, wondering how he'd misunderstood so completely. And he'd used my full name, which was not a good sign. "Not at all."

I came to stand close before him, jerking the pins from my hair and scattering them on the floor where they fell. When all the pins were gone, I raked my fingers through my hair so that it fell over my shoulders and down my back in a dark, glossy tangle. He'd always said he preferred it that way, that it reminded him of a wild wood nymph. I shook my hair again, my gaze locked with his.

I had his attention now, and I was quite sure there'd be no further apologies.

"Go on, Eve," he said, his voice low and gravelly. "Continue. Do not stop."

Without looking away I began to unfasten the long row of tiny covered buttons that closed my bodice. There was a rhythm to it, my fingers slipping each rounded ball of a button through the silk loop that held it captive. One by one by one, and not once did Savage's pale eyes blink or look away.

I reached the last button and shrugged my arms free of the bodice, letting it drop to the floor as I had with the hairpins. My corset cover was black silk and lace to match my drawers, with thin red silk ribbons threaded through the lace straps over my shoulders. There was another row of buttons to be undone here, too, an undergarment to slip free and fall.

My corset not only narrowed my waist, but it also plumped my breasts high. Beneath it, my thin linen chemise, edged with lace, did little more than frame my breasts and the shadowy cleft between them.

I'd tucked the pearl necklace that Savage had given me into the front of my corset and between my breasts, to keep it secure while riding. Now I drew the long strand free, the pearls slipping free one by one just as the buttons had earlier. The pearls were warm with the heat of my body, as if they were living things themselves.

"You wore the pearls," he said, clearly pleased. "I didn't realize it."

"Of course I wore them, Master." I let the strand drop, where it swung gently nearly to my waist. "They were a gift from you."

"Because you're mine," he said, explaining the obvious.

He caught the necklace in one hand and slowly began to wrap it around his fingers. The pearls clicked softly together, and with each loop the strand grew more taut, reeling me in until finally I'd no choice but to take another step closer, leaning into him. He closed the remaining gap and sealed his mouth over mine, kissing me with a hungry fury.

My hands remained at my sides, my fingers fanning out without touching him, and my eyes were closed to concentrate on his kiss. Yet even so I could feel the growing tension of desire in his body from how tightly he was pulling on the necklace and how the pearls were now pressing into the nape of my neck.

He was fucking me with his mouth, possessing me with his tongue, fast and forceful, and I greedily opened my mouth wider to suck him in. The more I wanted, the more *he* wanted, too.

My whole being was so intent on his mouth and his tongue and the giddy pleasure he was drawing from me that I didn't hear the interruption behind us. I don't think I would have stopped kissing him even if I had.

But Savage heard it and abruptly broke away, releasing the necklace to swing heavily against my chest.

"What the devil is it, Barry?" he demanded, wheeling around. "What do you want?"

Mr. Barry was his manservant, and Savage trusted him completely. I'd met Barry briefly at Wrenton, and likely he was the only servant on the staff who would dare interrupt his master like this. Even so, from the fury on Savage's face I hoped for Barry's sake that he'd a very good reason for coming into the bedroom at this moment.

"There is news, my lord," Barry said evenly. "A messenger has just arrived, and—"

"I'll come," Savage said curtly. He turned back to me, his mouth taut and his expression stormy. "Eve, dress yourself for dinner as we discussed. I'll return as soon as I can. Be here for me when I do."

Before I could answer he'd stormed from the room. Barry nodded to me and silently closed the door.

Slowly I sat on the bed beside the silk shift Savage had chosen for me. I'd wear it, of course, because he wanted me to but also because I'd nothing else to do.

I was left alone with my questions, and they were not good company.

6.

As Savage had asked (or had he ordered?), I shed my heavy riding habit and all the other layers of lace, linen, and silk beneath. I felt instantly lightened and grateful to be free of the confines of my clothing. I'd always enjoyed dressing fashionably and indulging in every new Parisian style, but from Savage I'd learned to appreciate my body as it was, without tight lacing to alter it to Society's view of beauty.

There was a small but luxurious bathroom connected to the bedroom, and I washed myself before I slipped into the silk shift that had been left for me. The silk slid lightly over my naked body like a whisper, exactly the way my Innocent's costume had done at Wrenton. I looped the necklace back around my neck, and the pearls settled familiarly across my breasts, brushing across my nipples just enough to make them tingle and stiffen.

I moved quickly, not knowing how long Savage would be away, and I didn't want him to find me not ready when he returned. I could only guess as to what I needed to be ready *for*—with Savage I never knew—but ready I would be.

I took one last look at myself in the tall dressing mirror,

imagining how he would see me. The shift was short, barely reaching to the middle of my thighs. The silk was so sheer that it was clear I wore nothing beneath it. My nipples were ruddy and pointed through it, and the dark curls low on my belly were a shadowy triangle.

When I'd first worn a similar costume last week (was it really such a short time ago?), I'd been ashamed to be so brazen, and unable to confront my own reflection. Now I boldly tossed my hair back over my shoulders, proud of my body and the pleasure to be discovered in it. Savage had given me that gift as my lover, and I would never be able to thank him enough for it.

I glanced at the clock, wondering yet again when he would return. He'd been gone forty-five minutes, and the time that had raced as I'd undressed now seemed to drag. Dusk was settling, and when I stepped to the window and pushed back the curtain I could see that the streetlights that ringed St. James's Square were already lit.

But there was more to see, too. A hackney cab was waiting at the curb before the house. As I watched, a man hurried from the house and climbed into the cab. The driver cracked his whip over the horse's back, and they quickly sped away. From the angle of the window, I could not see the man's face, hidden by the brim of his hat, but he had been well dressed, like a gentleman. His haste had given him an air of purpose, as if he was rushing off on a specific errand rather than leaving after a social call.

I frowned, thinking. It was clear that the gentleman must have met with Savage and likely was the "messenger" Barry had mentioned when he'd interrupted us. But what could have been the reason for such a meeting? Savage had left me as quickly as this man had in turn left the house, hinting at some great urgency between them. In fact, Savage had clearly appeared to expect the interruption.

But it made no sense. My father had always maintained that no important business affairs occurred after the noon-day meal. The morning was the time for male business, and besides, I had a difficult time imagining Savage, with his loathing for all things modern, being the same slave to the stock markets and bankers as my father and husband had been.

Nor did Savage need to be. He was unquestionably wealthy, with none of the telltale small signs of an aristocrat foundering on the edge of debt. Although he was a peer with a seat in the House of Lords, he had never mentioned an interest in politics or the workings of government.

Yet Savage had no personal reasons that I could guess for his abrupt behavior, either. His parents and his wife were dead, he had no siblings, and his only son was safely away at school.

There was, of course, the animosity he showed towards Lord Blackledge, but I doubted Savage would plot against the baron with another man. At least I hoped he wouldn't, considering that I'd be the cause of it. But what reasons could Savage have had, then, for this meeting, this urgency?

Still thinking, I let the curtain drop back in place. The bedroom was growing dim, too, and without thinking I went to turn on the light, groping about along the wall near the door where a switch would ordinarily be.

Chagrined, I remembered Savage's insistence on candles and noted how many candlesticks there were in the room. As a child I remembered some of my elderly relatives had had gaslight, but no one in New York lived by candles and I'd no idea how to light them myself. After I'd tied the satin robe over my shift, I rang for a servant.

A maid swiftly appeared, anticipating my request by shielding a lit taper in her hand. I watched her go about the room, lighting each candlestick. I thought that Savage, with his love of beauty, would have employed a charming young maid, but this woman was older, with ginger hair and pitted cheeks, and had clearly been hired for her brusque and near-silent efficiency, as she finished with the candles and drew the curtains, pointedly taking no notice of my state of undress.

She answered all the overtures I made to her with single-syllable replies, perfectly polite but volunteering nothing. I would have prized her if she'd been in one of my own households, but because I wished to learn more of her master (and mine) I now found her taciturn qualities maddening.

"Will that be all, ma'am?" she asked finally when her tasks were finished.

Enough discretion, I decided. I would ask her outright.

"Do you know where His Lordship might be at present?"

"His Lordship is at home, ma'am," she replied succinctly, rubbing her palms on the front of her apron.

I sighed, sensing my questions would accomplish nothing. "I know His Lordship is at home, meaning here beneath this roof. I wish to know where he is within this house."

"I do not know, ma'am," she said uneasily, her gaze darting everywhere but at me. "His Lordship don't tell me of his doings."

I didn't believe she was being stubborn but, rather, acutely literate.

"Very well," I said, determined to try another tack. "When did you last see His Lordship?"

"In the front hall, ma'am, when he arrived with you." She sniffed. "Will that be all, ma'am?"

"You may go." I had no choice, really. I didn't doubt that she was telling the truth. It was clear that Savage, who treasured his privacy as much as any man I'd ever known, expected his staff to do the same.

But there would be one servant who would know, and that would be Barry. I waited another moment or two after the maid had left me, tightened the sash of my robe, and then opened the door to my bedroom. Savage had said his rooms were directly across from mine, and resolutely I crossed the hallway, my bare feet sinking into the thick Persian carpet.

There were no footmen standing beside the bedroom doors to open them, as was often the case in grand houses, and I was glad of it, and not having to explain my intentions. In fact, the door that I guessed must lead to Savage's rooms was even ajar, as if he himself would be returning at any moment. For all I knew, he might already be within.

I knocked on the half-opened door, the sound echoing through the empty rooms. All I heard was the muffled sound of a carriage in the street and the ticking of a distant clock.

"Savage?" I called tentatively, pushing the door open farther. The candles had been lit for evening in here, too. Savage might think of them as casting a soft and romantic light, but alone as I was in the unfamiliar house, I was finding their flicker and the shadows they cast a little unsettling.

"Savage?" I called again, a little louder. "Mr. Barry? Are you there?"

Still, no one answered. Slowly I pushed the door open farther and entered the room, a spacious sitting room for a gentleman. A small table was set for our dinner, with two place settings of fine silver, crystal, and china and a large porcelain bowl of white roses. I smiled with anticipation and appreciation, too. It was hard to reconcile the gentleman who would arrange this with the man who'd nearly lost his temper and struck another in a stable yard earlier today. But that contradiction *was* Savage, the most complicated—yet fascinating—man I'd ever known.

There were many other things here that I associated with his varied interests and tastes, too: mahogany furnishings in the style of over a hundred years ago, a pair of cavalry swords crossed on the wall, books strewn everywhere, a small Roman bronze statue of a satyr ravishing a willing nymph, and a life-size painting of an opulently nude Venus over the mantel. Another door, half-open, must surely lead to his bedroom.

But what caught my eye and held it was a smaller painting hung between the two windows, a portrait of a young woman. Unlike everything else in the room, it was modern, and the sitter was stylishly dressed in a burgundy-colored velvet evening gown of a decade ago, not a century.

Drawn by the woman's face, I crossed the room to study the picture more closely. She was undeniably a beauty, with a mass of dark hair piled high over her pale oval face and her slender figure twisting gracefully to display her narrow waist below the exaggerated full sleeves of her gown. Around her throat was a priceless necklace of rubies and diamonds, and in one hand she held a white ostrich plume, the angular brilliance of the precious stones accentuated by the fragile white plume.

Or perhaps it was the lady herself who was most fragile of all. Despite her beauty and her jewels, her eyes seemed a fraction too wide, her lips almost quivering, and her fingers holding the quill of the plume were pinched too tightly together. To me, she looked as terrified as a deer startled by hunters, as if at any moment she must bolt and run away to save her life. It was not the way most ladies would wish themselves to be painted, nor the way that most husbands would want to remember their wives.

For of course she must be Savage's dead wife, Marianne, his doomed countess who had killed herself. She couldn't be anyone else, and I took a step closer, lost in the tragic sadness of her face.

I suppose some women would have been jealous to see a wife's portrait still hanging in a lover's private rooms, but I was not. How could I be, when the madness and suffering she had so obviously endured had only ended with the peace of death?

I stared at the portrait, unable to look away. What could have frightened her so much that it showed so clearly?

There were questions surrounding the death of his wife that were never properly answered . . .

Against my will, I remembered how Laura had wanted to warn me about Savage, repeating the old gossip about Lady Savage's death—all of which, of course, was preposterous lies. I trusted him. But the vulnerability that Lady Savage showed in this painting must have been a powerful attraction for Savage, given how much he liked to protect those he loved.

I smiled ruefully, realizing how I'd unconsciously included myself in that. He'd never once said anything of love, nor had I. It had never seemed to have its place between us. We'd agreed to be lovers without being in love. Having never been in love myself, I wasn't even certain I would recognize the difference.

Yet there was no denying that we were drawn together by more than physical amusement. Earlier he'd called me irresistible, and I felt much the same about him. The sadness and loss that we'd both had in our lives drew us together, and I'd an almost eerie sense that he understood me better than anyone else ever had or perhaps could. I longed to know everything about him, which was why I was intrigued by what I'd found in this room. When we'd left Wrenton, I'd agreed to another week in his company, no more, and I was determined to make as much of that time as I could.

I pulled the robe's sash a little more tightly about my waist, trying to sort through my thoughts about Savage, and myself. It was as if—

"Why are you here, Eve?"

Swiftly I turned around. Savage was standing in the doorway, his hand still on the doorknob.

I smiled with relief, glad he'd joined me. "I'm here to dine with you," I said, holding my hand towards the set table. "As you promised."

"I told you I would rejoin you in your room, not here," he said curtly. "I told you to wait for me there."

My smile faded. He wasn't as happy to see me as I'd been with him. Far from it.

"I'm sorry," I said contritely. "But I didn't see the harm in—"

"In prying?" he asked. Displeasure flashed in his eyes. "Is it the custom for Americans to wander about their host's home, inspecting his most private belongings for their own amusement?"

"I wasn't prying!" I exclaimed. "I simply came to dine with you, by your invitation."

Unconsciously my gaze flicked back to the portrait of his wife. It was only an instant—one guilty instant—but he noticed.

His brows drew together and he lowered his chin, never good signs with him. It wasn't the same fury that he'd shown earlier with Blackledge. This was more a cold, biting disappointment, edged with bitterness.

For me it was worse, because I knew I was the cause. Without a word I realized, too, that we were once again playing the Game, with me as his Innocent.

And now I'd disappointed my Master.

"I do not believe you deserve dinner now, Eve, not after this." He turned his head to call back through the open door. "Barry, here."

Instantly his manservant appeared in the doorway.

"Barry, please send word to the kitchen for Mrs. Wilson to stop her preparations," Savage said. "Mrs. Hart and I will not be dining at present, nor do we wish to be disturbed."

Barry nodded and backed from the room. Savage himself closed the door, turned the key in the old-fashioned lock, and slipped it into the pocket of his trousers. As he did so he watched me, making sure I understood that I would not easily be able to escape, even if I wished to.

Which I didn't, not while he was looking at me like this. His eyes seemed to darken beneath his brows, and the sharp planes in his face were taut and tense. I sensed how much that control cost him, and I sensed, too, where it would lead.

With Savage there was only one way, for all that tension to ultimately be released, nor could I wait.

I smoothed my hair back behind my ears, my breasts shimmying beneath the silk robe as I lifted my arms. Of course he noticed, and I wondered if he could also see how my nipples were tightening beneath his gaze.

I felt the first tendrils of desire curling within me, and this time I glanced expectantly towards the door that led to his bedroom.

He followed my glance and smiled: a tight, tense smile with no humor.

"Not yet, Eve," he said. "In time, perhaps, if it pleases me. But as your Master, it's my responsibility to correct you when you err, such as you have tonight."

"Yes, Master," I said obediently, unable to keep back my smile. I'd learned that Savage's "corrections" often led to a great deal of pleasure. "I have erred, and I deserve your punishment."

He frowned. "Don't be glib, Eve," he said sharply. "And do not try to seduce me, either. You must learn that there will be consequences when you disobey me."

I took a deep breath and lowered my chin. My heart was racing; his tone demanded that I obey. I had never seen him this serious, and I wondered how I'd inadvertently offended him so grievously.

"Yes, Master," I said, my smile gone and my bravado with it.

"Better," he said, the single word curt. "Now remove your clothes."

"But I already—"

"Do not argue with me, Eve," he said sharply. "You'll only make it worse for yourself."

"Yes, Master," I murmured. My hands were trembling, and I fumbled with the bow on my sash. At last I untied it, and I slid the robe from my shoulders. I began to walk towards a nearby chair, intending to drape the robe over it.

"Let it drop," he said. "I don't want you to look away from me. Now your costume. I want nothing in my way."

I nodded, and as I drew the simple shift over my head with a *shush* of silk I surreptitiously licked my lips from nervousness. I thought by now I was accustomed to being naked before him, and certainly it seemed a small thing considering all the other intimacies that we had shared.

But this felt different. There was a flintiness to his manner that brought his mastery to a new level, and I'd no notion of what might come next. He truly *was* my master. All I could do was follow his wishes.

I dropped the shift to the floor, settled the strand of pearls between my breasts, and shook my hair back over my shoulders so he couldn't accuse me of covering myself with it. There had been a time when I would have been too ashamed, too mortified, to be so exposed before a man, but because Savage made my nakedness his choice, not mine, I reveled in it. I was shameless, because that was how he wanted me, and because I was in his power it was thrilling.

Now I stood silently with my hands at my sides, waiting and clenching my bare toes into the plush carpet beneath me as the only outlet I had for my restlessness. I couldn't control how my nipples had pinched into tight little buds, but that could be blamed on the cool evening air. Still, I prayed that my expression was unflinching and that my cheeks weren't flushed and that he wouldn't be able to notice my growing excitement.

His glance raked over me, from my unpinned hair over my breasts and belly and the curls that crowned my mount to my bare legs and feet and back again. I must have passed muster. He nodded, though even by candlelight I saw the little twitch of arousal in the vein on his temple.

Good, I thought. Even if I'd displeased him, he wanted me. No matter what sort of punishment he'd planned, I'd have to remember that.

"Don't move," he ordered.

Methodically he unbuttoned and shed his riding coat

and the waistcoat beneath it, his gaze still locked with mine. He dropped the garments to the floor just as he'd instructed me to do.

His motions grew quicker, as if his very fingers had become impatient while he was looking at me. He pulled the links from his cuffs—the same links I always associated with him, black onyx discs centered with a curling snake with a diamond in its open mouth—and shoved his sleeves back to his elbows. He hooked his finger into the knot of his necktie and pulled it apart, then snapped the black silk through his collar and let it, too, fall to the carpet.

Finally he opened his collar and the top two buttons of his shirt with quick little jerks, but no more. Clearly this would be another instance where I would be exposed to him but not the other way around. He would keep his clothes, and his control, while I was stripped of everything.

A narrow upholstered bench with curving mahogany legs stood before one of the windows. He went to it now and picked it up with both hands, reminding me how effortlessly strong he was for a gentleman. He brought the bench to the middle of the room, about six feet from where I stood, and set it down with a muted thump.

I couldn't help myself from asking, "Whatever are you doing, Master?"

"Making preparations," he said absently, as if it were perfectly obvious. "Not that it is any of your affair at this time."

I didn't dare ask more but watched with growing trepidation as he reached into the pocket of his trousers and withdrew the key that he'd hidden there not ten minutes before. With a little clink of metal on metal he dropped the key in a silver bowl on the mantel.

"Take note of that," he said as he returned to the bench. "I have locked the door to keep us from being disturbed, but if you ever wish to leave this room and this house, you are free to do so."

"But I don't want to leave, Master!" I protested, surprised.

"So you have told me before," he said, squaring the bench with his foot so it aligned with the pattern in the carpet, letting me think that it mattered. "But you've also told me, Eve, that you never want to be my prisoner. I wish to make it clear that you are not. You may leave at any time."

I lowered my chin a stubborn fraction. I thought we'd settled this earlier, but apparently not. Did he doubt me? Had I failed him simply by coming into this room?

"Do you wish me to leave, Master?" I asked, my voice small. "Is that what you want?"

"Not at all," he said, his expression unchanged. "What I want is you, here and now."

I took a deep breath as relief washed over me. He was so good at masking his emotions that I seldom could guess his true feelings.

"But note this caveat, Eve," he continued. "If you ever choose to leave, then we are done. There will be no appeals, no beseeching, no tears, that will change my mind. Quite simply, if you leave, I can never trust you again, because you would have failed to trust me."

Slowly he sat in the middle of the bench, facing me with his long, muscular legs slightly spread. It was a flagrantly male way for him to sit, aggressively displaying his powerful erection beneath his well-tailored trousers. His need for me was written all over his face as well, in every tense muscle along his jaw and in the way his eyes were watching my every breath and move, like a hawk tracking its prey.

Oh, yes, he wanted me, and I felt his desire wash over my skin like a shimmering wave of heat.

"Do you understand, Eve?" he asked softly, his eyes hooded. "Will you trust me?"

"I wouldn't be here if I didn't, Master," I said, perhaps the most true thing I'd ever said.

I held my hand out to him, but instead of taking it he patted the bench beside him.

"Here," he said. "This is where I want you now."

I nodded and joined him, sitting close beside him on the bench. I began to put my arms around his shoulders to kiss him, but instead he took me gently by the arm and laid me across his lap. It was an odd position to be in, facing down at the carpet with my bare breasts pressed into the side of his thigh and the pearls hanging from my neck to the floor. My bottom arched over his other leg, with my own legs resting stiffly across the bench.

"This . . . this is strange, Master," I said, shifting uneasily. The wool of his trousers prickled against my skin, but much more unsettling was the hard length of his erect cock, pressing unmistakably against my hip. "I do not think—"

"I don't want you to think, Eve," he said, his voice low and seductive as he adjusted me to his liking. "I wish you only to feel."

I tried to do as he bid, and let out the breath that I realized I'd been holding in uncertainty. He'd asked me to do that before, and I'd only benefited. I told myself that this would be no different.

He smoothed my long hair to fall along one side of my face so that my entire back was exposed to him. He ran his palm along my spine, from the nape of my neck to the cleft of my bottom, and back again.

"Be easy, Eve; relax," he said softly. "Trust me. That's

all I ask of you, and in return I believe you'll be pleasantly surprised."

It felt good, that long caress, especially after wearing the heavy riding habit and corset. With his thumbs he kneaded the tension from my shoulders, and I automatically stretched across his knees and arched my back like a cat, and the small *hmmm* of contentment in my throat might even have been a purr.

He chuckled and repeated the long strokes. His hands dipped low along my ribs and over the sides of my breasts, and I shifted restlessly at the unfamiliar angle. He saw it and reached lower to scoop up the globes of my breasts to fill his hands. Lightly he squeezed and tugged my nipples to draw them out until they tingled and ached for more, and I moaned shamelessly in response. I began to twist around on his knees so I could free his cock from its trouser prison, but he pushed me back down with his hand on the small of my back.

"This is for you, Eve," he said. "I want to watch you respond as I give you pleasure."

"Then you've succeeded, Master," I said breathlessly, my voice muffled by hair. "You always please me."

He grunted, and his strong, knowing hands moved to my buttocks. Lightly he squeezed and massaged each cheek, lifting and caressing the flesh.

"You have the most beautiful ass, Eve," he said. "I don't think I'll ever tire of it."

How could he find my bottom beautiful? It was the one part of my body that was undeniably plump in proportion to the rest of me, and I'd always been grateful for full skirts that masked it.

Unsure of whether he was teasing me or not, I craned my neck to try to see his face. "That's a peculiar compliment, Master."

"Not at all," he said, continuing to stroke the full curves raised up before him. "Your ass is worthy of Venus herself. You are pure decadence, Eve, all for me to enjoy."

No matter what foolishness he was saying, his actions were having their effect on me. Liquid heat coursed through me, making my breath catch in my chest. Almost without thinking I spread my legs in blatant invitation.

"Greedy creature," he said. "I'd wager fifty pounds that if I touch your cunt, you'll be wet."

"Oh, Master," I said breathlessly. "That is not a wager I would take."

"No, I expect you wouldn't," he said. His fingers slipped lower, over the delicate little crease where my thigh met my buttock. He followed it higher and traced the crease slowly to prolong my sweet torment. With his other hand he pushed my thighs more widely apart and at last pressed one long finger into my slit.

I *was* wet, exactly as we'd both known I would be.

"Soaking," he said with satisfaction. "It's as if you hadn't spent at all this afternoon in the stable, yet I know you did."

"I . . . I cannot help it, Master," I said, which was true, but I also knew how much he liked hearing that from me. "Not when you . . . you do that."

"Or this?" His finger slid easily back and forth within my passage, so easily that he added a second beside it.

I could hear the sound of his finger stirring my juices, moist proof of his undeniable effect upon me. Even two of his fingers were a sad substitute for his cock, but they were better than nothing. Instinctively I tried to rock my hips to find a rhythm against them, but he held me firm with his other hand pressing my ass to make me lie still.

"No, Eve," he said firmly. "Not yet. Not like that. Not until I say it's time."

I whimpered plaintively. "But I cannot—"

"You can," he said patiently. "You must. It will be much better for you if you do."

I struggled not to move, my fingers gripping the carved edge of the bench from the effort. He'd drawn his fingers from my quim and slid the moisture he'd gathered from my passage over my outer sex. He parted my now-slippery lips and circled the pad of his thumb over my pearl with just the right maddening pressure.

My breath had become a series of shuddering sighs, my body tensing as the delicious pressure built inside me. When he eased his fingers back inside me, keeping his thumb on my pearl, I felt my pleasure cresting higher and higher, and I could no longer keep from rocking my hips up toward his hand.

"No, Eve," he repeated, raising his hand from my body. "Not yet."

I moaned with frustration, twisting across his lap and pressing my hip against his cock. He must have felt it as a kind of caress; that was what I wanted, to torment him the same way he was doing with me.

Yet he must have viewed it as something else entirely. Swiftly he lifted his fingers from between my legs. He raised his hand, and before I realized what was happening he'd slapped my left cheek: a quick, hard, stinging smack with his open palm.

I gasped with shock and tried to pull away, but he held me fast across his lap.

"What are you doing?" I cried, panicking. "No one has ever hit me, not once in my life. Father never permitted it."

"Your father isn't here, is he?" he said, his voice low and seductive, as if the very Devil himself were reasoning with me. "You wouldn't wish him to be. And this isn't hitting, not the way you mean it."

Part of me had already realized that. As soon as he'd spanked me he'd immediately placed his palm over the cheek he'd just slapped, gently stroking the same spot. It was almost as if he were trying to soothe away the sting he'd just caused.

And it worked.

My bottom felt warm, the skin tingling. To my surprise, that same warmth spread to my quim, my pearl throbbing in sympathy. I twisted restlessly against his lap, and that was all the invitation he needed.

Once again he slapped my bottom, this time covering both cheeks. This time, too, I caught my breath, but I didn't cry out.

Again, and again.

And again he paused, rubbing and kneading my heated flesh. He ran his thumb along the length of my spine, then rubbed my bottom again.

"Your ass is even more beautiful this way," he murmured, as if he meant to soothe me with words as he had with his hand. "Your skin is so pink and so hot, Eve. So very beautiful."

It *was* hot. I felt feverish, and although I longed for him to stroke me between my legs and ease that burn as well, I knew better than to ask. This was part of the Game, our game. He'd only tell me that it wasn't time, and that I must wait, and—

"Oh!" I couldn't keep that back. His hand had hit my ass with a glancing blow that cracked against my skin in a new way, and instinctively I clenched my muscles to brace against the next blow. I felt the tension increase in my quim, and I moaned softly in frustration.

"Don't pull back from me, Eve," he said, leaning over me. "If you wish to find the pleasure you crave, you know what you must do."

Panting, I squeezed my eyes shut, trying to decipher his meaning. So this was another puzzle, another challenge. I felt him sit upright, preparing to raise his hand again.

"I—I was wrong, Master," I blurted out. "I should have stayed in my own room. I should never have come here. Forgive me, Master; forgive me!"

He made a rumbling, wordless sound of approval as his palm smacked, then smoothed my bottom. I could have moved off his lap and away from him. He wasn't holding me so tightly that I couldn't have escaped. We both knew it and understood. If I didn't want to be here I could have plucked the key from the bowl on the mantel and left.

But I did, and I didn't.

"I disobeyed you, Master," I said in a whispered rush, wanting to please him. "I was wrong. I see that now. Forgive me, Master; oh, please, forgive me!"

He was holding my hips steady with one hand and caressing my bottom with the other, his hand dipping across the tender skin between the top of my leg and my cunt. I felt as if my whole being was centered on his stroking hand, the heat radiating from it like the rays of the sun. Even my toes curled and clenched, and the very soles of my feet felt on fire.

"You know you were wrong, Eve," he said, the tension in his voice unmistakable. "Coming in here where you didn't belong, before you were invited. Prying into matters that do not—cannot—concern you. You were spying. You know how wrong that is."

"I know it now, Master," I said, more eagerly than perhaps a true penitent would do. "It will not happen again; I swear it."

His hand fell again, harder, and I jerked from the impact.

"You would swear to anything now, Eve," he said. "I know you so well."

"Yes, Master," I gasped, my heartbeat thumping in my ears and my blood on fire. "You . . . you do."

"Yes," he growled. "I *do*."

My whole body tensed and quivered, waiting for his hand to come down even as I gasped and teetered on the edge of my climax. Yet still he held back, tormenting me by doing nothing.

"Please, Master," I begged, twisting over his knees. "Please, oh, please."

"Enough," he said sharply. "Stand, Eve."

Whimpering, I obeyed, though I couldn't believe he'd abandon me like this. Reluctantly I pushed myself clear of his knees and tried to stand, the necklace swinging heavily against my chest. My thighs were trembling, and I was close to tears. I kept my head bowed so he couldn't see the despair and disappointment that must surely be in my eyes. Still I knew he was watching me, studying me, taking note of how everything he'd done had affected me. I could only pray I'd done the same to him.

"Perfect, Eve," he said, his voice taut with desire. "*You* are perfect."

Then before I could react or respond he rose and hooked his arm beneath my knees. He lifted me into his arms as if I weighed no more than a feather, and I curled against his chest, weak with longing. He kicked the bedroom door open and carried me through the door and dropped me into the center of his bed.

7.

The coverlet had already been turned back, and I sank into the snowy white of fine linens. I'd a swift impression of the bed as being very large—although he'd dropped me crossways on it, I still wasn't near the edge—with an elaborate, old-fashioned canopy overhead.

But at that moment, I was more focused on Savage himself than his bedroom, and why shouldn't I be? I was naked in his bed, wild with desire, and he was standing not six feet away from me.

I understood now why he preferred candlelight, for surely there was no more beautiful sight in the warm, flickering light and shadows than the one before me. He jerked open the last buttons on his shirt and whipped it from his shoulders in a single fluid motion, a white flag of surrender that he flung to the floor.

I stared at him greedily, at his ridged, lean abdomen and his broad chest, the candlelight playing over the taut, bunching muscles exactly as I longed to do. He'd exactly the right amount of dark, curling hair on his chest, small whorls that accentuated the breadth of his shoulders and tapered to a thin, tantalizing trail to the waistband of his trousers.

"I didn't want it to be like this," he said, his voice thick, his gaze intense upon me. "Not this night. But I can't resist you, not now."

"You don't have to, Master," I said breathlessly, unabashedly pressing my legs together for relief. I pushed myself up on my elbows to watch him. He was glorious and male, putting ancient marble statues to shame. "I don't *want* you to."

He scowled, fighting with himself. "Oh, I know what you want, because we both want the same thing."

I nodded, without words. I was glad he found me irresistible, considering how I felt the same about him. With a crack he pulled his belt free from the loops and tore open the buttons on his trousers and shoved them down around his legs. His powerful erection tented the front of his drawers, the linen so thin that I could make out the bell-shaped head of his cock and the drop of moisture that had already soaked through the cloth.

But soon he jerked the drawers down, too, and kicked them aside, and he was at last as naked as I was. As primed as I was, my eyes still widened hungrily at the sight of him, a sight he'd denied me earlier.

"See what you do to me, Eve," he growled with a hint of angry despair, standing at the edge of the bed. "I'm your Master, and yet you control me."

His cock was ferociously hard and thick, jutting forward with the veins distended, and below his bollocks gleamed hard and full between his muscular thighs. He was so male I almost couldn't bear to look at him, he made me ache so with desire. How could he believe I controlled him when he was like this?

"You are my Master," I said, whispering my thighs

apart to demonstrate my obedience to him. The small motion reminded me of how he'd used my bottom and how sore it had become, and I winced, even though the memory alone made my blood quicken again. "All I can do is obey you."

He glanced down at my open quim and swore, his face hard and his eyes hooded. He climbed onto the bed before me, the mattress dipping beneath his weight.

"Turn over," he ordered. "I don't want to hurt you any further. On your knees."

He didn't wait for me to obey but caught me by my waist and flipped me over. I scrambled upright onto my knees, and he pulled me back across the bed until I felt his cock bump against my hip. I held my breath with anticipation, my heart racing, knowing that at any second that thick, heavy cock would be pushing into me.

"Your skin's so hot, Eve." He palmed my ass with surprising gentleness and trailed his fingers deeper, pressing between the slick, swollen outer lips of my sex. "You've bloomed like a rose for me. My God, I cannot wait to be inside you."

At his touch, I made a small strangled cry. He'd left me so aroused and on edge that even that slight caress was almost painful.

"Hush, hush," he said, his voice low. "You're shaking, Eve. Can't you trust me to give you what you need?"

"Y-y-yes," I stammered. "Yes, *Master*."

He parted the lips of my slit with his fingers and I felt the blunt head of his cock pressing into me. I closed my eyes tight the better to feel him, the better to imagine him poised behind me with his cock in his hand.

"You're so wet, so ready," he murmured. "For me."

He grasped my hips with both hands, his fingers sinking into my soft flesh to hold me steady. The impact of the first thrust made me cry out, a broken, strangled cry that was nearly a scream. He was so thick that he had to drive his way into my passage, opening my flesh to accept him.

One, two, three thrusts and he was buried deep, his balls pressed against my bottom. With a shuddering groan he paused to relish the sensations of us being joined.

"Put your shoulders down," he said roughly. "Lay your head on your arms, and lift your ass up."

I did as he asked, and immediately he sank into me even deeper. We'd never used this position before, and I was stunned by how completely he was able to fill me. As wet as I was, I had to stretch to accommodate his size, my passage yielding to the masculine force of his cock.

He began to move, a powerful glide of his hips. With each thrust he reached the end of my channel in a way that I thought was bliss, and yet his slow withdrawal, nearly complete, dragged across my inner nerves in new ways that made me shake with building pleasure. He reached around my ribs and cupped my breasts, pressing my nipples between his thumbs and forefingers until I cried out yet again. It was too much, all too much, yet still I rocked my hips to try to draw him even deeper, and it didn't begin to be enough.

I'd never felt anything like it. My bottom still stung where he'd spanked me, and yet now the burn turned to a liquid heat, coursing through my body as his belly slapped against my skin, just as his hand had done.

He slid his hands from my breasts to hold me in the place where my hips flared. He set a punishing pace, but I matched him, arching my back to take him deeper. I grabbed fistfuls of the sheets, mindlessly twisting them in my fingers as he slammed into me, and built the fire in my body higher and higher. I was drunk with his possession, and no matter how hard he drove into me, I craved more.

"Perfect," I felt him growl against the back of my neck, the tension in his voice and body echoing my own. "God, Eve, you feel so good."

I wanted to tell him that he was wrong, that he was the one who felt good. But I'd no words: my entire body was as tight as a bow with my coming climax, and the only sound I could make was a keening, yearning cry as the spasms began to rip through me.

He must have felt it, too, roaring with the force of his own release. He raised his right hand from my hip and slapped it hard against my bottom, in exactly the same place that he'd struck earlier.

And I screamed: not with pain or shock, but with pleasure so overwhelming that I must have lost consciousness for a moment, toppling forward only to be caught and held by him as he pumped furiously into me.

"Eve, Eve," he whispered harshly, breaking through my disorientation.

He was still holding me upright and tightly against his chest, his arm braced around my waist below my breasts. My heartbeat was still thumping in my ears, or perhaps what I heard was his; I was too dazed to be able to tell for certain. As our breathing slowed I lay limply against him, our skin slick with sweat, yet he continued to hold me with a gentleness I'd never expected from him. I still pulsed around him, little tremors that were only the last echoes of what had come before. I rested my head back against his shoulder, and he trailed small kisses along the side of my throat, nuzzling his jaw into my hair.

Finally his cock slipped free of my body with a rush of warm semen, and with a reluctant sigh I slipped free of his embrace. I began to use the edge of the sheet to wipe myself, but instead he reached into the drawer of the small table beside the bed. There was the pile of neatly

pressed handkerchiefs, each embroidered with his monogram, the same as he'd had at Wrenton, and he handed
me one. I should have grown accustomed to that by now,
but it still was a level of indulgence that startled even me.

Afterward I sat back on my heels and gathered my
damp hair into a loose knot at the back of my neck, tucking the ends in to make them stay. Now I noticed how my
bottom burned and I wasn't quite ready to sit on it yet.

Watching me, he reached out to touch one of my still-
erect nipples with his fingertip.

"Look at you," he said softly. "You are making it very
difficult for me to leave this bed."

"Then don't." I smiled tremulously. My emotions were
as tumbled as my body, the way they often were after we'd
fucked: joy and elation and satisfaction mixed with a hint
of melancholy. I couldn't say why. What I had with Savage was sex, purely carnal, and there was no real reason
for me to be so foolish and quivery afterward.

"Only for a moment." He winked at me and grinned,
unexpectedly, boyishly charming. "I give you my word."

He climbed from the bed and crossed the room, giving me a splendid view of his own muscular ass as he
walked. His cock hung heavy, but it was still thick, and I
loved seeing how it still carried the faint glisten of my
juices. I suspected that even after what we'd just done he
would be ready for more before the night was done, and
so would I. As I'd learned last week, he could be tireless;
it was one of his best qualities and one of the ways we
were so well suited.

He plucked a silk robe from the back of a chair and
threw it over his shoulders before he passed through the
bedroom door and back into the front room, tying the sash
around his waist. I heard him ring for a servant, and I
swiftly went diving beneath the sheets.

True, his manservant, Barry, had seen me quite naked in Savage's bathtub, just as my own maid, Hamlin, saw me that way whenever I bathed. But to have a servant witness me without a stitch in His Lordship's bed with his spendings on my thighs would have been entirely different.

Still, it was clear that Savage's servants were accustomed to his habits. Through the door I overheard him tell Barry to have our long-delayed dinner brought up as soon as it could be arranged, and Barry only murmured in agreement.

I sank a little lower against the pillows, pulling them up over my breasts and trying not to think too much of those habits. Of course a gentleman with appetites like Savage's would have brought other women here to this bed. No wonder Barry seemed so unperturbed. I couldn't possibly be the first, and yet that certainty punctured my earlier joy.

I sighed, staring up at the pleated silk canopy overhead. Like everything else in the house, it was a reflection of Savage's personal tastes: beautiful, luxurious, and costly, and the candlelight only added to the romantic, otherworldly quality. Beauty was important to him, beauty of every kind, which was why he said he claimed to be so intrigued by me.

Perfect, he'd called me. I wasn't sure I agreed with that, for like every woman I was acutely aware of my own flaws. But I had liked to hear it from him. I'd liked it very much. I smiled to myself, remembering, and let my fingers languidly wander over my nipple beneath the sheet, pinching and teasing the little peak as he had done. Certainly what we'd done together in this bed had been perfect, too.

And yet it wasn't. Over and over he asked me to trust him, and then in turn he seemed unable to trust me with even the most mundane aspects of his own life. At first I'd thought his accusations of me spying on him had been part of our game, but the longer I considered it, the less likely this seemed to be.

When I'd entered his rooms, I'd been looking for him, not for any secrets. Even if I had, there didn't appear to be anything in these rooms that required hiding. The only thing that he might have wanted to keep from me would have been the portrait of his wife, and even that had seemed more poignant than scandalous.

I'd respect his wishes. I was a private person myself and understood his need to keep things to himself, no matter the loneliness that often came with it. Besides, I'd promised him that I would. But that promise wouldn't be enough to keep me from wondering what had made him so sensitive and guarded and what, too, I could do to help ease his private demons. I knew they were there. I'd only to look into his pale eyes to see both them and the pain that they caused.

"We'll dine shortly," Savage said, returning. He was carrying two glasses of wine with the bottle tucked beneath one arm, and he handed one of the glasses to me. "No doubt my cook wishes to throttle me for delaying our meal, but she hides her displeasure well, and I'm sure what she sends up to us will do well enough. Which is good, since I am famished."

"So am I." I smiled, taking the offered glass as he climbed onto the bed beside me. "But it was all worth your cook's displeasure."

He smiled, too. He'd stopped calling me "Eve," which meant he'd put aside our game for now and I needn't address him as my Master—even though of course he still was.

It made for a kind of truce between us. The tension that

had lined his face earlier was gone, and I hoped I was the reason. Because he was more relaxed he looked younger. Having his hair mussed and the silk robe fall open over his chest only made him look more boyishly charming—and more wickedly attractive.

He tapped the edge of his glass against mine. "Then here's to displeasing Mrs. Wilson, repeatedly."

"To Mrs. Wilson's continued displeasure," I said, laughing softly as I raised the glass to my lips.

He did the same, his gaze locked with mine as he sipped his wine.

"I like that you wore my necklace," he said, glancing down to where it lay between my breasts. "I'd hoped you would."

"Of course I would," I said, cradling the globe of the wineglass between my fingers. "It was a gift from you."

His dark brows dipped together. "A gift should not come with an obligation attached."

"There was no obligation," I said. "I wore the pearls because they are beautiful, and because they remind me of you."

"Ahh," he said, noncommittal, though it was clear he was both pleased yet sheepish. The brows relaxed, too. "That was what I'd hoped when I chose them for you."

"Then your hopes are answered," I said, lightly running my fingers across the pearls. "You shouldn't have had any doubt."

"Oh, I have more doubts than you'll ever know," he said, striving to make a joke of it as he settled against the pillows beside me. "Hundreds upon hundreds."

"You shouldn't," I said softly. I thought again of his wife and how he still blamed himself for her death. "You've no reason to have any doubts at all."

"Do not be so blasted understanding," he said gruffly,

studying the wine in his glass instead of me. "I do not deserve that, especially not from you."

I set my glass on the table beside the bed and turned to face him. I didn't say anything. I simply waited for him to volunteer more, or not.

He grunted, still looking down into his wine. "Did I hurt you?"

"I was more startled than hurt," I said. The sting of his slaps had faded by now, leaving only a slight warmth that wasn't unpleasant. "I didn't expect you to do that."

"Nor did I, not at that moment," he admitted. His gaze slid back my way, watching for my reaction. "But you liked it."

"I did," I admitted slowly. "I don't know why, but I did."

"So did I." He grimaced. "God, you're making me hard again."

Automatically I glanced down at the front of the silk robe, where, in fact, he did seem to be stirring.

"I didn't lie," he said drily, following my gaze. "You have that effect on me."

I blushed at being caught. "I'm sorry if—"

"Don't be, because I'm not," he said. "As I've told you before, I find you irresistible. Not just in bed, either. I find you impossible to put from my thoughts."

That should have been a compliment, and from any other man it would have been. But he was frowning, as if he found my irresistibility more perplexing than enjoyable.

Once again he looked away from me, swirling the wine in his glass.

"I didn't want to hurt you, Evelyn," he said. "But there are . . . things that are better for you not to know."

The fact that he used my real name was significant. It was a sign that he was being serious and that those unknown things must be as serious as the things I already knew of him, of his temper and his wife and the man I'd earlier glimpsed hurrying from the house into the cab.

Yet I didn't dare ask, not after Savage had accused me earlier of spying. I felt terribly inexperienced and wished I'd had more friends and lovers, wished my husband had been more communicative when he'd lived, so that I might be able to know what was right to do and say.

All I could do was trust my own instincts and pray that they'd be right.

"You do not need to tell me further if you do not wish to," I said carefully. "Everyone has things about themselves they'd rather not share. If you wish to confide in me, then I'll listen, but if you don't choose to, then that is fine as well."

"I can't," he said, his voice dark and rough with despair. He emptied his glass and set it with a thump on the far table. "That is the difference. What I wish is of no consequence. For your own sake, I must tell you nothing."

"Then don't," I said softly. I laid my hand on his thigh in sympathy and solace, not desire, yet still I felt the heat of his skin through the silk. "It won't change the days and nights we have together."

"No, it won't." He sighed deeply, restlessly, and when he looked back to me his eyes were filled with sorrow and haunted by those secrets that he could not tell.

And yet he could, because he just had. Without words I understood and shared his suffering. I nodded in silent agreement.

He took my hand and raised it to his lips, lightly kissing the back of it. "That's what we have, isn't it?"

"Each day," I said softly, "and each night, with you."

He leaned closer, threading his fingers into my hair as he cradled my face.

"That, my dear, sweet Evelyn," he whispered, "is why I cannot resist you."

He kissed me then, as I'd known he would. But as he did I felt emotions I hadn't expected twisting within me. What if there was more binding us together than either one of us had anticipated or wished for? What if what we shared was more than this bed, more than the idle amusement of fucking?

What if he felt the same confusion that I was feeling now?

I kissed him fervently and was grateful that my closed eyes hid the sting of tears behind them.

When my eyes first fluttered open—or, more specifically, one eye, with the other still pressed shut against the pillow—the next morning, I'd no notion of where I was. The bed was large and unfamiliar, though very comfortable, the room unpleasantly bright with the sunlight that streamed through the open windows. Although so much sun meant it must be closer to noon than dawn, I still wasn't ready to wake, and I closed my eyes again, determined to slip back into blissful, unquestioning unconsciousness.

But even as my body longed to return to sleep my thoughts seemed to jump wide awake, and with them came a rush of memories of the night before. I was in Savage's bed, in his bedroom, in his house, in St. James's Square, in London. I hadn't returned to my suite at the Savoy but had stayed here. I'd spent the entire night with him, and during that night we'd done wild, wicked, glorious things to each other.

I lifted my head, shoved my hair back, and opened my eyes, looking for him. The place beside me was empty: the sheets were rumpled and the pillow hollowed, showing he'd been there, but he wasn't there now. Perhaps he was in the bathroom and would be back in a moment. I touched my fingers to the sheets to see if they were still warm from his body.

They weren't. Where could he have gone?

I blinked and squinted, for that infernal sun was very bright. What kind of servant would open the curtains in a bedroom before breakfast? Turning away from the window, I rolled over and began to sit upright.

"Don't move," Savage ordered sharply. "The light is ideal."

I froze as he'd ordered and shifted only my eyes. He was sitting in an armchair near to the bed. He was already dressed, though not in his usual impeccable manner, in a loose-fitting jersey and a pair of soft, wide linen trousers such as sailors wear, with turned-up cuffs. He wore no shirt, no socks, no shoes. The sleeves of the jersey were shoved up over his bare forearms, and his tousled hair fell over his forehead. He hadn't yet shaved, and his jaw was darkened with his beard. He looked more like a gypsy or Bohemian rather than an English earl, but mostly he looked devastatingly rakish and thoroughly desirable.

I was, in fact, so overwhelmed by his appearance that at first I didn't notice what he was doing. He didn't seem to require as much sleep as most people, and he'd often sat awake and watched me while I slept. Though it had startled me the first time I'd awakened and seen him beside the bed, it now made me feel protected, as if he wasn't just watching me but watching over me, too.

But this morning was different. Across his legs was propped a wide board with a sheet of paper pinned to it. Although I couldn't see the paper, I could tell he was drawing on it from the quick, sweeping motion of his arm. What took me longer to realize was that he was drawing me, his gaze darting from me on the bed to the paper and back again.

I blushed, suddenly shy. It wasn't because I was naked or even that he was drawing me that way. It was the fact that he was drawing me at all, preserving an image of me like this in his rumpled bed.

"What are you doing?" I asked, even though it was obvious.

"Trying to capture you," he said, scowling down at the sheet. "Trying, and failing."

He pulled the sheet from the board and tossed it to the floor and grabbed a fresh page from the table beside him. As he did I craned my neck to see the pages that were already scattered on the carpet around us, curious to see what he'd drawn.

"I told you not to move," he said as he began a fresh drawing. "The sun at this moment is exquisite, and I want to keep trying as long as I have it."

He drew with authority, decisive strokes of the chalk across the paper. I kept still as he'd ordered, but I didn't think there'd be harm in speaking.

"Have you done this before?" I asked. "Drawing people, I mean. Obviously you've never drawn me."

"Yes," he said, answering my question. "And you don't know that for sure, do you?"

My cheeks warmed again. "I . . . I suppose I don't."

"You needn't worry," he said. "No one else will ever see any of these pictures. Whether I keep them or destroy them, they'll never leave my keeping."

"I wouldn't be ashamed of them," I said quickly. "It's just that I'd no idea I was sitting for my portrait while I slept."

He glanced at me wryly. "You weren't sitting. You were lying, and in rather luscious abandon, too."

"I was asleep!"

"Then you were lusciously asleep." He chuckled. "Surely the celebrated Mrs. Hart has been painted before."

"Not for years," I said. "My last portrait was after my wedding, by Mr. Sargent."

"Oh, yes, it would be Mr. Sargent," he said, "who has turned more sow's ears into silk purses than any other portraitist in history. But then if one wishes to empty the silk purses of American millionaires and their dismal wives and daughters, I suppose that is what one must do. Present company excepted, of course."

"Of course," I said, aware that he was teasing. He didn't do it often, showing a playful side that few others would ever see in him, and I liked it. "But then I never knew you liked to draw in the first place."

"I wouldn't say I liked it," he said, scowling down at his work. "Nor that I do it for pleasure. Rather, I am driven to do it. It's a rascally demon that torments me by always holding satisfaction just beyond my reach, tempting my eyes with what my pitiful hands can't capture."

"Is that how you think of it?" I asked, surprised by his vehemence. Perhaps I shouldn't have been; he seemed to approach much in his life the same way.

"I do," he said. He paused, leaning back to consider his work. He whipped the sheet from the board and held it up for me to see. "Rubbish. Once again, I've failed."

"Oh, no, not at all!" I exclaimed. I don't know what I expected his work to be—I'd never known any gentlemen who were also artists—but his skill astonished me. Gentleman or not, he was talented, and to me his drawing looked equal to what I'd seen on display in museums and galleries. "It's very good."

He grunted in disagreement. "Chicken scratchings," he said with disgust. "A dilettante's scribbles."

"You are too harsh," I said, coming to the edge of the bed to be closer to both him and the drawing. "It's remarkable."

"For an amateur, you mean," he said gloomily. "A peer of the realm can never be regarded as a professional artist. I'm aware of that."

"It's remarkable for anyone," I said staunchly. "I saw at once that it was me, even though my face is turned away. I can tell that this is your bed, and—"

"Any apprentice draughtsman can do that," he said scornfully. "A mere factual cataloguing. A true artist discovers the soul of his subject, and makes it his own on the paper or canvas."

"Like lovers," I said without thinking.

Immediately his eyes turned wary. "What are you saying?"

I took a deep breath. Now that I'd begun, even though by accident, I'd have to continue.

"I'm saying that you've done exactly that to me already," I said carefully. I curled my legs beneath me, buying time to choose my words. "Last night, in this bed, and whenever else we come together. You find my soul, and join it with your own."

He didn't answer at first, his face impassive. He glanced at the drawing, then back to me. "You believe that?"

I nodded, self-consciously smoothing my tangled hair behind my ears.

"Do you believe it in reverse?" he asked. "Do you feel that when we fuck you lay some sort of claim to my soul as well?"

"I suppose I do," I said slowly. "You know how often you tell me to open my eyes, so that we can't hide from one another. Perhaps that's why you're not happy with your pictures of me. You've always drawn me asleep, or just now when my face was turned away. Perhaps if you were to draw me now, looking at you, you'd be better pleased."

He didn't answer, and my heart sank. I must have spoken too freely and presumed a closer intimacy than really exisited between us.

But then he nodded. Abruptly he dropped the last drawing and pinned a fresh sheet in place on the board.

"Turn a bit to your left, towards the window," he ordered. "Put your weight on your left arm."

I did as he bid, my heart racing. Did he agree after all? Did he feel the same as I did?

"Not like that." He rose suddenly, setting aside the board to lean over me. He placed both hands around my arm and gently guided it into the place he wanted. Concentrating, he next placed his fingers on the small of my back, making me arch my spine more gracefully.

I glanced down at my wrist. The fingers on his hand were covered with the black chalk, and each time he touched my arm he left an oval black smudge on my pale skin, like a visible map of his touch on my skin that I found both oddly beautiful and arousing.

Finally he stepped back, considering.

"Don't move," he said. "There's one more thing required."

He bent his head over my breast and sucked the nipple into his mouth, drawing so hard that he hollowed his cheeks. I hadn't expected him to do that, and I gasped, both with surprise and with pleasure. He massaged my other breast at the same time, his fingers squeezing and tugging at the nipple.

"I told you not to move," he whispered sharply, against my skin.

I shuddered, struggling to do as he bid even as I felt the pull of what he was doing deep within me, a subtle torment that drew on my very womb.

He shifted back and forth between each breast, licking and suckling until my nipples were bright red and tight, the areolas pebbled, and glistening from his mouth. Around them my pale skin was smudged with his sooty fingerprints, more signs of his possession.

"Are . . . are y-y-y-ou satisfied?" I stammered breathlessly, being careful not to break my pose.

"I cannot tell yet," he said, not committing one way or another. Yet he smiled wickedly to prove he knew exactly what he'd done and its undeniable effect on me. "You must look directly at me while I draw, and not look away even for a moment. I want to test this theory of yours."

He sat back down with the board across his legs. Instead of the earlier decisiveness that he'd shown while drawing, he now seemed in a kind of fury, his entire body behind the chalk in his hand and the marks he was making across the page. It was as if before he'd drawn with his intellect and now he drew with passion. When our eyes met I felt the heat of it, enough to feel I'd been scorched by his intensity.

I didn't move, but my anticipation built. I couldn't wait to see the drawing and if there was any difference. From what I saw in him, there should have been. Now he was making art with the same passion that he showed when he made love to me.

And it *was* making love and not just fucking. It was exactly as I'd said, a physical union of our souls as well as our bodies. Mine became a visceral response, and I felt each stroke of the chalk across the page as clearly as if it had been drawn across my skin.

I understood, and as I sat as still on the bed as I could my pulse quickened and my blood grew feverishly warm. It was as if he'd cast one more spell over me. My breasts grew heavy, and without looking down I could tell that my nipples were tightening into stiff little buds of desire. Although I'd promised not to move, my lips parted on their own, my breathing as rapid as my pulse.

All because he was watching me, studying me, seducing me, as he captured my soul with a swash of black chalk.

He worked fast, or perhaps it was the shifting morning sun that spurred him on. Finally he nodded with satisfaction and dropped the chalk on the table beside him before he turned the board for me to see his work.

"Oh, Savage," I murmured, stunned by the difference. Free at last to break the pose, I sat upright, rubbing my arms where they'd stiffened from my sitting so still.

"You see it, then?" he said, unable to keep the little note of triumph from his voice. "It's not perfect, not by a long ways, and yet it's closer than I've ever come."

I nodded, captivated by the new picture. The first one he'd shown me had been a pretty representation of the bed and the room with me in it, but this was only me, my eyes fathomless and hungry with longing. He'd made me look not like a lady but a vibrant, sensual woman.

Only Savage could make me feel that way, and only he could have drawn me like this.

"Do I really look like that?" I asked, almost in awe.

"In my eyes you do," he said.

Such simple words, yet made so rich by the way they reverberated with emotion. I didn't know how to answer, not with ordinary words, and instead I held my arms out to him, wanting him to join me.

He leaned the board with the drawing against the side of the chair, his gaze never leaving mine, exactly as he'd done as he'd drawn me. Quickly he pulled the jersey over his head but kept the loose trousers hanging precariously on his hip bones and against the jut of his aroused cock.

He came to join me on the bed, sinking into my embrace. He pressed his face between the globes of my breasts and I folded my arms around his bare shoulders, tangling my fingers into the black silk of his hair. I rocked backwards onto the tangled sheets, drawing him with me.

His hands settled on either side of my waist, and holding me that way, he lavished a trail of wet, hot kisses from my breasts down my belly. It was as if he was determined to remember and mark every inch of my body as he'd just drawn it, except now in this sensual, tactile way.

I arched my back against his mouth, reveling in the feel of his lips and tongue and the scrape of his unshaven jaw over my skin as he slowly worked his way back up my body. There were more black chalk smudges like leopard's spots on me now, and I did not care.

Liquid heat coursed through my body beneath him. His turgid cock pressed against my thigh through the thin trousers, hard and rigid with his need. There was no mistaking where this would lead, nor would I have wanted anything else.

He slid his hands along the outside of my rib cage and gently pushed my arms straight over my head. He rubbed his thumbs into the taut muscles of my armpits, holding my arms over my head as he straddled my legs.

His face was close over mine, his eyes quicksilver bright.

"Perfection," he whispered hoarsely. "My Innocent, my inspiration, my muse. My Eve."

"Yours," I breathed in return as he bent to kiss me. "All yours."

8.

"So this is where you've hidden yourself," Savage said as he entered the bedroom. We'd only been apart an hour at most, yet still I felt the familiar rush of pleasure and anticipation when I saw him again.

He was wearing the same loose trousers and jersey that he'd had on earlier when he'd drawn me and clearly, wonderfully, nothing beneath either. Without the burden of tailoring every muscle showed beneath the soft fabrics, and the dark curls on his chest peeked through the deep V-neck of his jersey. No man I'd ever seen could wear such casual dress with such seductive aplomb.

"I wouldn't call being in your bedroom hiding," I said, smiling at his return. He'd found me reading in the armchair beside the window, my feet curled beneath me. "It's where I've been almost the entire time. I wanted to be here when you returned."

He chuckled, clearly pleased with my answer and with me. His face was relaxed, almost happy, and I hoped I could take some of the credit for that.

He crossed the room and placed one hand on the back

of the armchair to brace himself as he leaned down to kiss me. Eagerly I opened my mouth for him as he deepened the kiss, sweeping his tongue against mine in a way that always made my core tighten with longing, and I wondered if it was possible for him to make me come by kissing me alone.

It was the middle of the afternoon, and he had gone downstairs to tend to a few pressing matters of business. Remembering how strongly he'd reacted yesterday, I hadn't pressed him for details. I'd reminded myself that he'd been right: whether his "business" had to do with the man I'd seen hurrying from the house yesterday or something as harmless as bills that needed paying, it wasn't any of my affair. Besides, this was already the second day of our week together, and I'd no desire to squander any more of it with his displeasure.

While he'd been downstairs I'd taken the time alone to bathe in the room across the hall. I didn't call for a servant but managed for myself, twisting my hair into a loose knot on my head. Without a fresh change of my own clothes I could have worn the scarlet robe that had been left for me. Instead I'd appropriated one of Savage's robes from his closets, a dramatic blue silk patterned with gold phoenixes.

The silk was redolent with his scent, a mixture of the spicy bay rum of his shaving soap and his own distinctive maleness. Wearing the robe was like wrapping myself in a memory of him: unique, enjoyable, but not the same as having the man himself. The silk slipped and slid across my naked body and I'd had to tie the sash twice around my waist to keep it from slithering off my body, but I liked knowing it belonged to him.

He liked it, too. As he continued to kiss me he slid the fingertips of one hand beneath the silk, pushing it so slowly over the curve of my shoulder and down my arm that it became another kind of caress. The silk whispered lower and lower until finally he'd bared my right breast completely. He scooped the rounded flesh into his palm, idly tweaking my nipple until it stood stiff. Impatiently I shrugged my other shoulder, trying to free my other breast from the robe for him, but he only broke the kiss and chuckled.

"Don't be greedy, Eve," he chastised softly. "Sometimes it's better to wait."

I sighed with longing. "So you say, Master."

"Yes, I do," he said, his smile wickedly indulgent. "I should draw you like this, with one perfect breast displayed against the silk. Ivory flesh crowned by a ruby jewel."

"Then why don't you, Master?" I asked. I'd enjoyed posing for him, one more layer to our games.

"Another time," he said, glancing down at the open book in my lap. "But I see how you've been amusing yourself while I was away."

I followed his glance down to the small book and blushed furiously. It had been the book's elegant brocade binding that had attracted me, sitting on the table beside the bed, and I'd chosen it hoping for something to read to pass the time. I soon realized, however, that I'd be looking at the book's pictures instead of reading it, for what few words there were on the pages were formed by Japanese characters, not Western letters, and I couldn't begin to make them out. But words were unnecessary, because the pictures—dramatic woodblock images of Japanese couples engaged in amorous play that filled every page— were vividly explicit.

So explicit, in fact, that when Savage glanced down to the pages I'd left open across my lap I tried to close the book.

He put his hand on the edge of the page to keep it open and twisted his head to see the illustration.

"The *shunga* are amusing, aren't they?" he said. "That's what these prints are called, you know. Erotic art to be enjoyed by every rank of society, and by both men and women. The Japanese are much more frank in these matters than the English."

I nodded, for that same frankness had also left me at a loss for words. Savage collected erotic paintings and sculpture, and it had been openly displayed about his rooms at Wrenton as well as here in his house. While at first it had embarrassed me, now I'd come to appreciate the pieces not only as art but also as arousing erotica. And wasn't that really what he and I had been creating together when he'd drawn me earlier this morning?

But everything that he'd shown me had been European, from a lush Italian Venus with her Mars to lascivious Greek satyrs and French shepherdesses yielding to shepherds. The figures shown had been mostly classically nude, and if they hadn't been engaged in pleasuring one another then everything could have been in any museum in London or New York.

The prints in this book were different. Here the couples were almost entirely clothed in swirling patterned robes much like the one I was wearing (or half-wearing, since I hadn't bothered to cover my bared breast). The swirling robes emphasized their contortions as they twisted and turned each other's bodies, their faces grimacing and their toes clenching. I knew exactly how they felt, that last frenzied moment when release seemed so close yet so agonizingly far.

But what I'd noticed first was how exaggerated the genitals were on both the men and the women. The men's cocks were enormous, with bulging, bell-shaped heads,

while the women's quims were shown stretching widely
to accommodate the men. The detail was astonishing, and
it had been impossible for me to look at the pictures without feeling that now-familiar warmth begin to gather low
in my belly.

"I'm surprised to see you blush," Savage said, looking
over my shoulder at the book. "There's no shame in such
a book."

"I'm not ashamed," I said defensively. "It's just that
they're very . . . very detailed."

He smiled. "That they are," he said. "But that's the
point. Books like this are called 'pillow books.' They were
owned by the highest-ranking courtesans, for their
amusement and inspiration."

I glanced up at him from beneath my lashes. "I do not
believe you would ever need such inspiration, Master."

He made a small grunt of amusement. "You flatter me,
Eve," he said. "But I am always willing to be inspired to
take new paths, try new things."

I turned the page in the book, back to a picture I'd studied earlier, and held it for him to see.

"Does this inspire you then, Master?" I asked. The
couple in the picture were on some sort of open-air balcony, with the moon overhead. The man crouched on his
knees with the woman's legs over his shoulders, and he
held her by his hips as he thrust his enormous cock into
her. My breath quickened merely from looking at it again,
and not from modesty, either.

"If it inspires you," he said, his voice low against my
ear, "then it certainly inspires me."

I laughed softly, running my fingers suggestively over
the image as if the printed man and his sizable cock were
flesh, not ink and paper.

"True, that fellow is endowed like the village bull,"

Savage said, chuckling with me, "but I know you, and I know the true reason why you like this picture."

He pointed to one corner of the image, where a small figure on another balcony half-hidden by trees was intently watching the couple in the foreground. I'd been so intent on the man and the woman that I hadn't noticed this detail until Savage pointed it out to me.

"You like to watch, Eve," he said. "I haven't forgotten that first night when you watched me in the garden with some other woman."

"I hadn't intended to watch you," I said, flushing at the memory. "I'd gone out onto the gallery to escape the bores in the ballroom, and you happened to be in the bushes with Lady Cynthia Telford."

"Was that who it was?" he asked, disingenuous. "I've forgotten."

"I haven't," I said, which was true. Seared forever in my memory was my first glimpse of Savage's cock, thick and hard and ruddy with lust as it had plunged again and again into her quim. With her bent over a bench her face had been hidden by her tossed-up petticoats, and Savage's, too, had been obscured by a branch. All I'd seen of him was his delicious cock, jutting forward from the front of his evening trousers, and how purposefully he'd used it.

He cocked a single brow. "I didn't expect you to be jealous, Eve."

"I'm not," I said. "Lady Telford is meaningless to me. What I meant is that I'd never forget seeing your cock for the first time. I knew from that moment that I wanted you."

"Did you now?" he asked, more surprised than I'd have expected and more pleased than I'd ever dare hope. "I'd no idea that the sight of my cock alone would have had that effect upon you."

"It did," I said, feeling bolder. "Granted, I hadn't seen many others by way of comparison, but I knew from that alone that you must be an extraordinary man. And you *are*."

"Thus I am extraordinary, and you, dear Eve, are irresistible," he said, tipping my jaw so I couldn't look away. "Perhaps I should arrange for us to meet in that same garden. Would you like that?"

"I . . . I do not know, Master," I whispered, though as I stared into his silvery eyes I did know: I would like to do that, like it so much that my heart raced at the very possibility.

He leaned a fraction closer to me, his fingers on my jaw moving in the slightest, coaxing caress.

"Imagine it, Eve," he said, lowering his voice seductively. "You would be the one with me in the shadows, with the risk that others might be watching from the gallery above. We'd hardly speak. There wouldn't be time before we were missed by the other guests, and besides, our tryst would be for the sake of passion, not conversation. You would be breathless with desire, and I would be hard for you the moment you found me."

I could picture it all exactly as he described it: the mysterious shadows that only happen in moonlight, the sounds of laughter and music from inside the house, the scent of the flowers from the garden. We would meet there because we couldn't meet anywhere else, not the way we wanted, and the moment he touched me I would be ready to melt for him, around him, just as I was now.

"We'd be clawing at one another like wild beasts, wouldn't we?" he continued, building the scene for us both. "Yet even then we'd have to be mindful of your dress, taking care not to tear it, so you could slip back unnoticed among the others. I'd turn you around and bend your over a garden bench. You were expecting this to happen. When I shove your skirts up over your hips, I discover that you've left off your drawers, and your beautiful ass and cunny are bare to the moonlight, and to me. You'd like to do that, wouldn't you, Eve?"

"Yes, Master," I whispered. "Oh, yes, I would."

He nodded, approving, yet still continued, for by now he was as caught up in describing the fantasy as I was in hearing it. His pale eyes had darkened, the way they did when he was aroused, and I could sense the growing tension in his body.

"I'd take you quickly, hard, and you'd push back against my thrusts, for you'd want it as much as I did. You'd have to press your hand to your mouth to stifle your cries, one to match each time my cock buried as deep as it could in your quim, smothering it all in the palm of your white kid glove. When at last we both came, I wouldn't be able to keep silent. I'd roar with it, overcome with how good it was—how good it is to fuck you."

I made a little purr of excitement, rubbing like a cat against his palm and twisting my thighs together in the chair as I sought relief.

"Would you like that sense of danger, Eve?" he asked, his voice rough. "Would you relish the chance that the proper Mrs. Arthur Hart of New York and Newport might be caught in a most compromising situation with me?"

"You know that I would, Master," I said, my voice husky with longing. "I would do whatever you asked, wherever you asked it of me."

He released my jaw and looked down at my bared breast.

"Your nipple is as hard as a ruby," he said, "and I haven't so much as breathed upon it."

"You do that to me, Master," I said. I closed the pillow

book with the *shunga* and set it on the table beside the chair; it had done its work most admirably.

I twisted sinuously in the chair to face him. "Your words, your smile, your eyes," I said. "Everything about you can seduce me. You must realize that by now."

He smiled, his eyes heavy lidded. "Then I'd wager a hundred pounds that you're wet for me now."

Shamelessly I swept the robe aside and parted my legs for him to see for himself. I *was* wet, exactly as he predicted, and I didn't have to look to feel the moisture that had already spread from my quim to my inner thighs.

His gaze flicked downward, unable not to, and I remembered how he'd said I was irresistible to him.

"Touch yourself," he ordered. "Show me how wet you are."

I didn't hesitate. I slid two fingers between the swollen lips of my quim and dipped deep into my passage. I shuddered at even that small intrusion, and when I withdrew my fingers they glistened with my honey-sweet juices.

That might have been enough to satisfy him, but I went further. I raised my fingers to his lips, where my scent would be unavoidable to him. He caught my wrist and inhaled deeply. Then he pressed my fingers into his mouth, sucking on them hard to taste my essence as his tongue lapped wetly around the tips.

"We needn't wait, Master," I said swiftly, hooking one leg over the padded arm of the chair in even more blatant invitation. "This room can be our garden, and if we leave this window open, there's a chance someone will see us from the house across the way, and—"

"No," he said, straightening and standing apart from the chair and from me. His expression changed, too, his eyes shuttering and looking not at my face but slightly to the left of it. "You tempt me, but it's not possible now."

"Why not?" I asked, disappointment at his sudden withdrawal crushing my desire.

"Because you've no place here this afternoon," he said absently, turning to look out the window at my side. The late-afternoon sun fell across his face, more shadows than light.

I shoved the robe back over my legs and pulled it to cover my breast and rose from the chair. It wasn't just that I found his sudden shifts of mood and humor frustrating. They wounded me, wounded me sharply, and left me feeling abandoned and filled with doubts. I told myself that it was his fault, not mine, and that I shouldn't blame myself, yet still I found it hard to stay beside him after what he'd just said.

I crossed the room to stand before the fireplace. I held the sides of my robe tightly closed together across my chest and stared blankly at the mirror over the mantel. Savage had tucked the picture he'd drawn of me earlier into the mirror's frame, a haphazard display. I'd admired it there this morning, but now its presence also stung, another reminder of how I'd believed things were between us and now apparently no longer were.

And how much I wanted it to be otherwise.

"I do not wish to trouble you, Savage," I said curtly. I did not want to let him see the pain he caused me. Fortunately, I was every bit as good at hiding as he was. "If you want me gone, then I'll go."

In the mirror before me I saw his head jerk up and turn towards me. "I never said that."

"I rather think you did," I said, unable to keep the bitterness from my voice. "If you could please send for one of your maids to help me dress, I shall be gone in half an hour."

"The hell you will, Evelyn," he said sharply. "If you

want to leave, then that is your affair, but you will not do so and blame it on me."

I saw him reflected in the mirror before me, growing larger and larger as he came towards me, so I was prepared when he seized me by the shoulders and spun me around.

Or so I thought. I tried to slip away, but he held me fast, his fingers digging into my wrists.

"Let me go, Savage," I said, fighting to free myself. "You're hurting me."

"You're hurting yourself," he said with infuriating calm. "Stop fighting against me."

I didn't. Instead I twisted and plunged, trying to break away. I hated him for being so much stronger than I was, and I hated him for using that strength to keep me still by force.

"One minute you wish me gone," I declared hotly, "and the next you want me to stay, and I . . . I won't oblige you, Savage. I *won't*. Now let me *go*."

"I never wanted you gone," he said, still holding me tight. "Listen to me. I said you've no place here, in this house, this afternoon. That is not the same thing."

"Then what else could it be?" I demanded, bitterness in my voice. "What other meaning could you possibly have had?"

"I meant that I had kept you here alone with me long enough," he said, his self-control only serving to make my own unravel further. "I meant that I didn't want you to think you were my prisoner in this room, in this house."

"Which is exactly how I feel at this moment!"

"Listen to me, Evelyn," he said deliberately. "I meant that I wanted to take you out to dine with me tonight, as my guest, so that the rest of London could see your beauty, and my good fortune."

I stopped struggling and stared at him, incredulous. "Why should I believe that?"

"Because, as I told you before, it is the truth," he said, watching me closely. "We have a table at Gaspari's at eight. If you do not find that agreeable, you may choose a different restaurant or hotel to your liking, and I will have it arranged."

I swallowed hard and didn't answer. For a man whose temper was usually so notoriously short, he was being restrained, even mild mannered. I was the one who'd lost control, the one who'd given in to my fears and passions. I was the dangerous one, not him. It all made me feel curiously off-balance, as if he truly did know some rare truth, some secret, that I didn't.

Nor did it help that he'd begun to stroke the insides of my wrists with his thumbs, directly over the pulse where he could feel my heartbeat, and know how distraught I'd become. He did it to calm my unhappiness but also to distract me, teasing me with a tiny light caress like that.

He knew me that well.

Exactly as I thought I'd known him.

"I want only to please you, Eve," he said, subtly shifting away from our everyday names and lives. "You have pleased me, and now it is my turn to do the same for you. You are not my prisoner, and never have been. Or haven't you realized by now that it's the other way around, and I am entirely yours?"

Perhaps he was telling the truth. Perhaps I had misinterpreted. Perhaps he never had intended to hurt me.

Perhaps he really believed that I wasn't his prisoner or that I'd willingly given him my liberty along with my heart and my soul.

I sighed, a deep, shuddering sigh that made the last of my frustration flutter from my chest.

"I cannot possibly dine at Gaspari's," I said in a small voice, wishing I didn't sound quite so petulant. "All I have to wear is my riding habit."

He smiled slowly, more relieved than I'd expected. Could he have feared that I was leaving, much as I'd feared he wanted me to do so?

"I'd anticipated you might say that," he said, "and therefore I've sent for your own maid to bring you the proper clothes from the Savoy, and to dress you here."

"You sent for Hamlin?" I asked, surprised.

"If that is your maid's name, then yes," he said carefully, as if wanting to not say the wrong thing. "I trust she can bring you a choice of dresses."

"Of course she can," I murmured. It wasn't Hamlin's choices that concerned me. As my lady's maid she knew my tastes, and she'd know what was appropriate for Gaspari's. I didn't doubt that she'd bring me not only the perfect gown but also the necessary shoes, stockings, undergarments, and jewels.

But I found the fact that Savage had sent for Hamlin to be thoughtful and generous in ways that touched me deeply. He could have just as easily expected me to be assisted by one of his own servants, yet instead he'd chosen the course that would please me the most, rather than what was easiest for him.

Far more important, it proved that he really had intended to dine with me all along, rather than send me away. He hadn't tired of me.

I was the one who'd misunderstood, and the realization humbled me.

"I'm sorry," I said softly, simply. "I was wrong, and now I'm sorry."

He smiled wryly. "I'll bet you don't say that very often."

"I don't," I admitted. "Or rather, Mrs. Hart doesn't."

"Ah, well, neither does His Lordship," he said lightly.

I smiled, too. "I'll bet you don't."

"No," he said. "Though perhaps I should."

His smile faded, his gaze so intense that he was nearly frowning.

"I'd never want you to leave, Evelyn," he said. "But there are things that I cannot explain at present—things that are better for you not to know—that may have led me to use the wrong words earlier."

I nodded, accepting, but he shook his head, refusing my acceptance until he'd finished.

"You and I are two of a kind, aren't we?" he said. "We say things, do things, in the heat of passion that later become regrettable."

"That's why I understand," I said. I'd often thought myself that we'd much in common, but to hear him call us two of a kind was almost sweet.

"Understanding does not excuse me," he said firmly. "Please, Evelyn, forgive me if I said the wrong things."

"Forgiven," I said softly. "Completely."

He was still holding me by my wrists, and slowly I bent my head to kiss his hands. His grip relaxed, and I slipped free and into his embrace. He folded his arms across my back as I pressed my face against his shoulder. The soft wool of his jersey pressed against my cheek, and beneath it I could hear the steady, reassuring beat of his heart.

My wrists stung as the blood raced back into my hands, but I didn't care, just as I told myself I didn't care about those mysterious things he didn't wish me to know. If I was meant to know them, I was sure he would share them in time. I'd trust him. We were two of a kind, weren't we?

For now, this was where I was wanted, where I was

safe, and where I'd stay. For now, this was where I belonged.

With this man.

I heard Hamlin arrive long before I saw her, briskly berating the hapless footmen who were bringing my things upstairs to the rooms across the hall from Savage's. She was not herself a large woman, but she'd a sizable presence among other servants, a useful gift for a lady's maid.

"Listen to that," Savage marveled. Despite his earlier refusal, we'd ended up again here in bed together, relishing each other's company. He was reading the evening paper with one arm draped over my waist, while I had been dozing against him with my head pillowed against his arm. We were naked, of course, and while we had agreed that it was most likely time to rise and dress for dinner, that agreement was as far as we'd gotten. It was cozy and companionable, and I was loathe to leave either Savage or his bed.

"I'm assuming that is your maid," he continued when I didn't reply. "Should you go supervise?"

"In time." I rolled over on my back and sighed, listening to Hamlin launch into another tirade about the cost of carelessness to Mrs. Hart's things. That two rooms and several closed doors separated me from her seemed not to matter; I could still make out every word of her tart Boston accent.

"I wouldn't have invited her here if I'd known she was such a tartar," Savage said. "My staff may never recover."

"Hamlin's protective of me, that is all," I said, finally sitting upright with my arms looped around my bent knees. "She has been with me since before I married, and I suppose I shall always be her 'poor, motherless lass.'"

"I can be protective of you, too." He tossed the paper

from the bed to the floor and ran his hand slowly and appreciatively down my bare back. "Nor will I make as much of a racket about it."

I arched my back, letting myself bask in his touch.

"We could dine here," I suggested, which sounded like a much more appealing prospect. "Gaspari's will go on without our presence."

"No, we must go," he said, swinging his legs over the side of the bed. He sighed and tossed me the blue robe. "Go dress. Don't keep that fearsome maid of yours waiting any longer."

I sighed, too, as I slipped the robe over my shoulders and headed for the doorway, silk billowing behind me.

"Wait."

I'd barely turned before he was kissing me again, as hungrily as if we'd been apart days, not minutes. He shoved aside the robe and his hand found the curve of my waist, sliding impatiently around to cup and caress my buttock, his fingers tensing and relaxing into my flesh. He stepped into me and pulled me close against his lean, hard, naked body as my open robe fluttered around us.

"Just watching you walk is enough to drive me mad, Eve," he said when we finally separated. "I don't want to let you go even for the time it takes you to dress."

"I don't have to go," I said breathlessly. "We needn't go out."

"No, we do," he said, his reluctance inexplicably clear. "It's better this way. Go dress, and return to me as soon as you can."

He kissed my forehead, a tender little mark of endearment before I left him to Barry, who was doubtless hovering in wait in Savage's dressing room just as Hamlin was doing for me.

Dutifully I tied the sash around the robe and headed

across the hall. I couldn't fathom why he remained so determined on this dinner at Gaspari's. His reason earlier—that he wished to show me off—seemed forced and unnecessary. We could just as easily have gone on another night or perhaps ridden in the park again tomorrow and achieved the same thing.

I was still searching for an answer as I opened the door to the bedroom that was ostensibly mine. Hamlin was busily laying out clothes across the bed, and she turned swiftly and ducked a curtsey as I entered.

"Good afternoon, ma'am," she said, her flinty eyes narrowing a judgmental fraction as she took instant note of how, at that hour, I wore nothing more than a man's robe. "I've brought you things, as was requested."

She pointedly omitted who had done the requesting, and I realized that whatever misgivings I'd had about her being here in Savage's house didn't even come close to the disapproval she was now exuding. True, she was the lady's maid and I was her mistress, but Hamlin had been with me so long that she'd earned—or, more rightly, claimed—a certain frankness with me that no other servants possessed. I'd told Savage that she was protective of me, but it went further than that. She often treated me like a spinster aunt with a favorite niece, and like that aunt she wasn't afraid to scold me if she thought I needed it, too.

"Thank you, Hamlin," I said briskly, striving not to give her an opening. "I have an hour before I'm to leave for dinner with His Lordship. Which dresses did you bring?"

"I've arranged them for your choosing on the bed, ma'am," Hamlin said, stepping to one side. "Since you didn't say which you wanted, I brought several suitable for dinner."

She had indeed. There were at least a dozen dresses laid carefully across the bed, a froth of silk, ruffles, lace, and beading, with one of my traveling trunks yawning empty to one side. They were all from the finest houses—Worth, Poiret, Doucet—but they were also all more suited to what I'd worn at home in New York as a respectable widow rather than what I wished to wear now. The sea of pale colors, demure grays and mauves, and cream-colored lace was elegantly genteel but hardly the thing to tempt the eye of a gentleman like Savage at a stylish restaurant like Gaspari's.

Which, I suspected, was exactly what Hamlin had had in mind when she'd made her selections.

Disconsolate, I halfheartedly sifted through the dresses. I'd have to choose one of them. The minutes were passing by, and I didn't want to keep Savage waiting.

Then, buried beneath the other dresses, I found the one I'd hoped was there: golden-yellow silk with an overlay of black lace, close-fitting and cut low in front and in back, with small wisps of sleeves that barely clung to my shoulders. It was new, and I'd yet to wear it. Tonight would be perfect.

"This one, Hamlin," I said triumphantly.

"Yes, ma'am." Hamlin pursed her lips, and I wondered if she'd brought the yellow dress by accident. "Shall we begin with your hair?"

"Yes, yes," I said, hurrying to sit at the bench before the dressing table. "I haven't done anything to it since yesterday, and it's quite the rat's nest by now."

At once Hamlin pulled my haphazard braid apart and began to drag my silver hairbrush down the length of my hair. Usually this was my favorite part of dressing, the comforting rhythm of the brush smoothing the tangles and unevenness from my hair, as if all the cares and worries of my day could be as easily brushed away, too. Seeking that solace, I closed my eyes and relaxed.

But this time instead of peace, my thoughts restlessly returned to Savage and whatever it was he did not wish for me to know. I knew it was not my affair, but there was something about the way he'd phrased it—*things that are better for you not to know*—that troubled me. He had every appearance of being a wealthy, powerful man with a title and property to insulate him, and yet I couldn't help but wonder if he was being threatened by secret danger.

Was that what he meant about protecting me?

My father had wanted to keep me safe, too, but he had done it with iron gates around our houses and armed Pinkerton men on our train. How could Savage mean to accomplish the same by taking me to a fashionable and very public restaurant instead of keeping me within his house? How could that be a safer place?

Unless the danger lay within this house, instead of outside of it. . . .

"That's not your robe, ma'am," Hamlin said, cutting into my uneasy thoughts. "I'd know it if it were. It's a gentleman's robe, not yours."

I took a deep breath that was more of a sigh and opened my eyes. So much for reveries.

"The robe belongs to Lord Savage," I said, trying to state a fact and not sound defensive—which of course I already was. "He was kind enough to make a loan of it to me while I am his guest."

"His *guest,* ma'am." Hamlin clucked her tongue. "No respectable unmarried lady is the guest of an unmarried gentleman, not in America, not in England."

"Hamlin, you forget yourself," I said as sharply as I could—which was nothing to Hamlin, now that she'd begun.

"What would your poor father say to that, ma'am?" she asked. "What would Mr. Hart himself say?"

"They'd say that you were speaking out of turn, Hamlin," I said. "You are fortunate that neither of them is alive to hear you address me like this."

"Oh, they're the fortunate ones," Hamlin said, undeterred. She began to pin my hair up, jabbing each hairpin into place for emphasis. "Being dead and buried, so they don't have to see the shame you're bringing on your self with this lord!"

"He is an earl, Hamlin, a peer of the realm," I said, "and deserving your regard."

"And I'm from Boston, America, where we don't have much use for earls and realms and such." She sniffed disdainfully, twisting my hair. "Where I'm from, ma'am, we haven't forgotten 1776 and what Paul Revere and John Adams and all those other brave lads did to toss that English king where he belonged, him and his tea, too."

Any other time I might have laughed at her version of American history, but now I was too agitated to find anything amusing in it.

"I do not require a history lesson from you, Hamlin," I snapped, "nor do I have any wish to hear your opinions on my private affairs."

"But they're not private any longer, ma'am, are they?" asked Hamlin as she pinned my favorite diamond star into my dark waves. "You haven't been discreet, ma'am. Every servant in the Savoy is whispering about what you and Lord Savage are doing together, and if waiters and chambermaids are talking, you know their betters are, too."

I sighed and turned around on the bench to face her.

"That defines backstairs gossip, Hamlin," I said sternly. "It's exactly how the most malicious tales and falsehoods are spread, whispered from one to another. Where are my underthings?"

"Here, ma'am," she said, and in uneasy silence we fell into our shared ritual of dressing me: drawers, chemise, petticoats, corset, corset cover, garters, and stockings, each to be pulled up or smoothed down, tied and hooked and buttoned into place.

All the layers made me feel like the weight of respectability was once again settling over my body, too, constricting me back into its expectations, and drawing me apart from Savage.

Finally came the yellow silk gown, falling over my head and body with a soft *whoosh*. At least that was as light as a rose petal, and when I looked at my reflection in the standing mirror I had to be pleased. The brilliant color would draw every eye, and the black lace made my skin even more fair by comparison. After days of going without a corset, it was oddly satisfying to wear one again, like returning to an old friend, and I reveled in the familiar way it narrowed my waist and plumped my breasts. Over my gown I'd wear a black velvet evening cloak embroided with glittering jet beads, the better to frame the brilliant yellow of my gown.

If Savage wished to show me off, then I'd done my part to make sure every eye would be on me. The only jewel I wore was the diamond star in my hair. I fastened the long strand of his pearls around my neck myself, and they fell familiarly over my breasts.

I glanced at the clock on the mantel, glad that I was ready early. Hamlin handed me my fan and draped my evening cloak around my shoulders, and I opened the door myself, eager to rejoin Savage.

"I don't mean just the backstairs talk, ma'am," Hamlin said behind me. "It's modern days now. Someone's bound to have sent telegraphs to New York, ma'am, and written about you in the newspaper columns. Everyone there will know by now, too."

Reluctantly I paused, and looked back over my shoulder. Hamlin's lips were pinched tightly together, and there were bright patches of emotion on her cheeks. She held my silver brush in her hands, preparing to put it away, and her fingers moved unconsciously across my monogram—the three letters that marked my married name—engraved on the back.

"It's not just the servants who talk, you know, ma'am," she said, returning to the topic that I thought we'd finished. "Mrs. Astor, Mrs. Vanderbilt, and all the others must already be talking about you and this earl. He's a wicked gentleman, ma'am. Everyone knows it. You're far too good for him, ma'am, and you'll ruin yourself if you keep company with him. Or worse, ma'am. Or worse!"

I hadn't expected such a tirade from her, and it shocked me. It was one thing to hear Laura's misgivings about Savage but quite another to hear them from my lady's maid.

"Hamlin, please," I said. "I've spoken to you before about indulging in that kind of whispering and speculation, and I—"

"But there's never been anything said of you before, ma'am," Hamlin said plaintively. "You've always been better and more decent than the other ladies. But now, because of *him,* you're—Oh, you're not."

To my horror, she burst into tears, standing before me sobbing with her arms hanging at her sides and my hairbrush clutched tightly in her hands.

I'd never seen her cry before, and it embarrassed me, especially because I was the reason for it. I went to the open trunk and found one of my handkerchiefs.

"Here now, take this," I said, pressing it into her hand. "You mustn't distress yourself, Hamlin, not over this."

She took the handkerchief and pressed it over her eyes. "How can I not be distressed, ma'am," she said, snuffling, "when I see what's become of you?"

"Nothing has 'become' of me" I said patiently. "I'm still much as I ever was."

"Forgive me, ma'am, but you're not," she said, her sobs fading to hiccups. "You're here in this man's house, as common and familiar as if you were his . . . his kept mistress."

I sighed, toying with my fan as I wondered how honest I should be.

"Very well, then," I said finally. "I am different, because I am *happy*. I'm happy in a way that I never was as a child, or as a wife, either."

She went very still. "That's not possible, ma'am," she said with startling vehemence. "Mr. Hart was a true gentleman, and kindness itself. He was very good to you, ma'am. No one could say otherwise."

"But that wasn't enough," I said softly. "Not at all. His Lordship makes me happier and more . . . more *alive* than I've ever been. If I must trade decency and the regard of self-righteous women such as Mrs. Astor for that, then I'll gladly do it, over and over, and without a single regret, either."

But Hamlin wasn't listening any longer. She was staring past me, and abruptly she bowed her head and dropped a curtsey.

I turned, and there was Savage in the doorway behind me. Gone was the old jersey and the rakishly unkempt look of a Bohemian artist. He was now impeccably dressed for evening, all crisp white and deepest black. His freshly shaven jaw gleamed above the white tie, and his hair was sleeked back as shiny as a raven's wing.

Ignoring Hamlin, his gaze roamed freely over me, lingering on the low-cut bodice outlining my breasts in black lace. He must have approved, because he smiled, slow and sinfully seductive and enough to make me melt.

"You're beautiful," he said. "No other woman in London can rival you tonight. Are you ready?"

I nodded and turned back to Hamlin. Her expression was like a mask, the emotions that had so recently spilled over once again carefully hidden.

"Have one of the men downstairs summon you a cab back to the Savoy," I said, finding the fare in my purse. "There's no need for you to remain here."

"As you wish, ma'am," she said with another quick curtsey. "Thank you, ma'am."

I pressed the coins into her palm. "Please don't worry about me, Hamlin," I said, lowering my voice for her. "I shall be fine in His Lordship's company."

She nodded, but I glimpsed something close to sorrow in her eyes as her fingers closed over the coins.

"As you wish, ma'am," she said again. "Whatever you wish."

9.

Gaspari's reminded me of Delmonico's in New York: a large, lavish restaurant with a great deal of gleaming dark wood and glittering chandeliers. The tables were covered with snowy linens, and the silver and china were of the first quality. Black-clad waiters with immaculate aprons hurried among the tables, carrying steaming dishes over their heads as much to display the savory contents as to protect them. Conversation and the clink of heavy forks and crystal created a well-bred undercurrent of sound, punctuated every now and then by the pop of a champagne cork.

Also like at Delmonico's, the diners were mostly male, a well-fed sea of black and white evening clothes and bristling whiskers beneath the haze of expensive cigars and cigarettes. I recognized their smugness and their arrogance, the sure signs of money and privilege. Because the hour was late for respectable women to dine the few ladies with these men—beautiful bright spots of silken plumage—were perhaps not ladies at all but actresses, opera singers, artists' models.

When I'd accompanied my father to Delmonico's, I'd

always looked at such women with curiosity and fascination, and with a certain pity, too. They were the women ladies called "fallen" in a melodramatic whisper, as if their taint could be caught like a cold. As a girl I'd wondered what they'd fallen from; later I'd learned it was from respectability and decency, marking them forever as the sort of women gentlemen didn't marry. Yet still they'd fascinated me, for they'd always appeared to be not only the most glamorous women in Delmonico's but also the ones who were having the most fun.

It came as something as a shock to realize that being here tonight at Gaspari's, in my golden silk gown and on the arm of a gentleman who had given me the pearls around my throat but would never be my husband, I'd become exactly the same as those long-ago women I'd glimpsed at Delmonico's.

And because that gentleman was Savage I didn't care one bit that I was. I'd been miserable in my respectable marriage. With Savage I felt vibrant, sensual, and happier than I'd ever been, and if that was the meaning of "fallen" then I'd embrace it.

Yet there was more than that: I was proud to be seen with him, proud to have nearly every eye in the large room turned towards us as we stood in the doorway. Savage had said he'd wanted to show me off, and he was doing exactly that.

Instead of offering me his arm he'd placed his hand on the back of my waist, a clear sign of not only familiarity but also possession. There'd be no doubt in anyone's mind that we were together, and even that little touch, the pressure of his spread fingers and open palm at my waist, made me glow and warm with pleasure.

"Your table is waiting, my lord," murmured the maître d'hôtel, bowing to one side before Savage.

"In a moment," Savage said, his gaze swiftly scanning the room like a hawk searching for prey. "Is His Majesty here tonight?"

"He is, my lord," said the maître d'hôtel. "He is dining privately with several gentlemen in the Salon Diamante."

Savage smiled. "Then we shall pay our respects before we dine ourselves."

"Very good, my lord," the maître d'hôtel said, and with another bow he turned to lead us through the crowded room.

"The king is here?" I said to Savage, my voice low so only he would hear.

"Oh, yes," Savage said nonchalantly, as if the King of England were no more than any other man of his acquaintance. "His Majesty has always been something of a gourmand, and he would steal the chef here away from Signor Gaspari if he could."

I slipped my hand into the crook of his arm, drawing him back.

"But I cannot greet the king, Savage," I whispered anxiously as he paused with obvious reluctance. "It won't be permitted. I haven't yet been presented at Court."

He smiled down at me indulgently, yet wicked enough to make me melt.

"You can, because the king himself will wish it," he said. "The formal presentation is only to please the punctilious fools at Court, nothing more. You'll be with me. You'll be welcome."

"You are certain?" Ever since I'd decided to come to England I'd been told that a formal presentation at Court was essential for any American lady wishing to make her way in London society. To breeze in upon the king while he was dining seemed impolite, even rude.

"Perhaps I should wait until after I've been presented,"

I continued, wavering beneath the weight of a lifetime of ingrained rules for good manners. "I've already received my invitation to the next Drawing Room, so it's not as if I'm not—"

"Stop," Savage said firmly, and though his smile remained, there was more than a hint of my imperious Master in his voice. "The king will not object. Old Bertie may have one foot tottering over the grave, but he still has an appreciation for pretty American women—a weakness I entirely understand."

I blushed, for even his most obvious compliments could do that to me, but still I hesitated.

"You are certain it would not be impolite?"

"Eve, Eve." He smiled and ran his fingers lightly along my jaw. "He will like you. He will like you to an exceptional degree, I am certain. How many times must I ask you to trust me, in this and in everything else?"

Although the maître d'hôtel stood waiting to one side, politely pretending not to listen, I knew he must be overhearing.

Nor was he alone. Even if the diners at the nearby tables couldn't hear Savage's words, surely they must be able to guess at the depth of our connection from the way he was touching my face, and from the way he was looking at me now they must see how I'd disappointed him.

My flush deepened, and not from embarrassment, either. I didn't care about discretion. He was my Master, and it pleased me that the others would see us together and realize our intimacy. What was it he'd once said to me—that I liked an audience? Perhaps he was right, and perhaps I did.

I straightened my back and raised my shoulders to lift my breasts, subtly presenting myself to him the way he liked.

"There've been too many times when I haven't trusted you as I should, Master," I murmured. "Forgive me, Master, for I have failed you again."

"Yes, Eve, you have," he said, a hint of disappointment in his eyes. Yet there was pleasure there, too, for I'd realized as well that he also enjoyed an audience. It was all part of the Game—*our* Game. Who would have guessed we'd be playing it here, in the middle of Gaspari's?

"I thought by now you'd learned how important it is to trust me," Savage continued. "I'm afraid that you must be reminded more forcefully. I have a special punishment in mind for you."

My pulse quickened with anticipation. "Yes, Master," I said. "That will help me to remember."

"It will," he said, leaving no doubt of what we'd do later. "Now come with me, Eve."

Once again he nodded to the maître d'hôtel, and this time we followed him. My hand remained in the crook of Savage's arm, and he kept me close as he led me among the tables and other diners—so close that he could continue our conversation.

"Do you already have your dress for your Court presentation?" he asked. "With all the prescribed fripperies?"

It seemed like a curious question for a man to ask, but I nodded anyway.

I'd had my presentation dress made as soon as I'd decided to come to London, for there were precise requirements to follow. The dress had been outrageously expensive, even for me, with a long train, elaborate beading, lace, and embroidery, all in formal white as if it were an extravagant wedding dress. I would also be expected to wear three white plumes in my hair to show that I'd been married, as well as long, formal gloves over my elbows, and every diamond and pearl I possessed.

"I should like to see you dressed to slay every other lady in the room, Eve," he said. "To which Drawing Room are you invited?"

I wasn't sure if he was teasing me or not. I didn't understand his interest; he'd made it clear that he'd little use for Court rituals, and I couldn't imagine him wishing to see me in the lavish but unyielding armor of my dress.

"Next Wednesday afternoon, Master," I said. "I will be attending with my sponsor, Lady Tremayne."

"Lady Tremayne?" he repeated with amusement. "That ancient relic? Don't be fooled by her aura of gentility; she was a greater reprobate than most of the gentlemen of her generation. Have her losses grown so bad that she's resorted to hiring herself out to Americans?"

"She accepted a gift in return for sponsoring, yes," I said. "I've only met her once, and she seemed pleasant enough."

"So long as you keep her from the brandy," he said drily. "But I believe you should attend only the actual presentation with her. After that you'll be mine for the reception. I am considering another way to test your obedience and your trust."

"At the Drawing Room, Master?" I asked, surprised. "At the Palace?"

"Yes," he said, and no more, letting my imagination race with possibilities—or the lack of them.

Laura had warned me that the Court presentations were notorious for being crowded and regimented, with everyone exquisitely dressed yet jockeying for the best places to see and be seen, and that the receptions that followed were little better. How could Savage mean to try me in there? It was one thing for him to contrive his tests at Wrentham or in his own house, but to do so at Buckingham Palace would be entirely another.

Yet as unsettled as I was by the prospect, I realized I was also excited by it. What *was* he planning? What would he expect me to do—and how?

The maître d'hôtel had led us from the main dining room, beneath a curtained archway, and through a door to a short hallway. At the end of the hallway was another door, with a pair of large, watchful men, simply dressed, on either side of it. From the way they glowered at Savage and me, I knew at once that they were some sort of private guards or policemen in plainclothes. My father had often employed such men from for protection, and so, I guessed, would the King of England.

Not that they intimidated Savage. Instead he greeted both men by name, and in return they both nodded with curt recognition and respect, too. I was impressed. He must truly be His Majesty's friend if the bodyguards knew him, and as the maître d'hôtel knocked on the door I felt a rush of excitement. I was going to meet the King of England, now, over his dinner, which was more than Mrs. Astor or Mrs. Vanderbilt or any of the pompous other ladies at home in New York had ever done.

"Must I make a full Court curtsey to His Majesty, Master?" I whispered urgently. I'd taken lessons to learn this skill and had practiced bending so low that the plumes that would be in my hair brushed the carpet before me. "I'm not sure there will be room if he's seated at the table, and—"

"No, no, nothing so grand," Savage said carelessly. "An American curtsey will do well enough."

I'd no idea what that might be, but before I could ask, the door had swung open and the maître d'hôtel was ushering us inside. Savage entered first, and I hung back: not exactly shy, but uncertain of my place.

Over his shoulder, I saw that the small private dining

room was even more lavishly appointed than the front room had been, with gold-framed mirrors and paintings and a thick Persian carpet underfoot and four waiters standing ready along the wall. A dozen gentlemen sat around the oval dining table, and it was clear from both their florid faces and the random blotches of wine on the cloth that they'd been drinking as much as they'd been dining and, from the tobacco smoke that thickened the air, that they'd been smoking a great deal, too.

All of the gentlemen were in evening dress, without any medals or ribbons to give away the noble ranks that they inevitably held, and yet at once I knew which one of them was the king. I'd seen pictures of him before, of course—he was stout, with popping eyes and a graying beard trimmed to a point—but it was more than that. The other men sat a little apart from him and had turned their chairs towards his to make him the centerpiece of their group. When he looked towards us as we entered, the others watched for his reaction, almost as if waiting for permission, before they, too, looked our way.

Not that the king himself noticed.

"Savage, you dog!" he called out, the corners of his beard tipping up as he smiled in welcome. "You're exactly what's needed. We need fresh blood and conversation for our motley company tonight. Come, join us. Another chair, here, for Lord Savage."

At once one of the waiters hurried to find a chair for Savage while the gentlemen at the table obediently began to move their own chairs more closely together to make room.

But Savage only smiled and bowed. "You're very kind, Your Majesty," he said. "But I fear I've only come to pay the briefest of regards, and then must retreat to a previous engagement."

He turned back towards me and took my hand, drawing me forward to join him.

"Sir, may I present Mrs. Hart," he said, leading me into the room and into the circle of light from the electric lamps. "She is one of your favorite variety of lady, another *belle américaine* visiting us from New York."

It struck me as a rather odd introduction, but then I'd little experience with how things were done before kings. I sank into a curtsey, bowing my head and praying I'd dropped low enough to please both the king and Savage. Without looking I heard the gentlemen push back their chairs and stand in my honor.

"Here now, Mrs. Hart, no more of that," said the king warmly. "Please stand, and come closer so we might see you properly."

Slowly I rose as he'd bid and circled around the table. He alone remained seated, as royalty should be, leaning forward towards me. Even with him sitting, I could tell he was shorter than I, much shorter than I'd imagined from the flattering pictures I'd seen, and much older. He didn't look well, either. His belly mounded heavily over his lap, his face was too flushed, he wheezed slightly with each breath, and his hand was unsteady, making the cigar in his hand tremble and scatter ashes on his sleeve.

"Oh, you are right, Savage; she is a most superb creature," he said, as if I were not a woman but simply an inanimate objet d'art to be admired and possessed. "American women truly are in a class of their own."

I decided to take this as a compliment, though I wasn't sure it was one.

"Thank you, Your Majesty," I murmured. "You are too kind."

"Not at all, my dear," he said, finally addressing me.

"I've heard you were the favorite at Wrenton last week. Now I understand why."

Word traveled fast through Society, and I should have known he would have already heard of what had happened with Savage and me at Wrenton—even if every guest had supposedly been sworn to secrecy. No doubt it had proved too good a story for someone not to share, especially with the royal ear listening.

Yet I didn't like the eagerness in his eyes as he studied me, his gaze fixed not on my face but on my breasts, raised by my corset above the deep neckline. He ran his tongue lightly over his pale lower lip with an unmistakable greediness and leaned forward towards me in his chair.

Like most women, I knew the different ways a man could look at me, the subtle degrees that ranged from polite admiration, to intriguing interest, to open, unabashed lust. That last was how the king was looking at me now—as if I were the next course on the menu for him to devour.

With any other man I would simply have removed myself from his company, adding a good slap or shove if he'd persisted. That was what American ladies did in such a situation.

But this was different. He was the King of England, and ordinary rules wouldn't apply. Beautiful women like Laura had considered themselves fortunate to have shared his bed, as if it were a great sign of favor. More confusing still was trying to determine what Savage, as my Master, wished me to do. Instead of jumping to my defense as he'd always done before he was standing silently behind me, saying nothing, doing nothing. Worse, I now recalled his curious introduction of me, telling the king that I was his "favorite variety of lady."

Was this another of Savage's tests for me? Did he truly intend to offer me to the king as a kind of gift—as if I were his to give? I know such things had been done in ancient times, but this was the twentieth century. I was an American lady, not some cowering peasant woman. I would do many things for Savage as part of our Game, but this . . . this I did not think I could do, not even for him.

When I looked at the king, with his trembling, vein-crossed hands and bilious pouches beneath his eyes, I could think only of my late husband, who hadn't been so very different. A dry, painful coupling without attraction, without love, without so much as a breath of desire or pleasure, with a man who, king or not, was still older than my own father . . .

No, I couldn't do this, even if my Master wished it.

Unconsciously I took a step backwards, already beginning to flee, when I felt Savage's hand at the back of my waist. The pressure of his hand was gentle, steadying, reassuring, and only then did I realize I was trembling, too.

"She is a rare lady, sir," he said behind me. His hand slipped from my back to my waist as he came to stand beside me, and I automatically leaned into him. "She has honored me with her acquaintance for only a short time, but already she has become an excellent friend."

"A friend," the king echoed. He said it sadly, with resignation, and the greedy lust faded from his rheumy eyes. He took a long pull on the last of his cigar and snuffed it out in the tray beside his plate. "You are a fortunate man, Savage, a young buck in your prime, and I know better than to try to poach. But if I were your age . . . ah, I'd give you a run for her!"

"I'm sure you would, sir," Savage said, his hand tightening a possessive fraction around my waist. "But I would fight you, and I would win."

He would, too. I'd watched him do it and knew how little it would take to make him do it again.

The king must have seen that in my face, for he laughed, a strange, small guffaw that had little humor to it.

"Yes, yes, I've heard all about the fisticuffs and blood-letting from Carleigh himself," he said, then glanced back at me. "Take care with him, Mrs. Hart, and I shall be sure to look over you as well. Never was a man so aptly named as our friend Savage."

Without looking I felt the tension in Savage's body beside mine and knew he wasn't smiling, nor would he take the remark as a joke. Perhaps the king hadn't intended it that way, either, and I was thankful when Savage only bowed and managed some sort of evening pleasantries that allowed us to retreat from the king's presence without incident or scandal.

The same maître d'hôtel reappeared in the hallway and ushered us to one of the best tables in the dining room, a corner table set apart from the others where I was framed and reflected by a pair of mirrors like a diamond in a jeweler's display. Most likely Savage had requested this table for exactly that reason, since he'd said earlier that he wished to show me off, but after what had just happened with the king I would rather have preferred a more private setting to recover myself.

Savage ordered dinner for us both, and when our glasses had been filled with wine and the waiters had finally left us he raised his glass to me, his pale eyes guarded and revealing nothing.

"You're quiet, Eve," he said. "I shouldn't think a lady from New York would be so overwhelmed in the presence of royalty."

I shook my head, wondering how best to explain. What

should have been a special, memorable occasion—to be presented so informally to the King of England!—had instead left me uncertain and filled with doubts.

"It was not . . . not what I expected," I said, which was true.

"Ahh," Savage said lightly. "I can understand your disappointment. I fear the king no longer cuts a particularly regal figure, does he?"

I shook my head again, my earrings brushing my cheeks. As difficult as the answer might be, I had to know.

"It wasn't that so much as . . . as the rest," I said softly. "Why did you take me there to him, Savage? What was your reason for it?"

"Why?" He set his glass down and placed his hand on my arm, his hand warm on my skin. "Because now you'll be safe from the worst slander at Court. I cannot protect you from everything, as much as I wish to. The king can. Now that he has met you and admired you, he will do as he says. He will not tolerate anything ill said of you in his presence, and will only speak well of you himself. It will make your life more . . . agreeable at Court."

"He will do that for me?" I asked, surprised. "I scarcely said a dozen words to him."

"It's not conversation that he admires in ladies," Savage said drily. "I know that being with me has come at a cost to your reputation. This will go a small way towards balancing that."

The unexpected kindness of it overwhelmed me. "That is so . . . so *good* of you, Savage."

His smile was tinged with bitterness. "You're alone in that estimation, too," he said. "The king certainly doesn't share it. I'll wager that he's already sent word to Scotland Yard to have me watched, to be sure I cause you no harm, but I can bear with that. It would not be the first time."

"It's not necessary, none of it," I said quickly, and covered his hand with my own. "You know I trust you."

"You will be one of the few who do, Eve," he said as our first plates were set before us. "You cannot know how much it pleases me, too."

When he smiled, the guard he usually kept so firmly in place was gone, replaced by a warmth and trust in me that I did not deserve. He raised my hand, his lips grazing the back in the way that gave me chills of pleasure.

"Now you must tell me, Eve," he said, turning to the elegant dish before us, "if the reputation of Gaspari's chef is better deserved than my own."

I smiled, yet in my heart I realized how I didn't deserve his gratitude. If I'd trusted him as I'd said, I wouldn't have suspected him earlier of offering me to the king. Savage had had only my well-being in mind, yet I'd suspected him, and now I felt despicable myself, low and unworthy of him.

All through the long meal I managed to keep this to myself, praising the food and wine and smiling when I should and returning every endearment that he offered, while he was his most charming, most irresistible self. Yet inside I was miserable, and as the last dessert dishes were cleared away I finally blurted out what had been worrying at me throughout the long meal.

"I must tell you the truth, Master," I confessed, my guilty words tumbling over one another. "I must be honest with you. I cannot keep it back. When you presented me to the king, Master, I . . . I feared it was another trial. I thought you wanted me to lie with him, there, and I . . . I would not have been able to do it."

His face went rigid. "You believed that of me? That I would give you to another man to enjoy, any man, even a king?"

"I thought it was one more challenge," I confessed. Tears stung my eyes, and I took his hand in my own to make him understand, my fingers moving restlessly against his. "I thought you were testing my obedience again."

His eyes had turned as hard as flint, and he pointedly pulled his hand free of mine.

"You are mine, Eve," he said. "*Mine*. Do you understand? I would never ask that of you, not as an Innocent, not as a woman, and if you do not trust me enough to believe that, then I—Damn, what is it?"

A waiter was hovering beside the table, his hands folded before him as if already begging forgiveness for the interruption.

"I am sorry, my lord," he said, "but there is a man here from your house who says he has an urgent message for you that cannot wait."

At once Savage stood, tossing his crumpled napkin on the table before me.

"Wait here," he said curtly. "Do not leave. We'll continue this when I return."

He didn't pause for my answer but turned and headed for the door, his tall figure in black cutting sharply back and forth among the tables.

I watched him leave and let my bitter tears spill over. I'd tried to do what was honorable and right by confessing, but instead I'd disappointed him, and worse, I'd wounded him, wounded him deeply. I knew him well enough to see that.

I bowed my head to blot my eyes with my napkin, not wanting the other diners to witness my misery. A woman weeping alone in a restaurant as a man stalked away: oh, yes, there was plenty of melodrama and gossip to be mined from that.

Yet it had been entirely my own fault. Over and over Savage had asked me to trust him, and I'd thought that I did, until I'd proved I didn't. I could have kept my fault to myself, but that would have been a lie by omission, only making things worse. It was as simple and painful as that. I wanted to be his in every way, yet still part of me held back, unable to let go and give him the complete trust he deserved.

He'd said he'd return, but I wasn't sure he would. I'd seen the pain I'd caused in his eyes, and I wouldn't blame him if he decided to abandon me here and never see me again. I suppose if I trusted him as he wanted I'd be sure he'd come back, but once again, I didn't.

I fumbled with the clasp of my beaded evening purse, hoping there was money inside. That was something that Hamlin, ever practical, always saw to—making certain there was enough at least for cab fare in every one of my purses—but in her haste to return to the Savoy this afternoon she'd left this particular purse empty. This disaster of an evening only continued to worsen, and I snapped the bankrupt purse close.

Still looking down at my lap, I dipped a corner of my napkin into my ice water and pressed it to my cheeks, hoping that would help me to keep back more tears until I could find my way back to my hotel.

"Take my handkerchief, Mrs. Hart," urged a man as he took the empty chair beside mine. "Please. It's never good for a lady to weep alone."

Swiftly I looked up and caught my breath with surprise and dismay. Beside me sat Baron Blackledge, offering me his oversized handkerchief clutched tightly in his plump fingers. His curling ginger hair gleamed with pomade, and his smile was far too broad as he pressed closer to me.

"Good evening, Baron," I said, striving to make my

voice frosty and unwelcoming. I wiped away the last of my tears and sat very straight. "I do not believe Lord Savage would appreciate your presence here at this table."

His smile only widened. "How can Savage appreciate my presence one way or another if he's not here?"

I slid my chair away from his, only to have him follow and place his hand firmly on the back of my chair to keep me from moving it again.

"His Lordship will return," I said as forcefully as I could. "I expect him back here any moment."

"No, you don't," he said. "You wouldn't be crying if you did."

I raised my chin with a final sniff. "My emotions have nothing to do with His Lordship's return."

"Oh, of course they don't," he said, his voice thick with sarcasm. "Not at all. That's why I saw Savage in the street, waiting for his carriage."

Before I could catch myself my eyes widened and my lips parted with alarm at this news. Blackledge saw my reaction and laughed.

"You thought I'd be fooled by your little fib, Mrs. Hart, didn't you?" he said, jeering as he wagged his finger in my face. "You thought I'd believe that Savage was coming back to rescue you. He's not, and now I'm here instead."

I swallowed hard. Because the table was recessed into the corner I was trapped between the mirrored wall and the baron's sizable body. I glanced past him, praying I'd see Savage returning. He'd told me to wait here, and I had. He had to come back to rescue me; he *had* to.

"I wish you to leave me, Baron," I said firmly. "Leave me directly, before I must summon the maître d'hôtel."

He didn't care. "You won't do that," he said confidently. "No lady likes to make a scene, especially not here at

Gaspari's. You'd do better to forget Savage, and come with me instead."

"No," I said, shaking my head for extra emphasis. He was right, of course. I didn't want to make a scene, especially not if the king and his party were still here in the restaurant. More important, I wanted to be there when Savage returned. *When*, I told myself, *when, not if.*

"I have no interest in doing anything with you, Baron," I said. "None at all."

With growing desperation I glanced about for one of the waiters who seemed to have inconveniently vanished.

"Oh, but I think you do," Blackledge said confidently. His eyes narrowed, watching me. "You can stop looking for help. I told the waiters that I wished to console you in private, and they've been tipped to stay away."

"You're a vile man, Baron," I said. "I despise everything about you."

He leaned into me, his face flushed with desire. "Don't you realize that the more you try to keep away from me, the more I want you? I know what women like you want, Mrs. Hart, and I'll give it to you, too, harder and hotter than you ever got from that weakling bastard Savage."

He circled my wrist with his fingers, squeezing so tightly that I gave a little cry of pain that made him chuckle.

"Let me go, Baron," I said, more panic than I wanted in my voice. "You're hurting me. Let me go *now*."

"Come with me, Mrs. Hart," he said, more a demand than an invitation. "My carriage is waiting."

His fingers were digging so tightly into my wrist that I was shaking from the pain. With my free hand I grabbed one of the dessert forks still on the table and stabbed it as hard as I could into his thigh beneath the table.

He barely flinched. Instead he smiled, almost laughing at me, with little flecks of spittle on his lips.

"Is that how you like it, Mrs. Hart?" he asked. "Is that how you play the Game? By God, you were meant to be mine, not Savage's, and nothing you can—"

"Release the lady, Blackledge," Savage said, suddenly standing before us. Outwardly he was calm, but I knew every muscle of his body must be tense with fury. "Let her go at once."

Still grasping my wrist, Blackledge smiled up at him. "Why should I, Savage? Why should I be afraid of you?"

"I don't give a damn whether you are or not," Savage said curtly. "But if you do not take your hand away from Mrs. Hart and leave us at once, I shall rip your arm from your shoulder."

"Don't, Savage, please, I beg you," I pleaded, unable to keep quiet any longer. "Not here."

"Don't fret, Mrs. Hart," Blackledge said with bullying bravado. "He hasn't the bollocks to do it."

"Rather I haven't your stupidity, Blackledge," Savage said, his voice clipped and purposefully low so others wouldn't hear him. "His Majesty is dining here tonight, and Gaspari's is crawling with men with Scotland Yard. They'd be at this table in an instant if I treated you as you deserve, and for the king's sake, I won't do that. Nor should you."

"His Majesty is here?" Blackledge uneasily peered around the room. I remembered how he was a much-lesser nobleman than Savage and clearly without the acquaintance that Savage had with the king, or the power that came with it.

"He is," Savage said. "In one of the back rooms. But you'll see his men scattered about if you care to look."

Swiftly Blackledge looked past Savage. He must have spotted one of the guards, because at last he released my wrist. I quickly pushed my chair apart from his, rubbing the place where his fingers had left their mark on me. Savage grabbed the edge of the table and pulled it forward, freeing me. I grabbed my purse and slipped around the far side of the table to join Savage. As much as I longed to, I didn't dare take his hand or arm, remembering how displeased he'd been with me before he'd left.

But still I stood close to him, by his side and a little behind him, taking comfort from even that slight proximity. His gaze was still locked with Blackledge's, and I wasn't sure their obvious hatred wouldn't yet erupt.

"I've warned you before, Blackledge," Savage said. "Keep away from Mrs. Hart. She has no interest in you, and never will."

"We're in London, Savage, and the Game is done," Blackledge said. "She's not yours any longer. You'll see. She'll be mine soon enough."

"The hell she will," Savage said curtly. "Mrs. Hart, if you please."

He crooked his arm for me to take, and I gratefully did, holding tightly as he led me through the restaurant, pausing only to settle my evening cloak over my shoulders. His carriage was waiting outside at the curb, and he handed me inside and let his footman shut the door after us.

Throughout he said not a word to me, nor did he so much as meet my eye. He didn't sit beside me in the carriage, as he usually did, but across from me on the opposite seat.

The carriage's curtains were drawn against the gaslights that Savage so despised, and in the murky shadows only his white collar and cuffs shone through the darkness, leaving everything else reduced to uncertain shapes.

It was not an auspicious beginning. As the carriage moved into the street I braced myself for more of the awful conversation he'd broken off earlier. I'd let him begin. I wouldn't dare start first, not until I could better judge his humor. I was so prepared for the worst that when he finally did speak it startled me enough that I jerked in my seat like a nervous cat.

"Did he hurt you?" he asked, his voice quiet. Not gentle, not soft, not charming, just . . . quiet. Subdued. "Do you need to see a surgeon?"

"No," I said quickly. "Not at all."

"Are you certain?" he asked. "You were holding your wrist as if it were broken."

"It's not broken," I said. "Only bruised, and that will heal soon enough."

He shifted restlessly on the seat, stretching his legs out before him and brushing against my skirts.

"A bruise isn't nothing," he said. "I don't want you to suffer at the hands of a brute like that, but I didn't want to thrash him as he deserves with the king so near. That would have been unwise."

"Yes, it would have," I said, figuring it was safe to agree. "I wouldn't have wanted you hurt, either."

"Oh, I wouldn't have been the one to suffer," he said with offhanded assurance. I'd already witnessed how frighteningly powerful—and violent—he could be in a fistfight, but Blackledge was a large man and a bully as well. I wouldn't want to see them come to blows, especially over me.

Savage paused, and I sensed he was watching me, or at least my shadow. "You were there when I came back."

"You saved me from Blackledge," I said. "Again."

He grunted. "I'm hardly a hero. I should have returned sooner. What he did to you—"

"It was nothing, Savage," I said. "I don't know why he persists in following me."

"He's obsessed with you," Savage said. "Which is understandable. It's the only thing I can understand about him."

I flushed in the dark. I understood, too, for I was obsessed with the irresistible man sitting across from me.

"I wish he weren't," I said. "I have made it as clear as I can that I will never have any interest in him."

"That only makes you more desirable to a bastard like that," he said. "The more you resist him, the more he'll want you. He's dangerous, Eve."

I shivered, remembering how the baron had enjoyed hurting me. "I'll still never agree."

"I wouldn't let him," Savage said, pausing for a moment. "I asked you to wait for me, Eve, and you did."

"Of course I waited," I said. "I wanted to."

"You trusted me." It was a statement, plain and unadorned, so why did it make my heart quicken?

"I did," I said. "I do. I do not know what became of me with His Majesty. He was so old and unwell that he reminded me of my husband, and being married, and . . . it frightened me, and unsettled me."

I let the words trail off awkwardly, not even sure myself of what I was trying to say. Again, the silence yawned between us, interminable in the darkness.

He drew in a long, deep breath, then let it out as a sigh.

"My poor Eve," he said, reaching for me across the seats. "No matter how we try to escape, the past always finds us, doesn't it?"

I curled against him, his mouth finding mine in the dark. He could say what he wanted about the past. *This* was my sanctuary, my solace, and in him I forgot Blackledge and the king and my husband, Arthur, and everything else and lost myself in desire. No matter what Savage said, the past would cease to matter. Here it was only the two of us, and the white-hot fire that burned between us. I prayed it was the same for him, too.

I loved how the darkness in the carriage heightened my other senses, making me doubly aware of his taste and his scent, the feel of his lips moving over mine, the rough wetness of his tongue as it slipped into my mouth. I relished the potency of his kiss, how it was enough to make me lightheaded with longing. I melted against him and over his lap as lust flared and the carriage rocked gently beneath us.

He unhooked my evening cloak and let it fall to the seat and then shoved the rustling skirts of my gown to one side so he could find the bare skin of my thigh over the top of my stocking, his hand covering as much of my flesh as he could. Our tongues twisted and tangled hotly together, and I felt his cock harden against my hip.

I reached between us, slipping my hand over the flagrant length of him, still shrouded by his trousers.

"Does this mean I am forgiven, Master?" I whispered breathlessly, slowly slipping the buttons free on the fly of his trousers. There were more buttons beneath that on his drawers, his impatient cock straining against the fine cotton. At last it sprang free, vibrant and hot in my hand, as hard as steel and as soft as velvet.

He grunted, his cock thrusting familiarly against my hand, and I smiled. There was considerable traffic tonight in the East End, and the carriage's progress was so slow that we'd have plenty of time before we reached St. James's Square.

"Am I forgiven, Master?" I asked again, my words husky as I stroked his cock.

"In part," he said. With his thumbs he eased the narrow straps of my gown from my shoulders and down over my arms until my breasts popped free of the low-cut neckline.

"Is this better, Master?" Shamelessly I sat back and shrugged my arms free of the straps. My corset supported the rest of my bodice and raised my breasts up like a lace-edged offering to him. "Is that enough for your forgiveness?"

He filled his hands with my breasts, knowing how sensitive they were. He pulled my nipples hard and rolled them back and forth with his thumbs until they stiffened, and then pulled them lightly, teasing me further. I moaned, straddling his thigh and rocking back and forth. Pleasure shimmered through my body. I moaned, unable to help myself, and arched my back into his hands.

"Better, but not enough," he said, his voice rough with the same stark wanting that she felt herself. "I warned you you'd be punished tonight, Eve."

"Whatever you ask, Master," I said. "Whatever you ask, I will obey."

10.

"You know what I want, Eve," he said, his voice low and seductively demanding. "What I expect."

I did. I didn't need to see his face in the darkened carriage to picture his pale eyes turned wolfish, daring me.

He'd promised to punish me when we returned home, and I knew what that meant, too. I'd disobeyed him; I deserved it. If in the process he helped me as his Innocent discover the pleasures to be found in my own body, then my punishment in a way became his reward, too. It was all part of the Game we played together.

And this . . . this would be the true beginning of to-night's adventures.

I slipped from his lap and knelt between his spread legs on the carpeted floor of the carriage. My skirts fanned around me in a rush of silk, and the long strand of pearls around my throat swung gently forward between my bared breasts. I placed my palms on his thighs to steady myself, feeling the tension in the long, corded muscles beneath the soft wool. I leaned forward, my taut nipples grazing against the plush of the seat's edge, and

he angled his long legs farther apart to give me more
room.

Blinded by the darkness, I moved entirely from instinct
and touch, and I let out an excited little sigh as my fingers
again closed around the thick tumescence of his cock. If
possible, his erection seemed to have become harder than
he'd been even a few minutes earlier, and his muttered oath
broke into a rough groan as my hand slid along his length.

Deftly I unfastened the last buttons at his waist and
opened his trousers completely. For a moment, I fanned
my fingers across the sleek skin of his belly and groin
and through the crinkling dark hair, as if to worship his
rising cock. I pushed the layers of cloth aside to free it,
and I dipped my other hand inside the gaping trousers to
cup his balls, primed and heavy with his waiting seed.
I'd done this to him, I thought with awe. He'd given me
this power. I felt as if I were holding his essence in my
hands, his virility, and my answering desire curled
through my belly to my sex.

He grunted, acutely aroused by my touch, and reached
out to dig his fingers into my hair, heedless of the carefully arranged waves. He held my face that way, lightly
stroking my cheeks with his thumbs. It was a gesture of
fondness, true, but also a way of urging me on, and I did
not disappoint him.

I parted my lips and drew the head of his cock into my
mouth. I'd come to love this first moment when I'd taste
him, when I'd join with him. I stretched my lips around
the crown, licking the salty drops that gathered like dew
on the little slit. I flattened my tongue and lapped it around
the head, wanting to cover as much of it as I could, and
he rewarded me with a grunt of pleasure.

"That's it, Eve," he said, his voice harsh and raw with
building tension. "That's it."

I held his balls gently in my fingers, marveling at how tight they were. I'd have to be careful not to go too fast; I wanted to take my time and make this last for him as long as I could.

Even though it was dark, I closed my eyes to concentrate. I drew him deeper into my mouth, caressing the underside of his cock with my tongue as I closed my lips around his turgid length. My cheeks hollowed as I sucked hard, the way he liked. I loved his taste and his scent, the fascinating mix of velvety skin over steely heat. I bathed him with the wet warmth of my mouth and closed my lips around his shaft to draw him deeper.

He grunted again, and his fingers tightened in my hair—another small reward to prove I'd pleased him.

It pleased me, too, as the familiar tingle grew in my sex. Unable to touch myself, I pressed my thighs together, hoping to find some relief that way. My time would come later.

He was pushing back and forth into my mouth now, and I worked to find his rhythm. I relaxed my throat, taking him deeper still as I'd learned to do, and sucked to make more delicious friction for him. He swore, his voice harsh, and his fingers fisted into my hair.

From outside the carriage came the coarse exclamation of another driver, a sudden reminder of where we were. I thought of how outside this enclosed little world of ours were other carriages filled with other people, riding home from their own dinners or perhaps the theatre.

What would they think if the door to our carriage suddenly sprang open? What if all of London could see us now, with me kneeling between Savage's legs, my dress pulled low to reveal my breasts and his cock buried deep in my mouth?

It aroused me to imagine it, having an audience like

that, and eagerly I bobbed my head over him, sliding my lips up and down his shaft.

"Not so fast," he said clearly through gritted teeth. He held my head to still me for a moment. He must be closer than I'd thought, and I paused, letting him take charge of his own pleasure.

No, I wasn't *letting* him do anything. He'd do exactly what he wanted, as he always did. My role was to obey him, and a fresh wave of desire rippled through me. I arched my back to rub my now-aching nipples over the edge of the seat, the bristling plush teasing them with a delicious torment.

"I said not to move, Eve," he ordered sharply.

I paused as he'd wanted, unconsciously making a hum of apology around him. The vibrations of it made him swear, and I ran my tongue lightly along the underside of his shaft to soothe him.

It didn't work. Instead he flexed his hips and began to fuck my mouth in earnest, and I could feel him pulsing between my lips.

"Your hand," he said roughly. "Use your hand, too."

I closed one hand around the base of his cock, pumping my fist there as I took the head as deep as I could.

"Yes, Eve." His voice sounded strangled now. *"Yes."*

He thrust hard and fast, his hips bucking off the seat. I tasted the moment when his orgasm began, the violent explosion that ripped through him and continued for seconds afterward, the animal roar that marked it.

I choked as he filled my mouth, yet still I held fast until he was done, making sure he'd found his satisfaction. I wanted this to be a gift to him, a gift of selfless pleasure. He shuddered one last time, gasping for breath, and his cock slipped free of my mouth, soft and heavy across my tongue.

He sat back on the seat, and without his support I dropped backwards heavily to the carriage floor. Breathing hard, I wiped my hand across my mouth and sat huddled with my arms across my chest, breathing hard. My body ached with unfulfilled desire, my muscles tight and my sex throbbing with empty longing, and all of it punctuated by the sound of the horses' hooves across the pavement.

"Come here, Eve." He reached down and pulled me up onto the seat beside him. I burrowed against him, my head resting over his still-racing heart and his arm around my shoulders.

"You've learned your lessons well," he whispered. "You've earned a reward for yourself, too, after your punishment is done."

I smiled against his chest, thinking of all he'd taught me and all I'd doubtless still left to learn.

"Thank you, Master," I murmured.

"No, I should be thanking you." He tipped my head up to face him and kissed me lightly. "You're a rare woman, Eve."

My smile was tremulous. "You're a rare man, too, Savage."

"Savage," he repeated, and belatedly I realized I hadn't called him Master. Yet he didn't seem perturbed that I'd dropped the guise of the Game. Instead he continued to stroke my hair, holding me close.

"You could kill me with that sweet mouth of yours, you know," he said after a while, "and I don't believe I'd mind."

He traced my lips with his fingers, and I flicked my tongue over his forefinger, enough to make him chuckle.

"Wicked creature," he said, teasing. "That's exactly what I mean."

"If I am wicked, then I learned it entirely from you," I said. "Entirely."

We laughed together, enjoying the closeness and affection of the moment.

"Perhaps that is so," he admitted, and then with a sigh of regret he slowly pulled my bodice back over my breasts. Considering how familiar he was with undressing me, he did it with unexpected clumsiness, a clumsiness that I found both touching and endearing and very unlike his role as my Master.

"As much as I'd prefer you to remain as you are," he explained, "I'd rather not have the footmen ogling you."

"Nor would I." I sighed, too, and slipped from his lap to the seat. "I suppose we must be nearly to your house by now."

He chuckled, tucking his cock back into his trousers.

"I'll wager we've been driving in circles around St. James's Square for the last half hour," he said. "My driver knows better than to stop before I've given him word to do so."

I smiled, despite a little twinge of unhappiness that punctured the playful intimacy of the last few minutes.

Now that he mentioned it, I realized we hadn't passed any other carriages or made any turns for a long while and that, in fact, we must be slowly circling the square's small central park. From the beginning, we'd agreed that our private version of the Game would only last a week and that there'd be no complicated lasting ties between us. Neither of us wanted that.

But I still didn't wish to be reminded that there'd been other women in his life before me and would likely be others after me, too. For now I wanted to believe—or at least to pretend—that I was the only woman who had played the Game with him, who'd shared his bed, who'd sucked his cock in the dark in his carriage.

I didn't want to believe I could be as easily replaced as the others had been by me.

Logically I had no reason to expect any lasting allegiance from him, but at the heart of it—in my heart, anyway—the real reason was much more simple.

I didn't want to be forgotten.

By now, he'd restored his clothing and I had done the same, at least well enough to make the short walk past the footmen, across the pavement, and up the steps to his house. He made three brisk knocks to the roof of the carriage, and at once the carriage's pace increased. Within two minutes we'd stopped, and the door to the carriage swung open.

I hugged my velvet cloak around my shoulders, and though once again Savage placed his hand on my back to guide me up the steps, the gesture seemed perfunctory now. The intimacy was gone, and I felt foolishly sad over its passing.

I expected that we'd immediately retreat to his rooms, but instead the butler was waiting for us in the front hall, a concerned expression on his face.

Savage recognized it immediately. "What is it, Parker?"

The man pointedly glanced at me before answering, hesitating as if I were some terrible imposition.

"Did you receive the message that was sent to you, my lord?" he asked.

"At Gaspari's?" Savage said, purposefully nonchalant, or so it appeared to me. "Yes, I did receive it, and acknowledged it, too. I've returned here as soon as it was convenient."

That soothed me somewhat. At least he'd put me before whatever this mysterious message might have been.

The butler nodded, hesitating again.

"I fear there has been a change in the original plans,

my lord," he said. "The, ah, delivery was made earlier than expected. They did not wait until tomorrow, as planned. He—that is, the delivery—arrived a short time ago."

Savage's nonchalance dropped away, his face unable to hide either his surprise or his concern.

"He's here now?" Savage demanded. "In this house?"

The butler nodded grimly. "Yes, my lord."

"Why the hell did they believe that to be wise?" Savage demanded. "They're paid to keep him there, aren't they?"

"Yes, my lord," the butler said patiently. "But under the circumstances—"

"The circumstances be damned," Savage said. "This is not where he belongs, and I'll see that he's sent packing as soon as it can be arranged."

At once I thought back to the first night and remembered the mysterious man whose arrival had so disturbed Savage and whom I'd glimpsed hurrying away from the house. Apparently he must have returned, and that return was not a welcome one, either. I could not begin to guess the nature of this business or why it had upset Savage, except that I probably had no place in it. Whatever had happened—or was happening—was beyond the Game.

I placed my hand lightly on Savage's arm.

"It sounds as if you've other affairs to occupy yourself tonight," I said. "Perhaps it would be better for now if I returned to the Savoy."

"No." He swung about sharply to face me. The expression in his eyes—unhappiness and sorrow—was at odds with the anger in his voice. "I want you here with me, Eve. I don't want you to go. It's not safe."

I frowned, taken aback by that. "If by that you mean Blackledge—"

"Of course I mean Blackledge," he said, but in a way that made it seem that the baron wasn't the only reason or even the primary one. "I cannot force you, but it would be best for both of us if you did."

"Very well, then," I said. "If you insist that I stay—"

"I'm not insisting." He took a deep breath, obviously struggling to control himself, and raked his fingers back through his hair. "I've no right to do that. I'm asking you to stay. Inviting you, as one friend to another. Please, do not leave. Stay."

There was no way I'd leave after that. I reached up on my toes to brush my lips across his cheek.

"I'll be upstairs, my lord," I said softly. "Join me when you are able."

"Thank you, Mrs. Hart," he said almost solemnly. "I won't be long."

It was an oddly formal moment, yet from the way he was looking at me it was also one I wouldn't trade for the world. My gaze held his a moment longer, and then I turned and climbed the stairs alone.

I didn't look back, and I didn't doubt that he'd follow me. It was only a matter of when.

It was still dark when I awoke to find Savage standing beside the bed, his face lit only by the flame of the silver candlestick in his hand.

"At last you're awake," he said. He'd removed his evening jacket and his tie but still wore his black trousers and the white shirt, the sleeves rolled back over his muscular forearms and the stark black and white made more so by the candlelight. "I've been waiting."

"You could have wakened me," I said, groggy. I rolled over to face him, pulling the sheet with me. "What time is it?"

"Nearly two," he said. "And I didn't want to wake you. You're so beautiful when you're asleep."

I frowned, not feeling exactly beautiful. "Were you drawing me again?"

"Not this time," he said. "I was merely watching, and imagining all the things I'd do to you when you woke."

At least that was enough to inspire me to try to wake the rest of the way, and I sat upright against the pillows. Earlier I'd undressed myself without a maid to help, and because of it I'd given only the most cursory brushing to my hair and hadn't bothered with a braid. My hair was now wild and unruly, a tickling tangle over my shoulders. Impatiently I shoved it away from my face, but with more patience Savage reached out himself to stroke it back from my forehead.

"Is your business with the gentleman resolved?" I asked.

He frowned, not understanding. "My business?"

"Whatever it was that so alarmed your butler."

"Ahh, that." He set the candlestick on the table beside the bed and walked across the room to where a decanter of wine and several glasses were kept on a silver tray. He might have watched me sleep, but I watched him walk, all coiled power and grace like some great jungle cat. No wonder I was awake now.

"My business, as you Americans call it, is resolved for the night," he said, handing me a glass of burgundy. "Forgive me if I alarmed you earlier, but it took me by surprise."

I took the wine and raised it towards him before I sipped at the deep-red wine. "So the man in question has left the house?"

"He will in the morning," he said. "I could not very well turn him out at this hour."

I couldn't help but feel he wasn't entirely telling the truth. I knew Savage well enough by now to sense when he was holding back, and he was definitely holding a part of himself away from me now.

"Are you sure?" I asked uncertainly, praying he'd confide in me. "If this man is a danger to me, as you implied, then—"

"He's not at all," Savage assured me, and smiled warmly. "You have my word as a gentleman on that. The fellow is troublesome and a great trial to me, but of no personal danger to you. You are safe in this house, and safe with me."

Slowly I smiled, too. It was true that I felt safer and more secure with Savage than I ever had before in my life, even more than when I'd been surrounded by my father's guards. There had been a terrible irony to our row at Gaspari's: Savage had accused me—rightly—of not trusting him in regard to the king when in reality there was no one I trusted more.

It wasn't just Savage's physical ability to defend me but a more intangible sense of well-being that I had when I was in his company. I couldn't describe it in words. It was more something I *felt*.

And if he said now that I was in no danger, then I'd believe him.

He gave me a nod of encouragement. "Now drink, my own dear Eve," he said. "Every drop. I want you ready."

"Ready?" I asked, looking at him over the rim of the glass. If he'd slipped back into the Game, then so would I. "What have you planned, Master?"

"As you should recall, Eve, you've had difficulty obeying me," he said. "I realize that it's a matter of trust. I believe I've come upon a way that will both punish you for being so forgetful and remind you to be more trusting of me in the future."

I smiled and drank the wine as he'd ordered.

As much as I'd wanted to give him pleasure and release in the carriage—and I had—sucking his cock had in turn aroused me more than I'd anticipated, and my body had ached with need and longing ever since. It didn't take much of this talk of his to make that need spark and grow.

I set the now-empty glass on the table and slid to the edge of the bed, letting the sheet fall away from my naked body. That was how he liked me best, and I saw how immediately his gaze flicked down to my breasts, rounded in full by the candle's light.

I reached out for his belt buckle, intending to undress him so he could join me in the bed. Instead he covered my hand with his and held it fast.

"Let me, Master," I said, trying to wriggle free. "I promise I'll be much more efficient than Barry."

"I'm sure you would be," he said, "but isn't this another example of you disobeying me?"

I pouted, looking up at him from beneath my lashes. "How can I disobey you if you haven't given me any orders?"

"You could anticipate my needs," he suggested, "the way a well-trained Innocent would."

"Then perhaps what I require is more training, Master," I said. "Perhaps that is all that's needed."

Although he continued to hold me by the hand, I sat back on the bed and let my knees fall open, displaying myself to entice him.

He grunted, his eyes heavy lidded as he glanced down at what I offered. What man wouldn't?

"You're right," he said. "You do need more training. But not here."

He pulled me from the bed and to my feet, and taking the candlestick in his hand, he led me into the sitting room connected to his bedroom. Expectantly I looked about for the long cushioned bench that we'd made use of the other night, but it was once again where it usually stood, beneath one of the windows. Instead he led me to a door beside the fireplace that I'd assumed was to a closet or cupboard of some sort. He released my hand, turned the key, and ushered me inside.

We stood in a small room with six walls instead of four. The ceiling was domed and painted a dark blue with stars set in the heavenly constellations. From the ceiling and the curious shape of the room, I guessed that at one time it had belonged to a gentleman of a scientific or philosophical inclination who had used it for his private thoughts and studies, or perhaps it had even been a personal chapel of some sort.

Clearly, however, since it now belonged to Savage, it was neither of those things now. Except for the wall with a large window, heavily curtained for the night, the walls were hung with mirrors. Even the door we'd entered through was covered, so that when he closed it the opening disappeared seamlessly into the others. There were several wall sconces with candles, and Savage lit these, one by one, with the candlestick he'd carried from the bedroom.

As he did the mirrors came to life, reflecting us endlessly in the small room. He was severe and masculine, almost ascetic, in his white shirt and black trousers, while I was as lushly female as any pagan goddess of love, my pale skin warm and glowing and my body displayed from every angle.

"Do you remember the room with the mirrors at Wrenton, Eve?" he asked.

"I do, Master," I said. I'd thought of it instantly. How could I not? He'd sat on the painted throne of a Renaissance prince, and I'd pretended I was his royal concubine,

straddling him to fuck him on his lap. The mirrors there
had reflected us, too, but they'd been old and mottled and
mysterious, the reflections wavy and defused. "I'll never
forget that. But these mirrors are different."

"They're new," he said. "Obviously. The effect is very
different."

I held my arms outstretched and turned, posing for all
the reflections of me in the mirrored walls. "It's like being inside some magical prism, isn't it?"

He chuckled, watching me twirl. But though the small
room was devoid of any furnishings, there was one other
item reflected in the mirrors that I'd never before seen in
any house, in America or in England. I wasn't exactly sure
what it was, beyond some sort of swing or sling.

Four long cords, covered in red velvet, were suspended
from a sturdy hook in the ceiling. Two of the cords met
to support a narrow seat that was scarcely more than a
strap of leather. A pair of large padded leather loops hung
from the second set of cords, and smaller straps with
buckles were attached to the cords a short ways above the
loops.

"You're admiring my new amusement," Savage said,
crossing the room to stand beside it. "I had it installed yesterday, specifically with you in mind."

I raised my brows, skeptical. The contraption did not
look particularly practical, nor comfortable, either. "For
me, Master?"

"For you," he said, "though I expect to benefit from the
swing as well."

He touched one of the cords, sending it silently
spinning.

I reached out and stopped it. I was beginning to imagine the possibilities, and my heart was already racing in
my chest, and not entirely from arousal, either.

When we'd been at Wrenton, we'd experimented with having me tied to the posts of he bed. I'd been completely helpless, restrained and unable to move, and completely at his mercy, too. I'd found it unbelievably exciting, and Savage had made sure that the pleasure was worth my initial uneasiness.

But being bound to the oak posts of a bed was very different from being trussed up and suspended in the air. There'd been no chance of falling from the bed. The thought of being buckled to the swing and hanging there in the air was . . . unsettling, in every sense.

"Is the swing to be part of my training, Master?" I asked, even though it was already clear that it was.

"Oh, yes," he said evenly. "What better way could there be to prove that you trust me?"

I looked at the swing again and swallowed hard. He was right. Words and protestations could go just so far. This would be a much more tangible way to prove how much I trusted him.

"You say the swing is new, Master?" I asked, stalling.

He nodded. "Yesterday. I've seen such swings before in my travels, of course—they're quite the rage in the more exclusive brothels in Paris—but I've never felt the desire to have one in my house until now. Yet in this room, with these mirrors to reflect your beauty and your passion, it shall be perfect. You see how you've inspired me, Eve."

I nodded. I'd regretted not being the first woman in his life. At least here I would be.

"We will experiment together, Master?" I asked, wishing I could keep the tentative quaver from my voice.

"We will, Eve, if you agree," he said, watching me closely.

Anxiously I smoothed my hair back behind my ears

and glanced at the swing again, trying to see it as an experiment to be shared with him, not a hazard.

"Is it my decision to make, Master?"

His smile faded, his gaze intense on me. "It's your decision, yes," he said. "Whether to obey me, or not. To trust me, or not. They're your decisions to make entirely."

I nodded. This *was* my decision.

And I'd already made it.

I nodded again and turned resolutely towards the swing. "How do I begin, Master?"

"I'll help you," he said, his smile warm with what I realized was relief. That made me smile, too. Had he really thought I'd refuse him? Hadn't he learned by now that I couldn't refuse him anything?

With both hands on my waist he lifted me so I was balanced on the leather seat and held tightly to the nearest cords. I wasn't so much sitting as perched with my feet dangling, like a trapeze artist at the circus. Most of my bottom hung over the back edge of the narrow seat, with the leather pressing against my quim. I shifted a fraction, startled by how good the pressure felt there, and unconsciously my lips parted with surprise and pleasure.

"You like the swing, don't you?" he asked, noticing. "I suspected you would."

He raised one of my feet, kissed the inside of my ankle, and carefully fed it through the nearest large loop until the loop hooked beneath my knee, and then repeated with my other leg. The loops not only raised my legs but also forced them to spread apart. With my knees raised I was also tipped farther back against the seat strap, and now my quim was blatantly open and exposed to him and my endless reflection. I thought I'd lost all modesty with him, but there was something about seeing my glistening, open quim in all the mirrors that made me suddenly shy again. I tried to close my legs, but the straps kept them firmly apart.

"Goodness," I murmured faintly with a small, nervous laugh. "I hadn't expected the effect to be like . . . like this."

"We've only begun, Eve," he said darkly. "Give me your hand."

I didn't give him my hand so much as he took it, unlocking my fingers from the cord and drawing them forward and up until he could secure my wrist with the leather straps, buckling it into place. He did it to my other hand, too, with startling efficiency. Finally he produced a belt that he fastened around my waist and threaded through two smaller loops on the cords. I might have inspired him, but from how tidily he'd handled the loops, straps, and buckles he'd clearly been thinking and planning for this moment for a long time.

He checked the last buckle again and stepped back to survey his handiwork. I was now secured in every way, effectively bound and trapped like a madwoman. Beyond an inconsequential wriggle, I couldn't move on my own, nor could I escape if I'd wanted to. I stared at my repeated reflection, swaying gently but helplessly. There was no question of toppling from the swing, as I'd first feared, but now I felt impossibly vulnerable and curiously close to tears.

"There," Savage said, his voice showing not only his satisfaction but his arousal as well. "What do you make of your swing now, Eve?"

"I think I look like a trussed hen," I said, my voice breaking. He was standing behind me, and though I could speak to his reflection, I tried to twist my head far enough around to speak to him directly. "That is, a trussed hen, *Master*."

"Oh, Eve." He came around and crouched before me so that our eyes were level. He smoothed my hair back from my face, and when he saw that a single tear had escaped from the corner of my eye he drew out his monogrammed handkerchief and carefully blotted the tear away. "Is the position painful to you? Are the straps too tight?"

I shook my head, not trusting my voice.

"Then what has upset you, my own sweet Eve?" he asked. "Have you changed your mind? Do you no longer trust me as you promised you did?"

"I trust you, Master," I whispered forlornly. "I'm sorry I've cried. I will be brave."

"That's not the point," he said with rare tenderness. "I don't want you to be brave. I want you to be ready to explore new pleasures, new experiences, with me. I want this to be something we try together. Uncertainty is natural. Fear is not, and I never want you to be afraid with me."

"I . . . I'm not," I said haltingly. I longed to touch him, too, to put my arms around his waist and press my body so close to his that he'd understand, really understand, how much he'd come to mean to me. "You always make me feel safe, Savage. It's just that . . . that this is so . . . so unusual that I do not know what to expect."

"Unusual," he repeated. "That's often the way it is with me, isn't it?"

He smiled crookedly, so endearing that I might have let another tear—this time from emotion, not anxiety— slither down my cheek.

"Do you recall the first time I told you to take off your Innocent's costume and stand naked before me?" he asked. "As I remember, you found that unusual as well."

I nodded, sniffing. "The first time you licked my quim and my pearl and made me come that way, I thought it was *very* unusual. I couldn't understand why any man would wish to do that."

"And look how far you've progressed," he said, faintly teasing. "You're sucking my cock in the back of a carriage. Whatever would Mrs. Astor say?"

I smiled, not at Mrs. Astor but at the other memories he was conjuring. He was right: I'd thought everything he'd suggested was strange the first time, until I'd learned how arousing and pleasurable it could be. Different positions, in a full tub, in a motorcar, with toys made for pleasure—it had all seemed strange at first, and now I wanted it all. I'd never even had an orgasm before Savage, and I would have called that "unusual," too, if someone had tried to describe it to me before.

"It's part of the Game, isn't it?" I asked softly. "Everything you've . . . we've done has been part of the Game."

"It is," he said, turning serious again. "And I want to share it all with you."

"You're the only one I'd ever play the Game with, Master," I blurted out. "I never would with any other man."

I feared I'd said too much, but he nodded, accepting.

"You're a special Innocent, Eve," he said. "There's no other who can compare with you."

He held my face steady in his hands to keep me from swinging away from him and kissed me, a long, seductive kiss that made my breasts tighten with wanting and my quim grow heavy. Without thinking I strained against the straps to reach for him, and to my surprise the effort seemed to make the passion within me twist and flare.

He sensed it as well, cupping one of my breasts in his palm and tugging lightly on the nipple until it grew hard and taut.

I moaned against his lips, and he pulled back a fraction, keeping our faces close and our foreheads nearly touching.

"Do you remember how I punished you the other evening, Eve?" he said, his voice rough. "How I spanked you the way you deserved, until your bottom was hot and bloomed like a rose for me?"

"And then when my punishment was done, Master, you fucked me," I whispered breathlessly, "and it was better than it had ever been."

I looked down, not from modesty but to see if this conversation was having the same effect on him that it was on me. It was: the front of his black trousers bulged outward with the force of his erection behind the black fabric.

"You must learn to obey, Eve, and to trust me," he said. "Are you ready now for that lesson?"

"Yes, Master," I breathed. "I believe I am."

"I'll judge that," he said. He licked his fingers to slick them with saliva and ran them across my wide-open quim. His touch was light, teasing, running his finger between my already-wet nether lips but not across my pearl. I gasped and tried to arch forward to reach his fingers.

But instead of coming closer, the slight motion of my body was enough to send the swing swaying back and forth, and away from his hand, and I groaned with frustration.

"That is hardly how a repentant Innocent would behave, Eve," he chided. "You must be grateful and obedient, not demanding."

"Yes, Master," I said, flustered and aroused from his passing caress combined with the swing's sway. I'd already realized that struggling against the restraints wasn't wise. Struggling tightened my muscles and only served to increase the tension building within me with no hope of release, and yet it was nearly impossible to keep still in this position. "I will try to be better, Master."

"Promises mean nothing, Eve," he said. "It's your actions that will convince me of your desire to change."

He was hardly unmoved himself. I could see the quickening rise and fall of his chest, the tension in his face, and the tiny beads of sweat that were gathering on his temples.

That and the pressure he must surely be feeling with his cock in the tightly confining trousers.

"Yes, Master," I said, struggling to keep my bound limbs from moving. "I will show you my intentions, Master."

"I trust you will," he said, reaching into his pocket. "But I don't wish for you to suffer. This should help."

He held up a short, thick dildo for me to see. The dildo was elegantly carved from ivory and complete in every detail, and though it was not so large as his own cock, I'd no doubt that it would stretch and fill my passage. The sight of it alone was enough to make my quim ache.

"I suspect you're already wet enough to take this," he said, holding the dildo to my lips, "but a quick polishing with your tongue wouldn't hurt."

He pressed the ivory shaft into my mouth, and as soon as I'd licked it as he'd instructed he withdrew it, dripping, from my mouth. He turned the swing so I was directly facing the nearest mirrored wall, steadying it for me to see my reflection

I was shocked by the change in my appearance: my eyes heavy with desire, my nipples red and pointed, my thighs white and pale in provocative contrast to the black leather loops that held them apart. In the center the darkened lips of my quim were swollen, with my pearl gleaming like a wanton jewel. Everything glistened with my juices, also soaking the short, curling hairs around it.

I'd never seen myself look so unabashedly lewd, so aroused. Perhaps neither had Savage.

"See how beautiful you are, Eve," he growled. "See how ripe and hot you are. By the time I finally take you, you'll be on fire for me."

As I stared he reached around my thigh and thrust the dildo into my quim, relentlessly twisting it to make the invasion more delicious. I cried out, not from pain but delight, as the ivory opened my swollen passage, and he pushed relentlessly until the dildo was buried to the hilt within me, with only its ivory bollocks dangling before me. Their weight served a purpose and held the blunt tip of the dildo pressed tightly against the most sensitive place in the front of my passage.

"Yes, Master," I gasped. "I . . . I will be ready to take you."

"You *will*," he repeated forcefully, his eyes dark with undisguised lust. "But first you must be punished."

Deftly he spun the swing around, and before I realized what he was doing he'd tipped me forward. My legs slipped higher into the larger loops to fit around my upper thighs, and the belt around my waist supported me instead, with my arms forced out before me. It was as if I were kneeling on all fours, except that I was suspended in the air. My breasts hung down and my bottom and quim were raised up. Even the slightest movement of the swing sent tremors from the dildo buried within me, making me perilously close to spending as I hung there.

"Perfect," muttered Savage. "You are perfect, Eve."

I lifted my head to see him standing behind me, his dark hair falling over his forehead. The small room hadn't seemed warm when we'd entered, but now it seemed as close and sultry as a summer afternoon. Savage had stripped off his shirt, and reflected in the mirrors were his broad shoulders and ridged abdomen, sleeked with a fine sheen of sweat. He turned and smiled wickedly at me.

And then I saw the flat wooden paddle in his hand.

11.

"What is that, Master?" I gasped anxiously, craning my neck to see better.

"It will do a better job than my hand alone," Savage said, turning the paddle in his hand as if admiring it. It was simply made from a single flat piece of dark wood, with the far end a wide, curved oval that would certainly cover more than even his hand alone ever could. "Mahogany. I promise you it's very smooth and well finished. I wouldn't want any splinters to mar that delectable bottom of yours."

"But . . . but that will hurt," I protested, panicking. "You said I should trust you!"

"You must trust me not to make it hurt more than you can bear," he said easily. "It's supposed to be a punishment, Eve."

"But if—"

"Shhh," he said, placing a single finger across my lips to silence me. "I said to trust me. I should think a half-dozen strokes will be sufficient to warm you. You are new to the paddle, and besides, your sin was not so grievous as to merit more."

In the mirror I saw how vulnerable I must be in this new position in the swing and how tempting a target. My hips and bottom were raised to the perfect height for his arm to wield the paddle. I watched him take a few preparatory swings, coming close but stopping, and tensed in anticipation.

He placed his palm on the base of my spine to steady me. I was trembling, making the swing shake with me.

He raised his arm and swung.

I yelped as the paddle struck my bottom, and I swung forward from the impact towards my wide-eyed face in the mirror before me. It didn't hurt so much as sting, much as his open palm had done to me the other night. But this time I felt it in my sex as well, as in response my inner muscles tightened around the dildo buried within me.

"That's one," he said unnecessarily, as if I'd somehow missed it. He grabbed the swing's cords to stop me from moving. "Now two."

The second time, I didn't cry out so much as gasp as the paddle smacked loudly against my skin. Afterward he pressed the paddle to the place he'd just struck, making small, soothing circles over my flesh with the polished wood. It was the same thing he'd done with his hand the other night, but the effect with the wood—harder, smoother, more rigid—was somehow more exciting.

"Three," he announced gruffly. "Jesus, your ass is so beautiful like this."

I couldn't tell if he'd struck me harder or if my flesh was simply responding to the paddle's effect. I know my quim was. With each blow I'd automatically clenched more tightly around the dildo, and the ripples of pleasure were making me feverish.

"Four," he said. Again, he stopped the swing's motion to smooth the paddle over my bottom. But when he'd done that this time he brought the paddle forward, rubbing it lightly over the globes of my breasts to tease my nipples. Already stiff and aching, they tightened further as he rubbed the paddle across them. I could not believe how good it felt. Liquid heat rushed through my belly, and I wasn't able to keep back a moan.

"You like that," he said. His voice was harsh, working for self-control. "Tell me you do, Eve."

"I do, Master," I said, my own voice unsteady. "I like that."

"What do you like?" he demanded. "Tell me."

I closed my eyes to gather myself. "I like how you're rubbing the paddle across my nipples to make them hard, Master."

"Very good." He leaned over me to sweep aside the now-damp length of my hair from the back of my neck and pressed his lips to my nape, not so much a kiss as a mark of approval.

Then he took the rounded edge of the paddle and lightly ran it between my shoulder blades, down my spine, and finally through the cleft of my bottom. Instinctively I tightened my muscles to close my legs, but with my thighs forced so far apart by the swing there was no hiding or escape.

He trailed the paddle's edge lower between my wide-spread legs, over my bottom hole. I moaned, and shuddered as he ran the paddle's edge across the end of the dildo, pushing it more deeply into my passage.

"Tell me that you like that, too, Eve," he ordered.

"Oh, Master," I gasped. "I . . . I cannot think!"

Because of the mirror I could see how he was staring, transfixed, at my bottom and my quim and how he was teasing me with the paddle. His face was fixed, every muscle tensed with barely controlled lust, and his chest and shoulders were sheened with sweat as if he'd run a mile.

His physical mastery over me was undeniable, and yet I was the one who'd done this to him. It excited me even more, seeing him watching me and seeing how his trousers were tented in front by his erection.

"Try," he said harshly. "Tell me."

I whimpered, twisting against my bonds.

"Tell me, Eve," he said sharply. "Tell me, or I'll stop."

"I . . . I like when you stroke me with the paddle, Master," I stammered, my voice strangled. "I . . . I like how you—*Oh!*"

He cracked the paddle hard against my bottom with the most force he'd shown yet.

"Five," he said. "Only one more, Eve."

I was on fire, my flesh burning from the paddle and my sex and ass so tight and on edge that I knew it would take next to nothing to make me spend. All of this felt so dark and dangerous and forbidden, so far beyond anything I'd ever imagined, let alone experienced, and yet I wanted more.

"Six, Master," I gasped, begging. "Six!"

The paddle cracked again on my ass, for the last time and the best. I sailed forward from the impact and my sex convulsed with the first tremors of my climax. I felt as if I were flying, ready to sail on the waves of fire and pleasure.

But Savage grabbed the cord and hauled me to a stop. He swore and yanked the dildo from my quim.

"*No!*" I cried frantically, in shock, writhing in my bonds. I was raw with need, desperate for release, and now he'd stopped me on the very edge, leaving me aching and empty. "Please, Savage, no!"

Gasping for breath, I lifted my head to search for him in the mirrors. He'd thrown aside the paddle, now abandoned on the floor. He was behind me, stripping away his trousers and his drawers in a single motion. I'd a flashing glimpse of his cock, impossibly hard and jutting towards his belly, the head purple-red with desire. He seized my hips to position me, centering that plum-like head against my weeping slit.

It was the tiniest sliver of a second, and yet I felt my whole being balanced on his possession of me. I'd never needed anything more than to have him join with me, to take him as part of my body.

And then I had him.

He held my hips and drove his cock hard into me. Even though I'd been opened first by the dildo, his furious need had made his cock far larger than the ivory shaft. As dripping as I was, I had to stretch and yield to take him, and it took several shoves before he was buried deep within me.

I scarcely noticed. I was overwhelmed with sensation. I'd been primed to such a fever pitch that I'd begun to come again as soon as he entered me, my sex unable to hold back. With my eyes squeezed shut I shook as my climax washed over me, and the convulsions that ripped through my body were so strong that they hovered on that finest of lines between pain and exquisite pleasure.

My cries mixed with his grunts, primal animal sounds that matched the force of our union. Suspended as I was, I felt weightless. He jerked me back onto his cock to match each of his thrusts, our bodies slapping loudly against each other.

I could feel another orgasm building within me, or maybe it was the first one recoiling to claim me again. I couldn't tell, and I couldn't care. Because of my position in the swing Savage's large hands were everywhere on my body, touching me, marking me, digging deep into my flesh to bend me exactly as he wished. He spread the cheeks of my heated, paddled ass even farther apart and found another inch of me that he could possess. I cried out with the sense of fullness, of completion.

This was what I'd wanted. This was what I'd needed.

He reached beneath me to take my breasts in his hands, squeezing and tugging at my nipples and sending fresh bolts of sensation directly to my sex. As I gasped with it my eyes flew open.

Before me in the mirrors, over and over, was the lewdest of tableaus: his cock, long and glistening with our juices, pounding into me and then drawing almost completely out before his hips flexed and jerked back into me again. His handsome face was fixed and hard, so intensely focused that he looked ferocious.

No, he *was* ferocious as he slammed into me. I was taut, tense, ready to break, and yet he fucked me harder, faster, hotter. At last he reached around me with one hand, and his thumb dipped between us, gathering our juices. He found my pearl and relentlessly rubbed the pad of his thumb across it with exactly the right, maddening pressure to slide over the engorged, slippery flesh.

It was, at last, too much. I felt the wave of my climax break and explode, shattering me into countless fragments of pleasure and release. I cried out as I rode it, rode him. My fingers and toes curling helplessly at the empty air, tears of emotion and release streamed down my face to drop unchecked on the floor beneath me.

Abruptly he stopped, buried deep, and with a guttural roar he came, too, his spendings so copious that I could feel his hot seed fill me and spill over. His hips continued to jerk, his fingers digging deep into my hips, until with a final grunt he was done. With his cock still buried in me he sagged forward and circled his arms around my waist to rest his cheek against my back. He was gasping for breath, utterly spent, and yet still he did not want to release me, nor did I wish to be released, not yet.

Finally his cock slipped from my sex, and reluctantly he lifted himself away. He didn't turn me in the swing but walked around to my face, quickly unbuckling my wrists from the straps.

I cried out as I lowered them and the blood returned, not realizing how much strain my joints had been under. Making little nonsensical soothing noises, Savage took each hand and rubbed his thumbs along the aching muscles of my arms to soothe them.

Exhausted, I let my head drop forward. He cupped my face in his hands and tipped it upward.

"There is no other woman in the world like you, Evelyn," he said, his voice rough and full of such unexpectedly raw emotion that fresh tears sprang to my eyes. "None."

I tried to smile, still overwhelmed. I hadn't missed that he'd used my real name, and I wondered if that meant the Game was over for now or if it meant—oh, I didn't know what it meant.

But there remained an inescapable feeling that things had just grown more serious between us. With any other man what had just happened could have been no more than the Game, but with Savage it had felt like something else, something that had bound us more surely together in ways that neither of us yet understood.

"I trusted you, didn't I?" I whispered. "I did everything you asked."

He nodded. "You did," he said. "I'll never forget that."

"Nor I," I said, and tried to smile. "You are always right about everything."

"Oh, Evelyn," he said. "The only thing I'm always right about is you."

He kissed me then, a slow, deep, inexplicable kiss that was full of both passion and promise. A promise of what, I could not say; but still I curled my arms around his shoulders, wincing at the effort, and kissed him back.

He unfastened the belt around my waist and lifted me from the swing. I cried out with discomfort. I hadn't been aware of any pain while I'd been lost to lust, but now I felt every stretched and aching muscle, my sex oversensitized and throbbing still, and my bottom burned so from his work with the paddle that I wondered if I'd be able to sit.

He didn't let me try but scooped me into his arms. I was so spent that I melted meekly against him, my head against his shoulder and my unkempt hair trailing over his arm.

I expected him to take me back to our bedroom as he had last night. Instead he carried me farther to his bathroom, a masculine space of polished black marble and gleaming chrome, and set me carefully on a bench covered in leopard-patterned silk. I sat gingerly on my sore bottom, leaning forward to support much of my weight on my thighs and hands.

There were already candles lit in here, too, and in my hazy state I still wondered if this was the work of his ever-present, ever-efficient manservant Barry; I didn't want to consider Barry also tidying up after us in the mirror-lined room, dowsing the candles, and wiping off the swing.

But it was Savage himself who opened the taps on the oversized tub, crouching beside it to test the water. I loved the play of the candlelight, burnishing the long curve of his back and the bunching of the muscles in his shoulders and his ass. He was so at ease with his body and his nudity that he'd made me that way, too. In the six years I'd been married I don't believe I'd ever stood naked before my husband, nor had I seen him that way, either. In New York society it simply wasn't done—nor had I wished it.

But everything was different here with Savage. Strangely content, I smiled as I watched him. "I never would have imagined His Lordship the Earl of Savage drawing me a bath."

He glanced over his shoulder and grinned wickedly.

"That's because Mrs. Hart deserves it." He took a large scoop of salts from a nearby jar and scattered them over the water. "This will help your muscles relax. I'm also told that ladies like it for their complexions."

That made me laugh. I loved the rare times like this when he relaxed and was almost playful. Was it part of the new level of trust we now had with each other? Because I'd made myself so vulnerable to him he felt he, too, could share more of himself?

"Listen to you," I teased lightly. "Now His Lordship is advising me on beauty regimens like a Jermyn Street apothecary."

He laughed, too. "What will you say when I tell you I learned of these salts from an ancient groom at Tattersalls, who swore by them to rub down the fetlocks of the nags in his care after races?"

"I suppose I should say nothing, and merely neigh." The tub was nearly full and I could not wait to sink into its depths, for I was not only sore but also sticky with sweat and Savage's seed. But as soon as I rose I winced, every joint aching in protest.

"Let me help you," he said, frowning with concern. He raised me up and lifted me into the tub as if I were a child and then climbed in after me. He sat back in the tub and drew me back against his chest. The water was exactly warm enough, and whatever the horse salts were, they did, in fact, ease the soreness in my stretched joints and everywhere else.

I sat between his outstretched legs, mine looking pale

and slight beside his. My breasts bobbed lightly in the water. Savage twisted my hair to one side and nibbled at the side of my neck behind my ear. I smiled and sighed with contentment.

The mantel clock in the sitting room chimed four times. Soon it would be dawn and another day begun. It would be my third day in London with Savage, and a small shard of uneasiness jabbed at my happiness.

We'd shared seven days together at Wrenton Manor and had agreed to another seven here in London. We had resolved to keep our liaison purposefully uncomplicated, based on pleasure and nothing more. It was only fucking, we'd reasoned, only sex, and seven days would be enough for both of us.

Except it wouldn't be. I could already tell that. How could I give up what I'd discovered with Savage in four days? How could I go back to my old life, a life that had been so unknowingly empty without him in it?

I threaded my fingers into his, wishing I knew the answer.

"What could be better than this, Eve?" he asked with purely male satisfaction, drawing me closer as if reading my thoughts. And I was once again Eve, his partner only in the Game.

"Nothing, Master," I said softly, sadly. "Nothing at all."

When I finally rose it was nearly noon and the bed was empty beside me. I wasn't surprised. Savage had warned me that there were matters requiring his attendance, which I'd interpreted to mean the mysterious man who'd appeared at the house last night and who was supposed to be gone this morning. Besides, after last night's activities I'd welcomed the opportunity to remain in bed to rest a little longer.

I *was* sore; there was no denying that. But there was also no denying that I'd do it all again without hesitation, and I smiled to myself at the memories. Part of me—the part that spoke in Hamlin's voice—told me I'd been exceptionally wicked last night, exceptionally wicked indeed, and that I should be ashamed of myself for willingly doing such licentious, shameful acts with a gentleman like Savage. But the larger part of me reveled in those same acts and hadn't found them shameful at all. They'd been wickedly pleasurable, or pleasurably wicked, and their very wickedness had been much of the pleasure.

Still smiling, I slipped from the bed and found my robe, folded neatly over the back of a nearby chair: more of Barry's work. As Savage had told me to do, I rang the bell for breakfast, or luncheon, as I supposed it must now be, and strolled out to the sitting room to wait for the footman and perhaps find something to read as I ate.

With the curtains open and the sunny afternoon outside the room seemed elegant but ordinary. The door to the mirrored room was closed, and even though Savage had repeatedly asked me not to prowl about his house, I saw no harm in venturing into the little room after last night. The door wasn't locked, and I opened it slowly, my heart racing at the memory.

But to my surprise—and disappointment—the room was not at all as I remembered. The swing was gone. In its place stood a small desk and chair, with a narrow case of books beside it, as if they'd always been there. The curtains were open, and the sunlight reflected from the mirrors as if they were a giant crystal from a chandelier. The mirrors that had reflected me naked and bound in black leather now only innocently showed me how unruly my hair was. The room had lost all its lewdness and looked almost ordinary, so ordinary that if my body didn't ache from the contortions I'd gone through I'd wonder if I'd dreamed the entire thing.

Then I looked up and saw the large hook in the ceiling beam, the hook that last night had held the swing. I grinned, satisfied. Savage—or more likely Barry—could put things back as they were by day if he wished. I knew what happened here by night. But why, I wondered, did they bother?

I returned to the sitting room, gently closing the door after me. I'd ask Savage later. The explanation could be as simple as not wanting servants other than Barry to be privy to Savage's more secret life. Many housemaids I'd employed would have shrieked in horror if they were confronted by that swing.

In fact, many ladies would shriek as well. In the beginning I'd felt trepidation, too, but I'd trusted Savage to lead me, and I'd be ever grateful I had. And hadn't Savage himself said last night that he'd never known another lady who'd dare to explore the swing with him?

I glanced at the portrait of Savage's late wife, her wide, frightened eyes staring back at me. Had he tried to introduce her to the pleasures he'd shared with me? Had she been unwilling, even frightened, by them? Could that have been enough to drive her to madness—or, even worse, did Savage believe his desires had been the cause of her death?

Poor lady, I thought sadly. Poor Savage, too, if that had been the case. As I'd learned for myself, being married was no guarantee of a match of appetites in the bedroom. Perhaps what I'd discovered with Savage was even more rare than I'd believed.

With a sigh I turned away and headed for the room across the hall where my clothes and other belongings had been put, hoping to find my hairbrush. I couldn't arrange my hair myself, but I could at least brush and braid it so

I didn't look as if I didn't care. I quickly found my silver hairbrush and comb and turned to cross back to Savage's rooms.

And nearly collided with a boy.

"Who are you?" he demanded imperiously. "Why are you here?"

"I should ask the same question of you, young man," I said, surprise making me curt. I guessed he was eight years old or so, dressed in dark knickerbockers to his knees and dark socks, a white shirt and silk necktie, and a tailored tweed jacket with engraved buttons. My first thought was that he wore quality clothing for a servant's child, and then, as I looked at him longer, I realized he wasn't a servant's child at all.

He had sharp cheekbones for a child, a full mouth that now was inclined towards sulkiness but would no doubt with age turn sensual, the kind of mouth that women would one day love to kiss. His black hair fell over his forehead, sleek and gleaming, and his eyes were the palest gray, the color of quicksilver.

He was Savage's son.

Suddenly it all made sense. The important messages that had drawn Savage away, that he'd never rejected or put aside, all were to do with this boy, his son, who for whatever reason had arrived here at home unexpectedly last night. Savage had only been behaving like a father. There hadn't been some mysterious, dangerous man in the house; there was only this boy now here before me.

"I asked you your name, madam," the boy said again. "Why are you in my father's house? And why aren't you properly dressed for this hour? Are you ill?"

"You ask a great many questions," I said, wondering how best to answer any of them. I tugged the sash on my silk robe a little more tightly, acutely aware of wearing nothing beneath it. Savage had said the boy was at school, as he should be, considering it was the middle of the term. I'd little experience with children, especially boys.

Especially boys who were far too much like their fathers.

The boy narrowed his eyes in a way that was all too familiar. "Are you one of my father's whores?"

Oh, yes, he'd been away to school, to learn such language from the other boys. I wouldn't let anyone address me like that, particularly not a child, whether he was Savage's son or not. I drew myself up and frowned down at him with all the considerable authority that I possessed as a Fifth Avenue resident.

"My name is Mrs. Arthur Hart, young man," I said, "and I am not a whore, but a guest of your father's. I do not believe he would approve of you addressing me with such rudeness, either."

The boy scowled in return, but his earlier bravado seemed to fade.

"My father's supposed to be here," he said. "If you're his guest, then you'd know that. He's supposed to be dining with me now."

"I don't believe he's at home at present, so he won't be dining with either one of us," I said, softening a bit. Why hadn't Savage told me his son was home? I remembered how critical Savage had been of his only son—criticism that, on first meeting, didn't seem merited.

"I am expecting my luncheon to be brought upstairs shortly," I continued. "I'm not your father, but you are welcome to join me if you wish."

His face lit. "I would be honored, Mrs. Hart," he said. "If Father returns, then I can go with him."

"True enough," I said. "But in the meantime, it would be a pleasure to have your company. What is your name?"

"Lawton," he said with undeniable pride. "More properly I'm Lord Lawton, and heir to the Earldom of Savage. That's my father."

"I guessed as much," I said, amused. "How do you wish to be addressed?"

"You may call me Lawton, as my friends do," he said with a breezy wave of his hand. "Are you American? Your accent is peculiar."

"I am better than a mere American," I said. "I'm a New Yorker."

His eyes widened, and for the first time he seemed his age.

"I've never met anyone from New York," he said. "Do you know Buffalo Bill?"

"I've met him," I said. "Annie Oakley and Chief Sitting Bull, too."

"Truly?" he said, impressed.

"Truly," I said, realizing I now had the upper hand. "Here's the footman with my luncheon. Is there anything else you'd like me to ask for you?"

"Cream tarts," he said without hesitation. "Mrs. Wilson says I've had enough for today, but if *you* order them, then she'll have to send them up."

I ordered the extra cream tarts, and then, to my amusement, I watched him eat three of them plus a good deal of what was supposed to have been my luncheon. Also to my surprise, I liked him, and he seemed to like me. I regaled him with tales of New York skyscrapers and my father's railroads, while he told me about school, which tutors were right tartars, which of the boys he liked and those he didn't, and which ones he categorized as bullies who needed to be put in their place for making life wretched for the smaller boys.

I avoided asking why he was at home in the middle of

the term, and he didn't volunteer an explanation. Most of all, he said nothing further of his father, except to look repeatedly at the clock on the mantel and wistfully wonder aloud where he could be.

I wondered that, too. I could occupy myself perfectly well until Savage returned, but I felt sorry for Lawton. I'd been the only child of a busy, powerful father, and I remembered all too well sitting dressed in the front hall and waiting eagerly for a promised outing or treat with him that never quite occurred.

"Would you like to go walk in the square?" I asked when Lawton had finished making a wreckage of the meal. "We needn't go far. You'll be able to see your father's carriage when he returns."

Lawton's smile was so much like Savage's. "I'm not permitted to leave the house alone, but I'm certain Father wouldn't mind if I were with you."

I excused myself to dress. I wore the simplest clothing I could find among my things, choosing a blouse, skirt, and jacket that were usually reserved for informal wear in the country—not because I wished to be informal, but because it was the easiest to put on myself, without a maid. I twisted my plaited hair into a simple knot and pinned a small straw hat on top of my head to keep away the sun.

When I was done, I looked more like the boy's governess than his father's lover, but under the circumstances that was probably for the best. I returned to the sitting room and found Lawton staring at some of the drawings of me that Savage had propped up on a bookshelf. I blushed; I couldn't help it. Fortunately, they weren't the most revealing ones, more drawings of my face, but it was still obvious that I hadn't been wearing any clothes when he'd drawn them.

"I'm ready," I said briskly, praying Lawton wouldn't say anything about the pictures, either.

But he did.

"Those are of you, aren't they?" he said, and I realized he was blushing, too. "Father always draws pictures of the people he likes."

"Then I'm sure he's drawn you, too," I said, pulling on my gloves.

"He did when I was little," Lawton said, looking down at the carpet. "Not now."

There was something so painful about his resignation that I longed to be able to take him into my arms and hug him. But I wasn't sure how an eight-year-old boy would respond to that, especially since he'd just been studying drawings of me naked.

I simply held out my arm, the way I would do with every other gentleman regardless of age. "Shall we go, Lawton?"

He stared at my offered arm and instead took my hand. I smiled, for his simple, gesture had made me ridiculously happy. Yes, he was a miniature version of Savage, but there was more. It wasn't until we were heading down the front stairs that I realized the true reason for my happiness: Lawton trusted me, the same way as his father did.

"Lord Lawton and I are going to walk about the square," I told the butler when we reached the hall and the front door. "We won't be far. We'll return as soon as we see Lord Savage's carriage."

Perplexed, the butler shook his head. "Forgive me, Mrs. Hart, but I am not certain that would follow His Lordship's wishes for Lord Lawton."

Lawton's small fingers tightened in mine, enough to make me want to stand up for him.

"Lord Savage can answer to me, then," I said firmly to

the butler. "You may tell him it was my idea to take his son outside for some fresh air. There's a beautiful afternoon today. It's not good for children to be closed up inside on such a day."

The butler bowed and murmured and moved aside, his disapproval palpable, but I didn't care. It was better for the boy to be out-of-doors, and it was better for me as well. My spirits rose as soon as we walked down the steps and crossed the road, Lawton's hand still firmly in mine.

It *was* a beautiful afternoon, too. The sun was warm on our shoulders, and the sky overhead was uncharacteristically blue for London. I only wished that Savage were with us.

St. James's Square wasn't what I would call a proper park (though I will admit that most parks paled beside the lushness of Central Park). This was really just an enclosure, surrounded by streets and houses on all four sides. There was a statue of some British king or hero in the center, some halfhearted grass, and a few straggly trees, enclosed by a black cast-iron fence: altogether disappointing for one of the most expensive addresses in London.

But there were a few benches and a narrow walk around the perimeter, and this was where I led Lawton. To my surprise and my pleasure, he continued to hold my hand, though I wasn't sure whether from boyish gallantry or because he liked the contact, as did I myself. We had the Square to ourselves except for two nannies with babies in prams and several elderly persons dozing on the benches in the sun. I asked him if he'd a pony at Thornbury House, his family's country house, and that topic lasted us for three turns around the Square, followed by another two turns devoted to various dogs.

Each time we passed Savage's house, however, both Lawton and I looked to see if his carriage was drawn before the door, to show he'd returned. Each time, it wasn't, though neither of us noted it out loud.

As we were walking along the far side of the square away from the house I noticed a hackney that seemed to be traveling at a different pace than the other carriages and wagons along the street. It was nondescript, a battered black cab with two large wheels, a single horse, and an equally nondescript driver riding behind, much like hundreds of others that clogged the London streets.

But I'd the uneasy impression that this particular hackney was following us. The driver was keeping close to the curb, about twenty paces behind us, and there he stayed, paying no attention to openings that appeared in the traffic that would have permitted him to go faster. That was not like any hackney I'd ever seen, and as an experiment I paused with Lawton, pointing out a cluster of starlings that had landed on the grass.

The hackney stopped, too.

We began walking again, and the hackney started as well.

My pulse quickened as I considered what next to do. This was exactly the sort of thing that my father had always feared for me, and now, during one of the few times I'd ventured into a city street unattended, I'd the uneasy feeling I was in danger. Although I glanced about for a policeman making his rounds, a customary sight, this time there wasn't one. I didn't want to alarm Lawton, but I knew we should make our way back to the house as swiftly as possible. We couldn't cut across the Square because of the iron railings that surrounded it, but I could hurry him along.

"Let's return to the house, Lawton," I said as cheerfully as I could. "It's nearly three thirty, and I'm sure your father will return in time for tea."

By way of answering, Lawton charged forward with his head down, trying to drag me along after him. I followed as quickly as I could, forcing myself not to look back over my shoulder for the hackney.

We turned the corner of the Square. Savage's house was in sight now, and we were almost there. I tightened my grip on Lawton's hand and stopped, intending to cross the street to the house.

But as I did the hackney came forward and blocked our way. I stepped back from the curb, pulling Lawton back with me.

"Stupid driver, to block our way," Lawton said indignantly. "He shouldn't—"

"Hush now; we'll just walk around him," I said, trying desperately not to panic. "This way, Lawton, and we'll—*Oh!*"

Two men with hats pulled low to hide their faces jumped from the cab, leaving the door open. Quickly they flanked me, one on either side, and grabbed my arms. The one on the right yanked my hand away from Lawton's and pushed the boy to one side.

"Stop, stop!" I cried, fighting to free myself as the two men tried to shove me towards the hackney's open door. I jerked back, twisting in terror. My hat slipped over my eyes for a moment and I couldn't see before it fell behind me. It was all happening too fast, and the two men holding me were large and strong. "Help me, please, someone!"

"You release Mrs. Hart!" cried Lawton furiously, and I'd a fractured image of him hurling himself at the arm of one of the men. The men shrugged him away and shoved him to the pavement.

"Not the boy!" I cried, thinking now of Savage's son rather than myself. "Don't hurt him!"

But Lawton wasn't hurt. Like a fierce little terrier, he popped up between the larger man's legs and bucked his head up into the man's groin. Caught off-balance and swearing with pain, the man released my arm and toppled backwards over Lawton, crashing on his back. In the confusion I jerked my other arm free and grabbed my skirts in one hand and Lawton in the other.

"Run!" I ordered breathlessly, already doing exactly that.

We were still in the street when Savage's carriage drew up before the curb. It was still rolling to a stop when Savage himself threw open the door to jump out and raced towards us.

"What has happened, Evelyn?" he demanded, seizing me by the shoulders to pull me from the street, away from traffic. "I saw you running—"

"Two men tried to kidnap me," I said, the words coming in big gulps. I was shaking from fear turned into relief. "There, those two, in the hackney."

Pointing, I turned back to where the hackney had intercepted us. It was gone, and the two men with it. All that remained was my crushed hat on the pavement. I looked down the street and caught only a final glimpse of the cab disappearing into traffic in the distance.

"Thank God they didn't," he said fervently, pulling me close and hugging me hard. His fear made me realize all over again the danger I'd been in. "I should have been here for you. I should never have left you as long as I did."

I closed my eyes, struggling to sort out what had just happened. It hadn't been random. Someone had been watching for me, waiting for me. My father had made many enemies in his life and he'd always worried that they'd try to take out their feelings against him upon me, but this hadn't been like that. Here in London there could be only one man, and that would be Blackledge. Was he truly that obsessed with me that he'd hire kidnappers?

"It . . . it m-m-must have been Blackledge," I stammered. "Who else would have dared—"

"It will not happen again," Savage said firmly. "I'll see to that. If anything had happened to you, I would never forgive myself. Never."

"But nothing did happen," I said, "because of Lawton."

I pushed myself away from Savage, looking for his son. Lawton was standing to one side, his face blank but his eyes filled with silent misery as he watched us. I placed my hand on the boy's shoulder, drawing him forward to Savage's notice—or, rather, so that Savage couldn't ignore him any longer.

"Lawton saved me," I said. "He knocked one of the men down, and that was enough to make them run away."

To my dismay, Savage frowned at his son as if he didn't believe it. "Is this true, Lawton?"

"Yes, Father," the boy said, his entire manner guarded. "I couldn't let them take Mrs. Hart."

Savage nodded. "No, you couldn't," he said. "Mrs. Hart is a dear friend to me as well as being a lady. You did well to defend her."

It was the chilliest of compliments, more fitting for a master to his servant than a father to a young son, and it shocked me.

"He did more than that, Savage," I said, eager to champion the boy and see him receive the credit due to him. "He had the cleverest move imaginable, ducking between that rascal's legs to knock him backwards. I don't know where a young gentleman could have learned such a trick, but I was most grateful that he did."

"At school, Mrs. Hart," Lawton said proudly. "The

upper boys bully us lower ones, but we learn ways to defend ourselves, no matter how much bigger they are."

But there was no pride in Savage's face.

"And that is precisely the sort of behavior that has landed you into such trouble at school, hasn't it?" he said grimly. "Come, inside. We needn't discuss this for the entire world to view."

The whole world wasn't interested, nor even the few passersby on the pavement who'd continued on their business, ignoring us, but that didn't stop Savage from ushering us inside the house in stony silence.

"Savage, please," I tried again once we were in the hall. "Lawton—"

Savage wheeled around to face me. "Lawton is no concern of yours, Evelyn."

"He is, considering how he just saved me!"

"If he had not left the house, as he'd been told, then there would have been no need for him to save you," Savage said, his anger barely controlled. "He must learn the consequences of his actions."

"He's only a boy!"

"He is *my* son, Evelyn, not yours," Savage said sharply, "and I will thank you not to interfere in his education. I will join you upstairs shortly."

He didn't wait for my reply but took Lawton by the shoulder and marched him into the drawing room off the hall. I'd one final look at Lawton, his black hair ruffled and his small face far more stoic than any child's had a right to be.

The door closed after them, and I was alone.

12.

I couldn't stay here in Savage's house any longer.

I didn't belong. As terrifying as the near kidnapping had been, these last few minutes with Savage and his son had been disturbing in a different but no less shocking way. I'd no real place in this household or in his Savage's, either. Hadn't Savage himself just made that clear enough?

I hurried upstairs to the guest bedroom. I didn't wait for a maid to help me but hauled my heavy trunk from beside the wardrobe. I threw the lid open and began throwing my clothes and other belongings inside. I didn't bother to fold or arrange them. My hands were shaking, and I was crying, and I didn't care. All I wished was to be gone from this place, and from Savage, as soon as I could.

I rang for a footman, and when he came I asked him to send for a cab for me to return to the Savoy. I could have asked for Savage's carriage to take me there, and perhaps after what had happened—or nearly happened—this afternoon that would have been the wiser course. But I wanted the break between us to be clean, without any chance of wavering.

I reached into my blouse and drew out the long strand of pearls that he'd given me. The pearls were warm with the heat of my body, and warm, too, with the memories they held. For a second, I cupped the strand in the palm of my hand, thinking. Then I resolutely pulled the necklace over my head and dropped it into a silver bowl on the table beside the bed, where it was sure to be found.

I latched the trunk shut just as the door behind me opened. Quickly I wiped at my tears with my fingers and turned, expecting the footman again to tell me the hackney was here.

But it wasn't a footman. It was Savage.

He stood in the doorway, his hand on the knob as his gaze swept the room, seeing the trunk and my preparations for leaving. I could tell from the tension in his body that his conversation with his son had not gone well and that this one, too, would not be easy.

"What the hell are you doing?" he demanded, though it must have been obvious. "You can't go, Evelyn. I won't allow it."

" 'Allow' it?" I repeated indignantly. "You have nothing to say about whether I stay or go, Savage, though the fact that you are ordering me to stay shows exactly why I am leaving."

"Then perhaps you can tell me," he said, his words clipped and irritated. "Enlighten me, please, since it pertains to me. Why would you leave now when we've four more days left in our Game?"

He stepped into the room, closing the door after him and standing before it with his legs spread and his arms folded over his chest. It was a defiant, hostile posture, meant to barricade the door, and all it did was make me more determined to leave.

"Because it's not the same here," I said. Deliberately I

folded my arms over my chest, too. "When we were at Wrenton, we could pretend the world began and ended with us. Nothing else mattered besides the Game. But here in London, there are . . . distractions."

His jaw tightened. "You mean my son. He'll be gone soon as I can arrange it, no later than tonight."

"He needn't go, Savage, and certainly not on my account," I said. "He has more right to be here than I do. This is his home, and there's no more important place to a child."

"Stop saying that," Savage barked. "It's not an excuse. Lawton must be responsible for his actions."

"I wish you would stop saying that," I said. "How old is he, anyway? Seven, eight, nine? How can a *child* that age be held responsible for anything?"

"Because he must," Savage said, his eyes glowing with determination. "He was sent down from school this week. Dismissed. Did he happen to tell you why?"

"No," I said. "I didn't think it was my affair to inquire."

"It's not," Savage said, "but you meddled so much that I'll tell you regardless. He was sent down for fighting, for thrashing another boy badly enough that he was taken to hospital, and the parents were clamoring for the police. Yet today you *encouraged* his violence."

I shook my head, refusing to see it that way.

"I agree that he should not be fighting at school," I said. "But surely there must have been other circumstances."

"No wonder he likes you," Savage said, goading me by turning what should have been a compliment into an insult. "You make excuses for him."

I refused to lose my temper. At least one of us should. "There's always another side to any story," I insisted. "Have you asked your son what happened?"

"I don't have to know the circumstances to understand

what happened," said Savage grimly. "I see it in his face every time I look at him. He is volatile, unpredictable, exactly as his mother was. He has her madness."

I stared at Savage, incredulous. "Do you know what I see when I look at Lawton? I see you, Savage. I see your eyes, your hair, your mouth, your chin. But most of all I see your passion, and now, it seems, your temper, too."

"You know none of this, Evelyn," he said. "You don't understand the history."

"I understand enough," I said. "He may be his mother's child, but he's also your son, Savage. Yours, through and through. Why is what he did to this other schoolboy any different from what you did—or attempted to do—to poor Mr. Henery at Wrenton last week?"

Savage drew back as if I'd been the one to strike him. "That has absolutely nothing to do with my son."

"Yes, it does," I insisted. "It has everything to do with it. If you'd bothered to ask him why he beat this other boy, I'd guarantee that he did it to protect another child, or perhaps a helpless animal that couldn't defend itself. He scarcely knows me, yet he came to my rescue this afternoon—a boy a quarter the size of those men! He could have hurt himself, or even been killed for my sake. Did he tell you that? Did you bother to ask?"

He frowned, taken aback, and I saw the first flickers of doubt in his eyes. "Lawton was in danger as well?"

"He was," I said firmly. "Perhaps more than I was, because of his size. They shoved him aside to get to me. Most children would have sat there crying on the pavement, but he jumped up and came to my defense as best he could, without a thought for his own welfare."

Savage's frown deepened, this time with remorse. His arms uncrossed and fell to his sides, and his shoulders lost their belligerence.

"I should have been there to protect you both," he said. "It's my fault. If only I'd returned sooner, then none of this—"

"Hush," I said, coming to stand before him. "I don't want to hear any of that, either. You're not my watchdog, and I can't live my life trapped in your house as if it were some castle with a gate and a moat to keep the world at bay. My father did that to me when I was young, and I vowed never to let it happen again."

Savage's hands settled familiarly at my waist. "I promised I'd keep you safe. Lawton, too."

"And so you have," I said, resting my palms on his chest. "But you can't do it alone, nor should you. Call the police. I'll tell them what happened, and swear to a complaint against Blackledge. If he's hiring thugs like those I saw today, then the police must be informed."

"No police," Savage said with a brusque, dismissive sweep of his hand. "That will accomplish nothing."

"Are you certain?" I asked anxiously. "Perhaps only a short conversation, to alert them about what happened?"

"They won't take you seriously, Evelyn," he said. "You can't identify the men or the hackney, and everything else depends on what Blackledge said to you alone, without witnesses. Although you and I know otherwise, there's no tangible way that today's attempt can be linked to Blackledge to satisfy a court of law."

"Then promise me you'll do nothing rash, Savage," I said. "Do not go after him yourself. These are dangerous men, and I do not want to lose you."

"I cannot promise that," he said, "any more than my son can, evidently. But I will be careful in whatever I arrange. Will that be enough?"

I nodded, running my palms up the broad planes of his chest to his shoulders. I knew I couldn't really expect him to promise more than that. As much as I might wish it, that need to protect was too much a part of him to be put aside like a change of clothes. All I could hope for was caution.

"Enough for me," I said lightly. "But I'd also ask that you not be so harsh towards Lawton. He's not mad that I could see, not at all."

"If you'd known his mother—"

"But I didn't, which means I'm not looking for madness where there's none," I said. "Recall that he's your son, too. He never forgets it. He idolizes you."

"Hah," Savage said grudgingly. "If he does, then he's an even greater young fool than I'd thought."

"Don't send him away tonight, either," I said. "Wherever it was that you were going to send him."

"To his aunt's house in Berkshire," Savage said. "I wasn't having him transported to Australia."

"Let him stay here, then," I said. "He shouldn't be turned out from his home."

Savage sighed. "He'll be here for another three weeks, then, until the new term begins. That was the best I could arrange today with that sly bastard of a headmaster. It cost me a sizable contribution to the building fund, too."

"I'm glad of it," I said softly, rubbing my fingers along the nape of his neck. "This house is large enough for him to be perfectly unaware of how the adults are amusing themselves."

He grunted, his hands sliding up the sides of my waist to the undersides of my breasts. "I already had Barry take down the swing. I didn't want to have to explain that it was an item meant only for adults."

"I should think that was why locks were invented for doors."

"Don't be smart, Eve," he said. "I'm serious."

"I am serious, too," I said, brushing my lips against his. "There will be other ways to entertain one another. You've always been inventive, Master."

"Because you have been receptive, Eve," he said. Our mouths clung, tasted, parted. He paused and pulled back, watching me through wary, heavy-lidded eyes. "Does this mean you will not be leaving?"

"Not this afternoon, no," I said slowly, surprising myself. I'd been so determined, but that determination had disintegrated and scattered as we'd talked. If he could pledge to change—or at least to make an attempt—then so could I. "No. I'll stay."

He gathered me into his arms, holding me so tightly that I scarcely noticed when he lifted me from my feet and carried me to the nearby bed. We sank down on the coverlet, our bodies already tangled together.

"What would I have done if I'd lost you?" he whispered hoarsely against my hair, desperation and relief oddly, endearingly, mingled. "What would I have done?"

"But you didn't," I said. I didn't care whether he meant that I hadn't been stolen away or that I hadn't left on my own, and I didn't care, either, that I was crying again. I was here, and so was he. "You didn't lose me at all."

The next morning, Savage suggested we take his open carriage and ride through Hyde Park. I was happy that he included Lawton in the invitation. I hadn't seen the boy since we'd parted in the afternoon; he'd been put into Barry's ever-capable care, an arrangement that apparently all parties found agreeable. I couldn't quite imagine the taciturn Barry reining in the high-spirited Lawton, but Savage assured me that Barry had "had a way" with Lawton ever since he'd been a baby and the two got on famously.

The two of them were in the front hall precisely at eleven when Savage and I came downstairs, and the carriage—an elegant barouche—was already at the curb. Savage was devastatingly handsome in a pale-gray morning coat with a tall silk top hat and pale-yellow gloves, all a welcome departure from his customary black that I was sure would draw the attention of every lady in the park.

But I would not be outdone. I wore one of my favorite carriage dresses, a closely tailored emerald-green ensemble with a boldly striped black-and-white skirt and an oversized black hat with a swooping brim and a white plume, trimmed with emerald ribbons. My parasol was black lace with green silk tassels that gave it a jaunty air. Around my throat, once again, was the pearl necklace that Savage had given me.

It was the kind of dress to be noticed, and this morning I hoped the entire fashionable world would take note of me. This was no ordinary outing, and Savage and I both knew its significance. It had been one thing to appear together late in the evening at Gaspari's, when by tacit agreement most diners would turn a blind eye to who was dining with whom. Even riding together on horseback would not have elicited much gossip, because truly, how much mischief could be accomplished with both parties on separate horses?

But to appear in a gentleman's carriage—even a barouche—was a bold statement indeed. I would be as much as admitting that the whispers about me taking the Earl of Savage as my lover were true. Having Lawton with us as our eight-year-old chaperone might mitigate my sins somewhat, but not enough to save my good name. I knew all this, and I'd considered it well.

And I did not care. Savage and I were both adults, both

independent, both widowed and now freed from unhappy marriages. We were hurting no one else by our actions and pleasing each other very much. I had spent the first twenty-five years of my life being respectable, good, and dull, and I was ready—more than ready—to be publicly scandalous, bad, and happy.

Savage had neatly summed it all when I'd finished dressing. First he'd let his gaze roam over me from head to toe, lingering upon the more interesting parts in the middle that had been spectacularly corseted. Then he'd smiled and bowed to me, his hat in his hand.

"I congratulate you, Mrs. Hart," he said, his smile sly. "You will make every lady in the park green with envy, and every gentleman sick with lust."

I'd one more goal, too. I wanted Blackledge to know that he couldn't intimidate me. I wanted him to see that I intended to go about my life as I pleased and that Savage and I together were prepared to stand up to him and his threats. I would not become part of his ridiculous *Arabian Nights* fantasy, where he could swoop in and carry me off simply because he wished it. I had every right to refuse him, and I would continue to do so until he finally understood and left me alone.

But when I stood on the step and looked at the barouche, I faltered. The carriage was entirely open, the brasses polished and the soft buff-colored leather seats sleek in the sun behind the matched pair of bays. There was a driver on the bench, of course, but no footmen, nor was there a place for any. We would be as exposed as if we were sitting on a bench in the park, and after the attack yesterday all I could think was how vulnerable I'd be.

"What is it, Evelyn?" Savage asked beside me. "Is the sun too bright?"

I shook my head, the brim of my hat bobbing before

me. "It's not the sun," I said. "It's just that . . . that the carriage seems very open."

"It is," he agreed. "That is why I've made sure we won't be alone."

He nodded towards the rear of the barouche. Belatedly I noticed two men on horseback, waiting about a length behind. They were dressed like any other gentlemen who went riding in the park, but there was a watchfulness to them that I remembered from the old days with my father's Pinkerton men, and I was certain that there were pistols beneath those riding jackets.

"You see, I kept my promise to you," Savage said, his voice low so that Lawton wouldn't overhear. "I told you I wouldn't try to protect you entirely by myself, and I won't."

Relief swept over me, and gratitude, too. He had listened to me after all. If Blackledge attempted something foolish, Savage wouldn't feel he had to jump in and risk his own life defending mine.

No, most likely he would, I corrected mentally. He wouldn't change that much. But at least if he did, he wouldn't be alone.

"Thank you," I said softly. "Both for those men and for understanding their necessity."

"You are welcome," he said gruffly, unexpectedly uncomfortable with being thanked. He might even have flushed.

He led me down the steps and handed me into the carriage. There was a brief moment of confusion when Lawton expected to sit beside me, but his father quickly directed him to the facing seat behind the driver while he and I sat side by side. I settled my skirts gracefully around my legs, tipped my parasol back over my shoulder, and at last we were off.

"Barry told me there were Punch-and-Judy shows in

the park," Lawton said eagerly. "May we please stop if there are, Father?"

"Stop bouncing about on your seat like a monkey, Lawton," Savage said irritably. "Sit still."

I glanced at Savage, not exactly warning so much as reminding, and he sighed dramatically.

"If Mrs. Hart wishes it, then we shall stop," he said with put-upon resignation. "You must learn always to bow to a lady's wishes, Lawton."

"Not always, my lord," I said, smiling. "Sometimes the lady prefers to submit to the gentleman's desires."

He raised his eyebrows and smiled in return. I'd clearly captured his interest.

"May we please stop for puppets, Mrs. Hart?" Lawton begged. "That is, if you like Punch and Judy, too."

"To be honest, Lawton, I've never seen a Mr. Punch show," I admitted. "You must be sure to point out the finer qualities of the production to me."

"You don't mind?" he asked, clearly surprised that any adult would ask for his opinion. "It's not always easy to figure out what's happening."

"I should be most grateful if you would," I said, smiling warmly to reassure him.

That was enough for the boy to launch into a detailed description of seemingly every puppet show he'd ever seen in his entire short life, so detailed that the only necessary replies were a few appreciative exclamations now and then.

I didn't mind at all. I liked listening to him, the boyish mix of being painfully earnest one moment and supremely silly the next. Wistfully I realized that if I'd a son of my own I'd want him to be exactly like Lawton. It wasn't just that I liked the boy. I liked his father, too, very much.

Beside me Savage had placed his hand over mine on

the seat and kept it there. It seemed like a small gesture, doubly muted since we both wore gloves, but somehow the very subtlety of it both touched and excited me. It was quietly, confidently possessive, proving that I belonged to him and that he was willing to let all London see it.

And all London did see it. Because the day was warm and sunny the park was crowded with carriages and riders as well as others strolling along the paths beneath the trees. Every well-bred head turned to look at us as we passed; we were that easy to recognize and that impossible to ignore. Like it or not, we were figures mentioned in the papers and scandal sheets, the Earl of Savage and Mrs. Hart, the American millionaire's widow.

Most we passed nodded graciously or raised their hats, as polite people did, although I could sense the eager curiosity behind their good manners. But there were a few others who pointedly looked away as if we did not exist, making their disapproval hard to ignore. When we stopped near the Serpentine because Lawton was clamoring for a flavored ice from one of the vendors, a photographer seemed to appear from nowhere and quickly took a picture of Savage and me walking arm in arm before he darted away.

"Ten guineas says that fellow will sell his work to the New York papers," Savage said drily as Lawton bought his ice. "They'll pay more for it there than in London."

"Earls are a rarity in New York," I said, striving to make light of it. "You're a curiosity."

"Oh, I doubt that," he said. "I believe they're more interested in the beauteous Mrs. Hart than the sort of raffish company she's keeping abroad."

"No one would think you're raffish today," I said. "You're looking thoroughly noble and handsome."

"And you, Mrs. Hart, are looking good enough to eat,"

he said. There was a small gap of pale, bare skin on my forearm, between the hem of my sleeve and the top of my glove, and he found it now with his forefinger, lightly burrowing into the fabric to touch me. For such a tiny caress, it was intensely arousing, perhaps because it was so small and so furtive. "I know that dress is intended to provoke other women to fits of rage, but all I can think of is how quickly I could remove it from your delectable person."

"My Lord Savage! Mrs. Hart! Good day to you both!"

Reluctantly I turned from Savage and watched as Laura, Viscountess Carleigh, waving enthusiastically as she climbed down from her carriage and hurried across the path towards us. I smiled with little enthusiasm of my own.

Laura was my friend, yes, and Savage's as well, but at that particular moment I would rather she had stayed in her carriage and merely waved and continued on her way. I say that not because of any dislike of her—far from it—but because I knew she'd ask questions about Savage and me. I suppose it was only fair, since she'd been the one to introduce us, but things between us were at present so special and yet so undecided that to discuss them with anyone else would feel like a kind of betrayal.

"Good day to you both!" Laura said again as she joined us, out of breath but beaming. I might be boldly dressed in green silk, stripes, and black lace, but she was all white lace, lawn, and fluttering ruffles, which did do justice to her fair skin and auburn hair. "I trust you are enjoying this beautiful, beautiful day?"

"I am, because it has been made more beautiful with you two ladies in it," he said gallantly.

"Oh, my lord, you are too kind," Laura said, simpering a bit as she twirled the handle of her parasol. "But I've a favor to ask of you. Would you permit me to borrow this lady from your company for a short while so we may discuss certain feminine topics of conversation?"

The only way to escape her would be to give in for a few minutes, listen to her gossip, then ease myself away.

"I won't be long, my lord," I said. "Only long enough to hear whatever Laura is perishing to tell me."

"If you must," he said grudgingly. "Go. Lawton and I will be waiting for you when you return."

"Is Lord Lawton at home already?" she asked cheerfully, looking about for the boy. "Our boys aren't due home from school until their term ends at the end of the month."

"He finished a bit early," Savage said, purposefully vague, and silently I praised him for saying nothing of the real reason for his son's return home. This was, in a way, genuine progress, but to be sure it remained that way I quickly took Laura by the arm and led her away for our "feminine conversation."

It didn't take long for her to begin, either.

"Whatever are you doing, Evelyn?" she asked, seizing my arm. "Everyone in London is speaking of you."

"I don't know what you mean," I said, smoothing my glove over the back of my hand to avoid meeting her eye.

"You're not making sense."

"Oh, you know I *am*," she said. "You and Savage. I've written you letters that you haven't answered, and called upon you at the Savoy even though I know you're not there. Your poor lady's maid is forced to tell me tales to protect you, but the truth's not been hard to decipher, has it? I do not know how these things are done in New York, my dear, but in London a lady does not take up residence in her lover's house."

"I'm not in 'residence,'" I said defensively. "I'm a

guest. Savage and I have chosen to continue to play the Game another week; that is all."

"The Game is reserved for the country, Evelyn, where there is privacy!" Laura said indignantly. "That is why we go to Wrenton, to be away from the prying eyes and gossips, and why everyone is sworn to secrecy."

I looked at her sideways, openly skeptical. "Do you mean to tell me that love affairs and liaisons are conducted only in the country? That in London everyone is chaste as nuns?"

"Of course not," she said. "But clever people act with a modicum of discretion. Why, look at you and Savage here today, free with one another's company in plain sight of everyone—even before his *son*!"

I stopped, forcing her to stop as well. "And where exactly is the harm in us being here together, Laura? Neither Savage nor I is married. We're respectably dressed. We're not rolling about on the lawn together. I believe we're going to watch a Punch-and-Judy show because Lord Lawton wishes it, but I don't believe anyone should be offended by that."

"You keep saying 'we,' but it's you who shall suffer," Laura said with unabashed vehemence. "Surely you must see that. When this little *affaire* with Savage has run its course—as it always does with him—then he will abandon you, and shift to another willing lady who catches his eye. He drove his poor wife to madness because of it. It's the variety he craves, Evelyn, the diversion of novelty. He will never be satisfied with one."

"Why do you think that I am not the same?" I shot back at her. "Why can't you believe that I, too, crave only novelty?"

"Because you're a woman, not a man," she answered without hesitation. "Women tire of sensual amusement, which is why the Game is so perfect. A week's adventure is sufficient for a woman. After that, we want more from life, and more from a man than his cock alone. You've been married. Surely you must know that."

"I have been married, yes," I said slowly. "And it is because of that that I want the same things that Savage does. I still do."

I thought again of everything that Savage and I had done together. Yes, much of it had been erotic, dangerous, and dark, and I had loved every moment of that. But there had been much that wasn't as well, quiet times when we hadn't needed a single word to feel completely and perfectly at ease with each other. Either way, I'd often sensed we were perhaps the two best-matched and best-suited persons under Heaven: sensed it and fought it, because it could not be true.

Thinking this way, I couldn't help but look back over to Savage now, standing in the shade of an oak tree waiting for his son to take his turn at the ice stand.

Savage stood with his weight on one leg, the other bent. His perfectly cut coat was open, and he'd hooked one thumb lightly in the watch pocket of his waistcoat. The sun through the leaves dappled his broad shoulders with light. His face was in profile below the sharp brim of his hat, a small smile on his face as he watched his son.

I'd often thought of Savage as some blatantly male jungle cat, all coiled power and muscular tension. Now that cat, though no less powerful, was relaxed, even content, as he watched his young son running towards him. I smiled, too, even though he wouldn't see me, and something squeezed tight in my chest.

Because in part Laura was right: I did want one man. I wanted Savage, the one man in London I'd sworn to give up in three days.

"With your fortune and your impeccable reputation, Evelyn, you could have made the most brilliant match of the season," Laura was saying, an unsettling counterpoint to my own thoughts. "You could have had your choice of titles. You might even have become a duchess. But now . . . what gentleman would wish Lord Savage's castoff? You've been so public that it cannot be overlooked. What decent man would want his leavings? What—"

"Thank you, Lady Carleigh, but I have heard enough sermons for today," I said curtly, unable to listen to her any longer. "I regret that my life is so distasteful to you."

I turned away, back towards Savage, but she caught my arm, and reluctantly I looked back over my shoulder.

"I'm sorry, Evelyn," she said, her cheeks pink. "I . . . I said too much, and went too far. My husband says it's my greatest failing, for he must suffer its effects the most."

She smiled brightly, trying to make a joke of what she'd said. I wasn't willing to forgive her yet—probably because most of what she'd said had been painfully true.

"You were the one who introduced me to Savage," I said. "Why did you do it if you believed him to be such a disreputable gentleman?"

Her smile faded, and she nervously twirled her parasol again, the white lace spinning behind her head.

"Because I thought you understood the rules," she said. "I thought you both did. I never thought it would go this far. Savage himself has never dared continue the Game in London with any other woman."

That was interesting. He'd told me I was the first, the only, woman to have been brought back to his house, but I hadn't been sure I should believe it.

"Why is it so difficult to believe that we so enjoyed one another's company that we decided to continue the Game?"

"Because it's simply not *done*," she said emphatically.

"Not by Savage, or any other gentleman, either, and I . . . and I . . ."

She was looking past me, squinting a bit. I began to turn to see what had caught her attention, and she took my arm again to stop me.

"Do not look back, but there appears to be an odd sort of man watching us," she said, lowering her voice and leaning forward. "Perhaps we should walk back to my carriage and my driver, and let Savage come to you there."

"A thickset, menacing man in a homburg hat?" I asked.

Her eyes widened. "Yes," she said. "Do you know him?"

"He's one of the guards that Savage hired to watch over me," I said with a careless little shrug. "He feels it's necessary, and I agree."

I didn't want to tell her how I'd been nearly kidnapped or how Savage and I suspected Blackledge was behind it. Laura enjoyed her gossip, and I'd already given her enough fodder today.

Still, she looked at me curiously. "Savage hired a guard to protect you?"

"Two, actually," I said. "I'm sure the other fellow's about as well."

She arched a single painted brow.

"How . . . protective of Savage," she said. "And here I would have thought you'd require guards to protect yourself from him!"

I gasped, stunned by her audacity. "Laura, please. I thought I'd told you before that I'm not—"

"I know, darling, I know," she said blithely, fluttering her fingers. "You're not afraid of the man even though he may—*may*—have caused his wife's death. But you will not listen, so I will not warn."

"Thank you," I said, not entirely mollified. I was tired

of people warning me against Savage, especially Laura. Again, I began to turn away, and again, she stopped me.

"I know tomorrow you will go traipsing off to Court to be presented," she said. "Will you have a seat in Lady Tremayne's chariot to the Palace?"

I raised my chin. I know what she was really asking. She didn't truly care about Lady Tremayne but was intensely curious as to whether I'd be joining Savage at the reception afterward.

I'd no intention of obliging Laura, not after all her so-called "warnings."

"I will, yes," I said evenly. "Her Ladyship is expecting me."

"And afterward?" Laura asked. "There is the reception, of course, another tedious affair that Carleigh and I must also appear at for appearance's sake. But there are also several private balls that Savage usually attends as well. I'm sure you've been invited to at least one or two of those yourself, yes?"

"Oh, yes," I answered blandly. "But I have yet to decide what my plans shall be. It's not my choice."

She raised her painted brows. "Does Savage now rule your social calendar, too?"

I smiled with rare sweetness and shook my head. "It's His Majesty himself has taken a particular interest in my presentation, and of course I must oblige his wishes for my plans after the ceremony. Good day, Laura."

This time when I turned away, she didn't try to follow or stop me, though I could have sworn I heard her sputtering with frustration behind me.

I headed back towards Savage and Lawton beneath the tree. They couldn't see me as I came through the trees, yet I could observe them easily. They were standing slightly apart, together but not together, as they watched the parade of carriages and horses. Lawton's face was stained by the cherry-colored syrup of the ice and Savage's was carefully impassive, but at least he wasn't berating his son for untidiness.

As I watched, Lawton laughed and pointed at a bustling stout man walking a half-dozen little dogs with curling tails, their leashes tangling together as they darted back and forth. I wasn't surprised Lawton was entertained; the man looked very silly, herding his little pack of dogs, and I remembered how enthusiastically Lawton had described to me every dog, large and small, that he'd encountered over the last month. That made me smile, too, recalling our meal together.

But I was surprised by what happened next. Savage, too, looked in the direction that his son was pointing, and he laughed as well. Not an uproarious laugh—Savage never did that, especially not in public—but enough to make his face relax and his amusement show.

Slowly, gently, he rested his hand on his son's shoulder. Startled, Lawton twisted around and looked up at his father, no doubt expecting another reprimand. When he saw Savage's smile, he grinned, and that single quick shared moment was one of the most beautiful things I'd ever witnessed.

Then Lawton caught sight of me coming towards them and ran towards me. The moment was done, and when I glanced back to Savage his face had once again assumed its usual reserve.

"A man told Father and me that the puppet box is just beyond those trees, Mrs. Hart," Lawton said eagerly. "We were waiting for you to come with us."

"Have all the female topics been successfully exhausted?" Savage asked drily.

"Entirely," I said, regretting that I'd interupted his time

alone with Lawton. "It didn't take long. Shall we go to puppets?"

With Lawton chattering at my side the three of us traipsed across the lawn to where the puppet box stood. With Savage's permission Lawton took a seat among the other children towards the front while Savage and I stood apart, away from the others but still able to watch. The show was already under way, beginning with a raucous musical performance by a man with a banjo and a woman in a short dress covered with bells who sang to various puppets as they appeared, much to the shrieking delight of the young audience.

"I saw you with Lawton," I said softly. "I'm glad of it, for both your sakes."

"The boy has been on his best behavior today," Savage said grudgingly. "I, however, have not."

"No?" I asked, surprised.

"No," he said, taking advantage of the noisy performance to stand more closely to me. "Do you know how hard it has been to be in your company and not touch you, Evelyn?

"Then touch me," I said, shifting closer to him. "I promise you I won't object."

"You never do, do you?" he said. His hand was around my waist, pulling my hip against his, and then his fingers slipped lower, over my ass. "I'd kiss you, too, but I can't reach you beneath that damnable hat."

I smiled archly. "Try harder, Master."

"A challenge, ma'am?" he said. He swept off his own hat and ducked beneath the brim of mine and kissed me, swiftly, surely, and enough to leave me breathless before he returned his hat to his head before anyone else watching the puppets took notice.

I grinned and touched my gloved fingers to my lips.

"You liked that, didn't you?" he said, his eyes shadowed beneath the brim of his hat. "I know you like the idea of being caught, but I never considered an audience of puppet voyeurs."

"I never considered it, either," I said, teasing. "Imagine the possibilities."

"My dear, I have been imagining them all morning," he said, his voice low and moody. "If we weren't surrounded by children, I'd drag you into those bushes, toss up your skirts, and fuck you the way I want and the way you want. Don't deny it, either. You know you want it, too. That kiss proved as much."

"You don't have to prove anything," I said breathlessly. My skirts had fluttered to one side in the breeze, conveniently covering his crotch. Behind their cover, I found the column of his cock beneath his trousers. He was already hard, and he sucked in his breath at my touch.

"Don't, Evelyn," he warned sharply, "else I'll spend."

Reluctantly I withdrew my hand.

"Poor Mr. Punch," I teased. "All he wants is to come out and play with Miss Judy."

Savage took a deep breath, and another. "You are trying me. My God, *puppets*. If Miss Judy isn't careful, Mr. Punch will take her back into the bushes, children or no children."

I glanced at Savage from beneath my lashes. "When we return to your house—"

"Don't test me, Evelyn," he growled. "If you push me too far, I could be capable of damned near anything."

I smiled again, pretending to watch the puppets. I hadn't lied to Lawton. I really never had seen a Punch-and-Judy show before, and I was stunned by how little there was to it. Mostly it seemed that the two puppets shrieked in high-pitched voices and then struck each other with wooden sticks. The more violent and shrill the puppets were, the more the audience loved it, and they weren't entirely children, either.

My gaze kept returning to Punch's long stick. It was made of wood, and its shape wasn't that different from the paddle that Savage had used to punish me when I'd been on the swing. In fact, the longer I watched, the more convinced I became that Judy's shrieks might be more of pleasure than outrage.

I glanced again at Savage, wondering if he was thinking the same thing.

"Perhaps it is just me," I whispered, "but does it seem to you that Judy might have been a naughty Innocent in need of Master Punch's correction?"

"I told you, Evelyn, do not begin," Savage said, testy. "Our time together is precious to me. This is not how I had planned to pass this day with you, either."

That sobered me. Was he thinking of how we'd only three days left as well?

"You've made Lawton happy," I said, which was true. He was boisterously delighted with the puppets, roaring with laughter among the other children on the bench. "He'll remember this day."

Savage made a noncommittal growl. "What did Laura want from you?"

"Nothing of any note," I said. "Nothing I haven't heard from her before, either."

His gaze slid back towards me. "No doubt she was offering advice to you about me."

I nodded. "She likes to advise."

"She always has," he said. "It's not one of her more attractive qualities."

"She thinks it's caring for her friends." Without thinking I looked over my shoulder; the guard was there where I'd expected him to be, far enough away not to be noticed but close enough to be ready if needed. "She noticed the guard following me, too."

"Of course she did," Savage said. "I'm sure she had an explanation for his presence as well."

I didn't want to repeat her unkind comment. "It doesn't really matter what she said."

"But I can guess," he said. "Most likely she said something about how you'd hired the guard to protect yourself against me. That was it, wasn't it?"

I blushed, startled that his guess had been so accurate. "I told you, it doesn't matter."

"But it does," he said, bitterness washing over him. "She's not alone in her opinion, either. After Marianne's death, there were many in London who decided I was the monster, the murderer of my own poor wife."

"Oh, Savage," I said, placing my hand on his arm in sympathy. "How cruel!"

"There were never any charges, of course, because there was no crime," he said. His eyes were unfocused, looking back to another time through his memories. "But because there were so many high-placed meddlers who insisted on my guilt, the police tried their best to make me confess. It was not a pleasant experience."

"That's why you didn't want to call them yesterday," I said softly, understanding now. I understood, yes, but I couldn't begin to imagine what he must have gone through. He'd already blamed himself for his wife's death; to have the law and Society blaming him as well must have been unbearable.

"The police wouldn't believe me if I accused Blackledge," I continued. "Instead they'd think you were the one at fault."

He let out his breath; I hadn't realized he'd been holding it in.

"Something like that, yes," he said, his voice flat and distant.

"That isn't fair," I said. "None of it. That you should be persecuted like that for—"

"You've only my word, you know," he said, purposefully not meeting my eye. "Has it ever occurred to you that everyone else might be right, and that I might be lying?"

I didn't hesitate. "No, Savage, it hasn't," I said. "I trust you too much for that."

"Perhaps you shouldn't." He pulled out his watch to check the time. "Surely these blasted puppets must be nearly done."

I took his arm, though it wasn't offered. "Don't turn me away," I said gently. "We need one another too much for that."

Still, he would not look my way.

"Don't resort to music hall sentiment, Eve," he said. "You know what brought us together. Sex, and nothing more. That's what we need. A good fuck."

I'd heard him say much more explicit things than that, and I'd found them wildly arousing. But this time anger gave his words an edge that wounded me with their coarseness, exactly as he'd wanted.

I began to pull my hand away from his arm, but he caught it and held it, lightning fast.

"You're not going to slip away from me again, Eve," he said. "You're going to stay, and you're not going to say anything to upset my son. Then, when we are home, you are going to be punished until you give me exactly what I want. No, what I *need*. Isn't that what you said we shared? Need?"

I shook my head, unsure what to say or do. Was this part of the Game, too?

"Did you see the crocodile eat old Punch, Mrs. Hart?" Lawton said as he bounded up to us. "He *devoured* him, exactly as he deserved for being so mean to Judy. That will teach Punch, won't it?"

I felt the pressure of Savage's hand, reminding me to pretend that the brightness hadn't vanished from this day, that the trust I'd felt in him had been shaken, that though I knew I should return to the Savoy, I wouldn't.

I wouldn't leave him. No matter what he said, I couldn't, because I knew he needed me. He *did*.

Nearly as much as I needed him.

"Yes, Lawton, Punch did deserve his punishment," I said, my smile forced and brittle. "But I'm not sure Punch will ever learn, nor will Judy."

13.

"I want you to go to the bedroom and remove your cloth-ing, Eve," Savage said curtly. "Every last stitch. Wait for me there."

I nodded and left him alone in the library. At least he'd waited until Barry had taken Lawton away for his dinner before he'd given me orders. Of course I obeyed. It didn't even occur to me not to, not today.

In hindsight I realized I shouldn't have told him what Laura had said. Her waspish comment had been enough to unleash Savage's old demons from whatever well-hidden place he usually kept them, and it was clear they'd still held their power over him. I'd never seen him look so utterly alone and bereft as he had this afternoon. There in the middle of the sunshine, with laughing children around him, he'd been trapped in the darkness of the past, and if I could ease any of that pain by being Eve to his Master I'd gladly do it.

Alone in his bedroom, I pulled off my clothes as quickly as I could, not knowing how soon he'd join me. I didn't want to give him any excuse for displeasure by not having done what he'd asked, and I didn't even take the time to fold or drape my clothes over the back of a chair. Instead I left a riot of silk and lace scattered across the floor, emerald green and black, to mark my path. I sat on one corner of the bed, where he'd see me as soon as he entered the door.

I waited, and I waited. I watched the shadows lengthen in the Square outside the window and the color drain from the sky with the coming dusk. I suppose I could have looked at the clock to see the time, but somehow the hour itself didn't matter. I sensed that the waiting was part of my punishment, too, and I'd bear it along with whatever else he contrived for me.

I stared from the window, thinking. He was like a complicated puzzle to be solved, and each small scrap of himself or his past that he grudgingly exposed was another piece to fit into place.

Now I realized that it wasn't just his wife's madness that he feared had been passed along to his son. Savage feared that Lawton had inherited his father's violent temper, too. To have his son dismissed from school for fighting must have seemed an ominous sign, and having to face the school officials on Lawton's behalf would have been a terrible reminder of Savage's own ordeal with the police after his wife's death. He'd accused me of making excuses for the boy when I suspected Savage feared he would do the same himself.

That was likely why he'd been so hard on Lawton, not wanting him to repeat his father's own misdeeds. Now that I'd seen them together, I didn't doubt that he loved Lawton, yet there was a desperation to that love that made it so painful and so sad as well.

I was so lost in my thoughts that when Savage finally opened the door I started and gasped from surprise as I twisted around to face him.

He didn't join me at first but stood in the doorway, quickly taking in my scattered clothing on the floor that proved my haste. He nodded, approving.

"I'm glad to see you've obeyed me at least in this," he said. He'd changed his clothes, too, into the loose linen trousers and jersey. His feet were bare, and the heaviness of his cock was outlined through the soft linen. His expression was impassive, carefully betraying nothing.

"You say you trust me, Eve," he said. "Now is your chance to prove it."

"Yes, Master," I murmured, and began to rise from the bed. "Will you be using the swing again for my trial?"

"Stay where you are," he ordered, going to the large chest beneath the windows. "The swing was about sight, and watching your correction reflected a hundred times over. This one is about patience."

So the long wait had been part of my challenge. At least I'd passed that much of it. Not asking questions would likely be part of the test, too, trust and patience, and even as my curiosity—and my excitement—rose I waited for him to explain.

"Trust, and patience," he repeated, returning from the chest. In his hands were a black scarf and a coil of thick black cords. "I know how much you like to watch, Eve, but since this punishment will be about pleasing me, not you, I'm going to make sure you don't see any of it."

Dropping the cords on the bed beside me, he folded the scarf into a long rectangle.

"Close your eyes," he said, and when I did he covered them with the scarf, wrapping it tightly around my head and tying it in the back. The pressure of the scarf across my face was unsettling, and the darkness was as complete as if I were blind, and instinctively I raised my hands to the scarf to loosen it.

"Don't touch it," he barked. "You are not supposed to see. That is the reason for the blindfold. Now climb into the middle of the bed, and kneel there."

Not being able to see made me clumsy, and I moved awkwardly across the bed on all fours, not knowing if I'd reached the center of the bed or not.

"On your knees, Eve," he said, correcting me. "Put your hands behind your back. Cross your wrists."

I did and felt him wrap the cords around my wrists, holding them together. The cords must have been silk, strong but soft against my skin. Tentatively I tried to move my hands, flexing against the bindings: tight, but not cutting. He'd tied me at Wrenton once, and I'd learned then that as long as I didn't fight against the cords they'd leave no mark on my skin.

Of course I'd learned that the hard way. When he'd fucked me, I'd been unable to keep still, and the cords had left bruises that shocked my maid. But no matter how I resolved now not to repeat my folly, I suspected I wouldn't be able to keep still this time, either.

"They'll hold," he said, reading my thoughts. "You needn't worry about that."

He pulled my ankles together, and automatically I widened my knees to keep my balance.

"That's good, Eve," he said. "Exactly what I wanted from you."

But I hadn't expected him to tie my ankles together, too. I felt the cords tighten around them, pressing into my tendons. My knees pressed into the soft mattress, and I arched my back to steady myself.

"Very good, Eve," he said. "You anticipate my wishes so well."

I felt the mattress give as he climbed on it beside me, and my heart quickened, sure he would take me now. Without thinking I blindly turned my face in his direction, my lips parted in anticipation, and he laughed softly.

"Don't be so eager," he said. "Recall that half of this challenge is to test your patience."

After a warning like that, I wasn't prepared for him to lick my nipple lightly, then draw it between his lips to suckle. He flicked his tongue over my sensitive flesh, teasing it until it hardened, then sucked with more intensity until I felt the pull of it deep within my womb. He then moved to my other breast and repeated teasing me with his tongue while keeping the first nipple taut by pinching and tugging at it with his fingers. His mouth was wet, his tongue soft and teasing, and his hair fell forward and flicked against my breast. He didn't touch me anywhere else, and craving more, I arched against his mouth and moaned, twisting against the cords that held me away from him.

But instead of giving me what I wanted he pulled away. I cried out softly in protest.

"Patience, Eve," he whispered close to my ear. "That is what I wish to see from you now. Patience."

His fingers on my breast again, I sighed happily. But instead of his mouth or tongue I felt something hard and cold, something tightening around my nipple. Whatever it was fastened around the base of the tip with a little click, enclosing it and squeezing it tightly in its grasp. He repeated this with my other nipple, clipping the ring around it, and then hung something—a chain?—from one to the other, so that it fell softly across my rib cage.

The squeezing sensation of the rings around my nipples

stopped just short of being painful. They held me suspended at the same point of arousal that Savage's tongue had done, turgid and stiff and aching for more. Even the slightest movement made the chain suspended from them swing against my rib cage and tug the rings on my nipples with extra pressure I arched my back further to try to keep the swinging chain still, whimpering at the sensation.

"Beautiful," murmured Savage as he rose from the bed, making the mattress shift again so that I nearly toppled over, spreading my knees farther apart to keep my balance. The small motion sent the chain swinging again, and I gasped at the fresh pressure on my swollen nipples.

"It's a pity you can't see yourself now, Eve," he continued, his voice now behind me. "You'll just have to imagine how you look from my description of your new adornment."

"My adornment, Master?" I repeated uncertainly.

"Yes, Eve," he said, and I heard the pleasure in his voice. "I had those rings on your nipples made especially for you. I know how fastidious you are about your jewelry, so I made sure these would be to your taste. They're white gold, as is the chain, and the outsides of the rings are outlined with diamonds. There's a small diamond pendant suspended from the center of the chain, too—that's the weight that you feel. It's in the shape of a perfect, sparkling drop, though I shall leave it to you to decide whether that makes it a drop of dew, a tear, or perhaps a drop of semen."

"Yes, Master," I whispered, struggling to keep the chain from moving.

He'd described the jewels so well that I imagined them easily on my body, and from how they felt I could picture my body, too, my eyes covered with the black blindfold, my wrists and ankles bound with the black silk cord, my skin so white and my nipples red from the diamond-studded rings around them, my dark hair tangled down my back.

That was how I must look to him and how he'd made me look. He'd created that image for us both, and I found the idea that he'd done that to me incredibly arousing.

I was his Innocent, to do with what he pleased. I was his Eve.

"Yes, Master," I breathed again, the chain with the diamond droplet trembling against my chest. "I am yours."

"You *are*," he said, his voice rough as he made the two words sound more like a declaration. "Now bend forward."

I took a deep breath and leaned forward, whimpering as the chain and the pendant began to swing freely.

"Lower," he ordered. "I want your cheek to touch the bed."

I sank forward as he bid until I felt the linen of the sheet beneath my face. I turned my head so my cheek lay upon the bed, exactly as he wished, my hair falling forward across the blindfold. My breasts now pressed against my bent knees and the chain fell between them, which brought some relief to my aching nipples.

Where before I must have looked like an offering to him, now I must look bowed and subdued, a conquered supplicant. At least that was how I felt, bent there before him with my body sorely aroused, and completely at his will.

"Now stay there until I tell you otherwise, Eve," he said roughly. "Do not move. Show me patience. Do not move at all."

I held as still as I could. I'd expected to have to remain like this while he'd prepared to join me, and my ears strained for the sounds of him undressing. Instead I heard nothing beyond the beating of my own heart.

No, there was something else: the rustle of paper, the scrape of chalk across it. He was drawing me like this. I'd inspired him.

I didn't dare move, nor did I want to. My muscles ached and my nipples pinched, yet all that mattered was that this was how he wanted me.

I heard one sheet of paper tossed aside, the drawing finished one way or another. I heard him swear, biting off the words in frustration, and begin a fresh sheet and then another after that. I'd no idea how long I remained like this before him. Blindfolded, I couldn't tell if the afternoon had become evening, though once I heard the scrape of a match, smelled the acrid flash, which meant he'd lit candles. For all I knew, it could have been midnight. Yet still I was the captive of his desire and his art, my body hanging on the edge of wanting.

At last unable to keep quiet, I let out a long, shuddering sigh. I heard him swear again and throw aside the paper, and then he was suddenly leaning over me. The hard muscle of his bare chest pressed into my back as he leaned over me, covering me, sweeping my hair aside so he could see my blindfolded face.

"Do you know how you torment me, Eve?" he rasped above my ear. "Day and night, you give me no peace. No matter how I challenge you, it's never enough. How can I be your Master when you do this to me?"

"You . . . you are my Master," I insisted. "You are!"

"Show me," he growled.

Before I could answer he'd grabbed me by the hips and lifted me back to my knees. With my wrists still bound behind my back my face remained pressed to the sheet, the way he wished me to be. I whimpered with excitement, knowing how exposed I was to him now, and shifted my knees as far apart as I could to open myself further to him.

"Enough," he ordered sharply, though enough of what, I didn't know. It didn't matter. That mastery, that command, excited me wildly.

He slapped one buttock and reflexively I jerked my head to one side. He gripped my hips again, opening my buttocks with his thumbs the way he'd open a piece of ripe fruit to be tasted. He held me that way, ready, and plunged his cock deep into me, and I bit my lip to keep from crying out.

He stretched me wide, enormous with need, and drove into me to bury himself. Once he was fully sheathed, he paused, breathing hard as he bent over me. His cock throbbed high inside me, and his balls, full and heavy, pressed against the outside of my quim. I arched my back to take him the last fraction deeper, and he groaned, his fingers tensing into the soft flesh of my hips and buttocks, holding me.

"Fuck me, Eve," he ordered with a vicious desperation as he began to pump his cock into me. This *was* fucking, pure, primal, and stark, and each thrust rocked me so hard that I gasped with his complete possession. Bound as I was, I was helpless before his driving need, and it was like being taken by the night itself.

And it was glorious. As violent and demanding as this possession was, I never felt in danger. Instead I felt more a part of him than ever before, more truly his, because at that moment nothing in his world mattered more to him than me. Everything had narrowed to his possession of me, and my own feverish desire rose to match his.

I felt his cock lurch within me, and I rocked back and cried out with excitement, mindlessly pulling against the silk cords. His hands slid forward, tugging just enough on the chain to draw on my nipples, and I cried out again, desperate for release. He shuddered against me, his hands positioning me, and in response I felt myself begin to tighten around him.

He pounded into me mercilessly, mindlessly, and his shout when he came triggered my own orgasm, too. I thrashed beneath him and bucked with him, my head thrown back and even my fingers spread and trembling with the force of it.

Afterward he held me, both of us panting and exhausted and slick with sweat. He kissed the nape of my neck, another more tender mark of possession, and I felt weightless, as if I were suspended in his arms.

I was his, completely. I was his.

With a sigh he finally withdrew from me, sitting back on his heels, and without his support I slumped to my side, panting. Quickly he untied the silk cords around my ankles and wrists, massaging the places where they'd cut into my skin. He laid me onto my back and gently stretched my aching limbs. I wept, from the sensation of the blood rushing back to my hands and feet but also from the tenderness he was showing me.

I'd almost forgotten the nipple rings until he carefully removed them, too, and I gasped, my hands fluttering up to soothe my sore breasts. Gently he pushed my hands aside and licked each of my nipples in turn, his laving tongue the best balm imaginable.

At last he untied the blindfold, slowly pulling the silk band from my eyes and smoothing my hair back from my face. I blinked, wincing at the sudden brightness of the candles, and then smiled. Savage's face was all I saw before me, his hair tousled and his eyes filled with raw emotion that cut straight to my heart.

"You're mine," he said softly, bending to kiss me. "All mine."

I couldn't agree more.

"Of course you must go to Court," Savage said late the next morning. We were still in bed, a place I'd decided I'd rather stay than go to the Palace and be formally presented to the king. From the moment I'd decided to come to London, this day had been one I'd anticipated more than my own wedding day. A Court presentation was a significant milestone for anyone, but for an American widow like me the invitation from the Lord Chamberlain was an almost unimaginable honor.

Yet over the last few days that honor had paled and lost most of its allure for me. How could a complicated ritual like a presentation possibly compare to the time I spent here in Savage's company, in his bed? As the days passed, each minute with him was becoming increasingly precious to me, especially lying curled here beside him.

"There will be so many other women—most of them younger than me, too—that I doubt anyone will miss me at all," I reasoned, hoping he'd agree. "All I've heard is that there's such a tremendous crush for a few seconds' time before His Majesty and then it's done. Surely no one will take notice if I send my regrets."

Savage grunted, never a good sign.

"To begin with, there could be a hundred younger women there at the Palace today and not one of them would have your beauty or grace," he said, tracing lazy circles over my bare shoulder. "Of course your absence would be noticed."

"You're flattering me," I said unhappily. He was looking wickedly seductive, his jaw dark and unshaven and his silvery eyes heavy lidded, and the musky scent of our combined bodies clung to his skin. None of it made me want to leave him or his bed.

"I'm telling the truth," he said, nibbling at my shoulder. "Besides, once you've accepted your invitation, the only excuse that's accepted is death, and fortunately, you are very much alive. Believe me, His Majesty will be looking for you amidst the milk-faced girls and their mamas."

"You're flattering me again," I said, pulling my shoulder away. "Please, Savage, don't make me go."

"I'm afraid you have no choice," he said, leaning on his bent arm to look at me. "You go off with your hired marchioness, make your curtsey at the Palace, and I'll be waiting for you at the reception afterward, where I promise you I'll have an excellent—most excellent—reward for us both."

I sighed again, tipping my head to one side to look up at him from beneath my lashes. "Why can't we skip the parts about the marchioness and presentation and the Palace, and have the reward here instead?"

He smiled indulgently. "Do not tempt me, Eve," he said, tracing his fingers over my lips. "This is for the best. You've come all the way from New York to secure your place in Society here in London. I'm not about to stand in your way, as much as I might wish to. You need to make alliances of your own, without me."

He rolled to one side, away from me, and left the bed. Most times I'd enjoy the sight of him walking naked across the room, the play of the powerful muscles of his back and buttocks. But now I could think of nothing beyond what he'd just said, and I sat upright in the rumpled bed.

"Without you?" I asked uneasily. "What is that supposed to mean?"

"It's not supposed to 'mean' anything," he said, an unmistakable touch of irritation in his voice as he shrugged into his dressing gown. "I cannot be everything to you, just as you cannot be everything to me. You know that."

"I do," I said softly, understanding now. We'd two more days together. That was all. Just two more days.

"Your maid is probably here already to help you dress," he continued, "and I've also arranged for a hairdresser familiar with Court attire to help her prepare you. You don't want to lose your plumes before the queen."

"No," I said, reaching for my own robe—or, rather, the Chinese silk robe of his that I'd worn while I was here. In two days I'd be leaving that behind, too. "Thank you for thinking of that for me."

"One more thing." He scooped something from the table into his hand before he joined me again by the bed. "Beneath all your finery, I want you to wear these."

He held his hand out to me, and in his open palm were the nipple rings and chain that I'd worn last night. I hadn't seen them before, of course, having been blindfolded, but I recognized them from his description: gold bands studded with diamonds. They looked like miniature wedding rings, except for the little hinged clips that tightened them into place.

"You wish me to wear these beneath my Court gown?" I asked. Remembering how they'd felt made me blush furiously and also spurred the first twinges of excitement.

"It's not a wish, Eve," he said with that sardonic smile that meant he expected to be obeyed. "It's an order. Consider it the first of the day's events."

"Yes, Master," I murmured. I looked down at the jewels in his palm, surprisingly delicate for what they'd done to me. They must have been costly for erotic playthings and had obviously been bespoke from some skilled and very discreet jeweler. The chain with the diamond drop slipped swinging from my fingers, and the dangling stone danced in the light. Last night Savage had likened it to several things, but today to me it could only be a melancholy teardrop.

"I'll put them on you now, before you go to your maid," he said. "Open your robe, and prepare yourself. The rings won't fit unless your nipples are erect."

I nodded, pulling the front of the robe open so that my breasts were bare. I cupped my breasts in my hands and lightly pinched my nipples between my thumbs and forefingers. My nipples were still sensitive, a little raw, from wearing the rings last night, and I couldn't help but wince a bit at my own touch.

Yet I knew how much he liked seeing me pleasure myself, and I'd lost all of the shyness I'd once had about doing it. Now it excited me to watch him watching me. His heavy-lidded gaze was intent on my hands on my breasts, framed by the brightly colored silk, and I teased my nipples as much for his pleasure as for my own, flaring my fingers across my flesh. We fed upon each other's excitement that way, and my breath quickened as my nipples puckered and stiffened. His breathing had changed, too, and I glanced down at the front of his robe, already knowing his cock would be tenting the silk above it.

"That's enough," he said roughly. He brushed my hands away and quickly clipped the rings to my now-stiff nipples. Again, I gasped at the pressure of the gold bands surrounding them. The pinch was subtle, more of a tight squeeze, with the pressure accentuated by the tug of the weighted chain.

He led me to the mirror. He grabbed my long hair in his hand and twisted it over my head to uncover my neck and shoulders.

"Look at yourself," he said. "See and understand how beautiful—and desirable—you are to me."

I didn't just look at my reflection. I stared. Framed by the open robe, my skin glowed like ivory. Fascinated, I now could see how the rings looked in place. The tips of my nipples were as red as berries, and their arousal was enhanced by the stones around them. I raised my chin a fraction, arching my back to make the chain swing and the stones sparkle, and my breasts swayed like ripe, jeweled fruit. I looked like a pagan goddess, adorned and worshiped.

No, it wasn't just what I appeared. With Savage that's what I'd *become,* and I reveled in it.

I shook my hair free of his grasp and turned around to face him, making a shimmering offering of myself to him. He captured my jaw with one hand and kissed me deeply, possessively, his mouth grinding over mine as his other hand thrust into my robe and over my hip to caress my buttock. I melted against him, certain he'd sweep me back to the bed and that my presentation at Court would be forgotten.

I was wrong.

With a groan he pulled back and away from me. The effort it took was clear, especially in the way his gaze remained on my breasts, yet from the way he crossed his arms over his chest I knew he wouldn't change his mind.

"Go dress now, Eve," he ordered. "Even as you bow before the king, you'll feel those rings, and remember you're mine."

"I never forget, Master," I said softly, wishing it weren't quite so painfully true.

"I'm glad." He smiled crookedly, and that alone was enough to make me melt inside. "So long as you remember, you'll be rewarded later tonight."

Reluctantly I left him, tying my robe closed before I went across the hall to the room where I'd dress. As he'd said, Hamlin was waiting for me, along with another maid to assist her, and the special hairdresser. All the various pieces of my Court attire—petticoats, lingerie, corset, stockings, shoes, gloves, plumes, and veil for my hair, feather fan, cloak, handkerchief, and of course my dress and train—were arranged in waiting around the room. Everything was of the finest quality, exquisitely and extravagantly embroidered, beaded, and lace trimmed, and all purchased for this day alone. Most likely I'd never wear any of it again, either.

Also on the bed were the jewels I'd wear, still carefully arranged in their plush-lined cases. There was a choker of diamonds and a slightly longer necklace, also of diamonds, to go beneath that, both made for me for this day by the Maison Cartier. Beside the necklaces was the drum-shaped box that held my diamond tiara, created by Mr. Tiffany from stones my father had purchased long ago.

Last, but certainly not least, was the pearl necklace that Savage had given me, looped sinuously in its case. It must not have been easy for Hamlin to bring Savage's pearls in place of the ones that my husband had given me at my wedding, though perhaps the mercenary fact that Savage's gift was more valuable than Arthur's had been might have been enough for her to put aside her old loyalties.

But then in many ways this was more Hamlin's day of glory than mine. Dressing me for Court must be the ultimate creation for a lady's maid, and even Hamlin couldn't be her usual dour self in the face of such a challenge.

"Come now, ma'am; come," she said, hurrying me into the bathroom where I heard the splashing sound of the tub being filled. The small room was already steamy, and the flowery scent of bath oil perfumed the air. "There is so much to do to prepare you, and we've only a few hours."

She drew the robe from my shoulders, the same way she'd done thousands of times before, and I climbed into the tub, sighing gratefully as I sank into the warm water.

"Let me soak a few minutes, Hamlin," I said. "You'll have time enough, I'm sure."

She didn't reply, and I glanced back at her. She was tightly clutching the robe in her hands and staring in horror at my breasts with the nipple rings and the diamond teardrop hanging between them.

"Another gift from His Lordship," I explained, trying to sound blasé even as I blushed.

"Yes, ma'am," she said, disapproval roiling through the two words. "That . . . that rigmarole must be removed before you bathe."

"It's not rigmarole, Hamlin," I said. "It's a diamond-studded jewel, and it's not to be removed. I intend to wear it beneath my chemise and corset today."

"To the Palace, ma'am?" Hamlin exclaimed in disbelief. "Before Her Majesty?"

"Yes, and before His Majesty, too," I said firmly. "It is not your decision."

"No, ma'am," she said grimly, putting aside the robe and coming around to the back of tub to begin washing my hair. "But I will say that I've never seen the like."

I was certain she hadn't, but with everything else happening to me today Hamlin's lack of worldly experiences was among the least of my concerns. I closed my eyes, letting the warm water relax me, and tried to let my thoughts relax, too, the way I usually did in the bath.

Yet my thoughts kept returning uneasily to something Savage had said: *I cannot be everything to you, just as you cannot be everything to me.*

What had he meant by that? In the same breath he'd spoken of how I should form other alliances, too. Variety had been one of the main rules of the Game as it was played at Wrenton. No one was expected or encouraged to keep the same partner. Savage and I had already pushed the boundaries by being exclusively attached for nearly two weeks. I was acutely aware of how we had nearly reached the end of our agreed-upon time together, but was he pushing me to find another lover, another gentleman to amuse me? Or was it that he himself had already set his sights on a new lady?

I knew the rules. I knew his penchant—and his reputation—for variety. I knew that we'd never promised anything to each other beyond sexual diversion and pleasure.

And yet, and yet . . .

If I was honest to myself, I also knew I didn't want to find another man. I didn't want to explore more sexual games with anyone other than Savage. I didn't want our time together to end.

I didn't because I loved him.

I'd never loved any other man, but I loved Savage, loved him more than was wise, more than I could easily undo or forget.

I could tell myself that he loved me in return, and deep down I did believe it. In a thousand small ways he'd told me he cared for me, but he'd never once said the magical word, nor had I. I also told myself that too many men would speak of love carelessly, without any meaning, while Savage had not spoken it but shown that he treasured me and that we belonged together.

That meant more, didn't it? Weren't actions supposed to speak louder than any mere words?

Then why hadn't he ever said it aloud? Why hadn't he

freed me to speak my own heart's longings to him in return?

Why had I let myself be drawn into this miserable Game that could be at once so full of unimaginable pleasure yet so inexpressibly painful, too?

Admitting all this to myself hurt, and I groaned aloud, making the chain between my breasts tremble and send little ripples through the bathwater.

"Are you unwell, ma'am?" Hamlin asked with concern as she held the towel open for me.

"I'm perfectly well," I said, rising from the tub with a scattering of droplets. "I'm only concerned about whether I'll be dressed in time."

That was as good as a dare to Hamlin, and for the next two hours I was at her complete mercy. That was how long it took me to be powdered, coiffed, corseted, dressed, and bejeweled. Most time-consuming of all was the arrangement of my hair and headdress. My hair required extra pins to offer a secure base for the tiara and the veil that floated behind, and finally the three white ostrich plumes. The hairdresser Savage had hired knew all the tricks of this complicated arrangement and used needle and thread to sew the tiara and plumes into my hair so there'd be no question of anything falling off as I curtseyed.

When all this was complete, I stood before the tall dressing glass while Hamlin and the other women hovered proudly around me. There was no doubt that they'd made me an imposing figure, tall and regal and glittering with gold-thread embroidery, diamonds, and pearls.

But I'd grown so accustomed to wearing next to nothing with Savage that the formal dress felt stiff and confining, like a trap of silk and steel bones, and the train—all eleven feet of it that Court dress required—dragged like a gilded weight behind me. The diamond choker forced me to hold my chin high, and already my neck was beginning to ache from the effort of holding so much atop my head. The only things that felt familiar were the nipple rings, now well hidden beneath layers of clothing yet their pressure still somehow oddly comforting because they'd been put there by Savage.

"Oh, ma'am, you shall be the most beautiful lady there," Hamlin said, sighing with happiness. "You'll do all of us Americans proud, you will."

I didn't care about doing anyone proud. All I cared about was finding Savage before I had to leave for the palace with Lady Tremayne. It wasn't that I wanted his admiration. Rather, we'd been together so much that it felt wrong to be apart and I longed for the comfort and reassurance of his company, if even for a few minutes before I had to leave. I looped the train over my arm the way I'd been taught and hurried across the hall to look for him.

"Savage?" I called eagerly as I walked through his rooms. "I want to show you all my noble splendor."

But to my surprise, there was no answering voice and no sign of him at all. Disappointed, I couldn't help but wander into the bedroom where we'd shared so much. By now, the bed was neatly made, with all traces of our earlier passion—and of us—tidied away. How easily it had been done! I didn't want to believe he'd left the house without wishing me well, and unhappily I turned, preparing to go downstairs alone.

As I did I noticed one of the drawings he must have made of me last night, now propped on the bookshelf near his side of the bed where he must have seen it as soon as he awakened. I frowned, drawing closer to study the drawing. This one wasn't like the other pictures he'd made of me—not at all.

The lines were sharp and aggressive, the shadows harsh and black in comparison to the pale vulnerability of my skin. Clearly this hadn't been an easy drawing for him to make, any more than it was easy for me to see it now. Somehow the reality of my posture was more shocking in the drawing than it had been to experience: on my knees, blindfolded, with my wrists and ankles bound and the pendant dangling from the rings on my nipples. At the time, I'd felt bowed and submissive and entirely at his mercy, yet that wasn't how he'd drawn me. Instead the arch of my back and the turn of my head seemed boldly defiant. I didn't look like a captive but a rebel, ready to run away at the first chance.

Was that truly how he saw me? Independent, rebellious, and ready to flee, no matter how he tried to restrain me?

"Mrs. Hart, ma'am," said Savage's manservant, standing in the bedroom's doorway. "If it pleases you, His Lordship would like to see you in the library downstairs before you leave."

Relief swept over me.

"Thank you, Barry," I said, returning the drawing to the shelf where it had been standing. "Show me the way, please."

I walked down the stairs as swiftly as I could beneath the burden of my formal clothing and followed Barry to a room that faced the garden at the back of the house. I'd been a guest here for nearly a week, yet I'd rarely ventured from Savage's private rooms upstairs. I'd seen next to nothing of the house or its obvious treasures, and I couldn't have found the library without Barry's guidance. Now the manservant knocked, and at the muffled assent from within he began to open the double doors himself for me.

I hung back a second, just long enough to drop my train

from my arm to the floor and to sweep it gracefully behind me. When we'd been at Gaspari's, Savage had told me that he wished to see me dressed to slay every other woman at the Drawing Room, and I wanted to give him that moment now.

The doors opened, and I glided through them. He was standing in the center of the room over a large desk strewn with papers and maps. He was in his shirtsleeves, the cuffs rolled up to his elbows over his forearms and the collar unbuttoned at the throat, and his smile when he looked up to see me made my heart skip.

"Evelyn," he said. "Eve. You are . . . *magnificent.*"

14.

I blushed, pleased by his response. "You approve, then?"

"How could I not?" Savage left the desk to come walk around me, considering me from every angle. "His Majesty may suffer a complete apoplexy, having you at his feet."

"You know it's only for a few seconds," I said almost apologetically. "So much effort and expense, and for what?"

"For the chance to be received in every fashionable house in Britain," Savage said with just the proper tinge of mockery. "That's every American woman's dream, isn't it?"

"Every New York woman's," I admitted. "I'll be forever guaranteed a place in Mrs. Astor's ballroom after this."

He stopped his circling to stand directly before me. His dark hair was neatly slicked back now, the waves tamed, and his jaw was so newly shaven that it gleamed. He looked almost civilized, standing there surrounded by books and paintings.

I wasn't fooled. Nor did I wish to be.

The next moment he proved it. He leaned forward to kiss me, taking care not to touch any of my finery. With us joined only by our mouths, he kissed me purposefully, his tongue penetrating my mouth to duel wetly with mine. All sensation focused on the forceful possession of that kiss, desire stabbing directly to my sex. Obeying the unspoken order, my hands fluttered uncertainly at my sides and clutched at the air to keep from touching him.

Without warning he deftly plunged his hand down the front of my low-cut bodice, beneath my corset and chemise to find my right breast. He plumped the flesh against his palm, testing it, then grazed his fingers over my nipple. Instantly he found the tip, made swollen and extrasensitive by the gold and gem-studded circle tightened around it. I broke away from his kiss and gasped, but I didn't pull my body back, and he smiled wickedly.

"You wore the rings as I asked," he said, his voice low, satisfied. "You obeyed me, Eve."

"Yes, Master," I whispered, dizzy with desire and bewilderment. How could such a slight touch from him be enough to do that to me? "I always obey you."

"Almost always," he corrected. "But in this you couldn't have done better. This evening you'll be surrounded by crowds of others, none of whom will guess that beneath your dress you're wearing these rings, or that when you make your curtsey before the king and queen your breasts will be aching with excitement."

"No, Master," I breathed, feeling that arousal even now. "I will know, but no one else."

"Except for me," he said, the pad of his thumb rubbing back and forth over my trapped nipple. Such a tiny caress, and yet I felt the pull of it in my quim, that familiar building heat and tension. "I'll know, too. It shall be our secret, Eve, won't it?"

"Yes, Master," I barely managed to say, my breathing ragged. "Only ours."

"Exactly." With unnerving aplomb he slipped his hand free of my bodice and smoothed the layers of silk and lace back into place. "But your obedience tonight guarantees that you'll receive your reward after you've been presented."

"Thank you, Master." I let out my breath, belatedly realizing I'd been holding it as long as he'd teased my nipple. I'd half-hoped he'd change his mind and fuck me there in his library, but instead he walked to the far side of the desk, his mind clearly shifting back to other matters with disappointing swiftness. He bent over the papers, poring over them.

The large mahogany desk now stood between us, a physical barrier, but there was also to be another, less visible one between us. He'd withdrawn from me as completely as if I'd already left the room or, worse, he'd dismissed me. He'd done it before, not that that made it any more pleasant. This time, however, I was determined not to let him withdraw from me again.

"Would you please summon Lawton to join us?" I said as if our conversation were continuing still—which, to me, it was. "He'd asked if he could see me dressed for Court, and I promised him I wouldn't leave before he did."

"Lawton?" Savage repeated, glancing up with surprise. "I'm sorry, Evelyn, but he's no longer at home."

I took a step forward, forcibly closing the gap between us. "Where has he gone? To the home of a friend?"

"I've sent him to Berkshire," Savage said. "You may recall I've an aunt there, who has agreed to look after him until the next term begins and he can return to school."

I couldn't keep back the little exclamation of disappointment.

"I'm sorry," I said wistfully. "I didn't have a chance to say good-bye."

"I know," Savage said, glancing up at me again. "That was intentional. Lawton had become entirely too attached to you, and I thought it best that he be removed before he was hurt."

"*Hurt!*" I exclaimed, feeling a bit hurt myself. "How could I hurt him? Your son is a charming boy. He and I got along wonderfully well."

Something flickered across Savage's eyes that I couldn't read, or perhaps I'd just imagined it.

"That's exactly the reason," he said evenly. "You liked one another too well."

"How can that possibly be?" I asked. "He is your son, and—"

"Lawton *is* my son," he said bluntly, "and not yours. There's no question he liked you, as any motherless boy would. But he's too young to understand that your presence in his life will only be temporary, and I didn't want him to feel it was his fault when you inevitably left him behind."

I began to protest, then stopped. Of course. These last two days with Savage would have also been the last two I'd have had with his son. *His* son, not mine. There would have been no reason to see Lawton again, and Savage was right to spare the boy—a boy who was not my own, nor ever would be, as Savage had so pointedly reminded me.

I looked away, hiding the disappointment that must surely be in my eyes. Lawton might be a motherless boy, but I was also a childless woman, and perhaps I'd been equally guilty of becoming too close to him. No wonder the sting of his sudden departure seemed so sharp.

But now that I was turned away from Savage I noticed other things that I hadn't when I'd first entered the room. Mingled in among the letters on his desk were train schedules and maps. On the floor were several leather-bound trunks, their lids open, half-packed with the kind of books gentlemen took to amuse themselves on long journeys.

I could guess what this meant, but I had to know for certain.

"You've sent Lawton away," I said slowly. "Are you leaving London soon, too?"

He stood upright again to confront me, his expression enigmatic and impossible to read.

"Yes, I am," he said with that same maddening evenness. "I have some affairs that need my attention in France. I have passage booked to Calais for tomorrow evening, and then the train to Paris. I would imagine you've made similar plans for yourself."

"Oh, yes," I lied, praying the faintness of my voice didn't betray me. How had the time passed so fast? I'd made no plans at all for myself, and now the finality of my life without him in it seemed to yawn before me like the edge of a cliff.

We'd agreed that our version of the Game would end on this date, and I'd known that from the beginning. But what if he was leaving now for the same reason that he'd sent Lawton away? What if he feared I'd leave him—and hurt him—first?

Unaware of my thoughts, Savage had pulled his watch from his pocket, flipping the gold case open with his thumb.

"It's nearly four," he said. "I'm surprised Lady Tremayne is this late, considering you'll have to wait at least two hours in line along the Mall for your turn to enter the Palace."

"I saw the drawing you made of me last night," I said.

He tipped his head to one side, considering me. "Did you like it?"

"I didn't," I said honestly. "Not at all."

I sensed the subtle change in him, a tension in his body that hadn't been there before. His half smile had a snarl to it, a challenge.

"Was it the pose you didn't like?" he asked, his voice low and slightly mocking as he raised a single dark brow. "Or perhaps you didn't care for seeing yourself blind-folded and bound to my wishes?"

"But I wasn't," I said. "That is, I was blindfolded and you'd tied the cords around my wrists and ankles. Yet the way you drew me wasn't how I *was*."

He shook his head once, decisive. "You're mistaken, Eve."

"I do not believe I was," I said. This time I was determined to follow the truth, even if it countered his memory of it. There was too much at stake for it to be otherwise. "I did bow to your wishes. I obeyed you in every way, exactly as an Innocent should. But you didn't draw that. Instead you drew not what you saw, but what you feared."

He lowered his chin, his expression darkening. "You're making no sense," he said. "I'll concede that the drawing was flawed, as my work always is, but it was as true as I could make it."

"But it wasn't," I said. "Once you said that a true artist must capture the soul of his subject, and make it his own. The drawing you made last night had none of me or my soul in it, but all of your fears that I would rebel, and leave you."

"Don't be ridiculous," he said sharply. "Whatever has given you such ideas?"

I raised my own chin to match his, my heart racing.

"Perhaps I couldn't see, but I heard how you fought with the chalk," I insisted. "I heard the force of your drawing, and I heard you swear with frustration. I heard you fight with the truth of what you saw, versus the drawing you had to make. My soul was lost, but yours was laid bare in black chalk."

"That's all nonsense." His handsome face was frozen, rigid with self-control and denial, yet in his eyes I saw the unmistakable flicker of despair that proved my words had struck home. "This is not the Eve I've known."

"Because here, now, I am Evelyn," I said. "Eve has her place, just as there will always be a place for you to be my Master. But we could have more, Savage, if we dare, if we—"

The servant's knock on the door could not have come at a worse time, yet Savage seized upon the interruption, barking for the footman to enter.

"Lady Tremayne's carriage has arrived, my lord," the footman said. "Her Ladyship sends her compliments to Mrs. Hart."

"Mrs. Hart will be there directly," Savage said, then looked back to me. "Go. You can't keep her waiting."

I didn't follow the footman, waving for him to go without me.

"Is that the end of it, then?" I asked Savage wistfully. "You've nothing more to say to me?"

He smiled, a forced, tight smile, and exhaled. "I will join you at the reception after the ceremony."

I swallowed the lump in my throat.

"How do I know you'll be there?" I asked, unable to keep the bitterness from my voice. "How can I be sure you won't run away tonight instead?"

He was looking at me as if memorizing my face, as if trying to preserve this moment in his memory. That and the unmistakable desperation—or was it despair?—that he couldn't keep from his face did little to reassure me.

"I promised you seven days, Eve, and seven nights," he said. "I don't say things I don't mean."

I wanted to remind him of all the times he'd told me I was his, that I belonged to him and no other man. I thought of how he'd let me glimpse his darkest secrets and how we'd come to share so much more than sex alone.

But I hadn't questioned him then, and I didn't now. I'd still had some semblance of pride left to me.

"Good-bye, Savage," I said, the words brittle, and turned away. The only sound was the rustle of my silk train as it swept over the parquet floor.

I was nearly to the door when he called my name. I paused, hating how the sound of my name on his tongue was enough to make my heart beat faster. Against my better judgment, I couldn't help but turn and look over my shoulder back at him.

"Don't doubt me," he said. "I will be there."

But I did doubt him, doubted him very much, and I left without replying. He didn't follow, either.

Hamlin was waiting with my cloak and plumed fan and to make the final plucks of adjustment to my dress. One of the footmen carried my train for me down the steps of the house. I bowed my head with the towering plumes to climb up into Lady Tremayne's carriage and with a sigh settled my train across my lap as the door was latched shut.

"Good day, Mrs. Hart," said Lady Tremayne, burrowed into the far corner of the carriage. Being an older widow, she was permitted to wear dark colors and sleeves to Court, and both made her almost disappear against the tufted maroon upholstery of the carriage's seat. "You look as excited as I to be heading to this foolishness."

"Good day to you, my lady," I said hastily. "Forgive me my ill manners. I was preoccupied with the preparations for the day."

" 'Preparations,' my foot," she scoffed. She could have been the younger sister of the old queen, small and stout and swathed in old lace, if the old queen had had rheumy eyes and smelled faintly of brandy with an overlay of brandy-sugar drops. "If I were a guest of the Earl of Savage, I'd have much more interesting things on my mind than dragging a Court train through the Palace."

I flushed, grateful that the shadows in the carriage would likely hide it. "His Lordship has been most kind to me."

"Oh, I am sure he has, a pretty American lady like you," she said shrewdly. "If even half of what is said of that man and his attributes is true, then you have had a merry romp in his company, Mrs. Hart. A merry romp indeed."

I raised my chin defiantly. I wasn't ashamed of anything I'd done, and I refused to let her think I was. "There is no harm in merriment, my lady."

"Hah," she said, not in the least offended. "I never said there was. Still and all, I should have asked for a larger . . . remembrance for this day's work had I known of your antics. If I am to present you, I must vouch for your reputation as a respectable widow, you know."

I sighed, thinking how this day could not sink much lower. "Would another fifty pounds suffice, my lady?"

"Oh, you Americans are so vulgar about money!" the marchioness exclaimed, waving her fan grandly before her. "We needn't haggle like fishwives, Mrs. Hart. I shall leave the exact figure of remuneration to your generous discretion."

I said nothing more, and neither did she, though I mentally added the additional sum to the already-ridiculous cost of my presentation. It was a long time for silence. As everyone had warned me, the traffic along Pall Mall leading to the Palace was indeed staggeringly slow. I wondered if Savage's guards were riding somewhere behind me or if I'd lost their escort along with Savage himself. The fading afternoon sun was still warm, especially dressed as I was. Making the wait even more disagreeable were the people who lined the pavement to gawk at the extravagantly dressed ladies in their carriages and who offered loud, coarse, and often cruel appraisals of the dresses and jewels as well as the ladies themselves.

Lady Tremayne coped with this unpleasantness by falling asleep, leaving me to stare resolutely ahead and try to ignore it all. This was not so very difficult. Because of Savage my head was full of far more than the hecklers on the pavement.

No matter what he'd promised, I didn't believe he'd come to the reception after the presentation. What I did believe was that that kiss we'd shared in his library would be our last. I realized now that there had been a poignant finality to it. At the time, I'd thought he hadn't embraced me to save my dress or for the sake of the Game, but now I sensed it was another of his ways of drawing apart from me, of saying farewell, as much a step in separation as the desk had been.

My role as Eve to his Master was done. Our game, our affair, or whatever it had been had lasted thirteen days, but one day short of what we'd promised each other. If we'd both dared and been more honest, it might have lasted far longer than that. But neither of us had been that brave, and now it was over.

The knowledge pressed like a leaden weight upon me, dull, heavy, and unforgiving. There wasn't so much a pain as a hollow sadness that was beyond the showy emotion of tears and full of regret for what might had been. I tried not to think of his smile, his touch, the way he looked at me, and how he'd loved me. Because there *had* been love between us, too. I don't think I'd imagined it, yet that was also done now. Already I felt the emptiness that he'd left in me, a void that I doubted I'd ever be able to fill.

I'd make only the briefest appearance at the reception, and then I intended to return alone to the Savoy. I'd leave London as soon as I could arrange it. I'd no wish to remain here in a world that was so much Savage's, even if he, too, was leaving. Paris was of course out of the question, but Florence might be a haven, or Venice, that city of lost souls.

I felt the pressure of the rings on my nipples, his last gift to me. I considered removing them now, here in the carriage while Lady Tremayne slept unawares. If I was no longer Eve, then I'd no right to be wearing them. But my hand reached for my bodice, then stopped. Savage had put them there. If that was our last shared intimate act, his final caress, then I wanted to prolong it as long as I could.

By the time our carriage finally reached the Palace steps, I felt as distanced from myself as Savage must have. It was almost as if I were in a play and I were in the audience, not on the stage.

With Lady Tremayne at my side I joined the long line of other women waiting their turns. With my train looped over my left arm the line inched through the various antechambers and into St. James's Gallery. The marchioness and I continued our silence, for which I was grateful in my present mood.

I was only vaguely aware of the distance the other women were keeping from me. Because of Savage I'd become that scandalous American lady, and I imagined what they would have thought if they could have seen the rings squeezing my nipples beneath my dress. Whispering, sharp-eyed mothers in line around me were pointedly shielding their virginal daughters from my taint.

At any other time, I would have laughed at their vigilance. So would Savage, and I pushed back the little rush of sadness that he wasn't there with me. Not that he could be, of course, considering that Drawing Room presentations were for ladies only, but for the last weeks we'd been so nearly inseparable that it felt odd not to have him with me.

Finally Lady Tremayne and I reached the entrance to the Throne Room, and even I couldn't help but feel awed by all the crimson and gold. Three pages arranged my train behind me, Lady Tremayne handed a card with my name to the Lord Chamberlain at the door, and with a deep breath I glided across the room towards the king and queen, seated on their thrones.

As the Lord Chamberlain announced my name I curtseyed before them as I'd practiced, so low that my knee nearly touched the floor. My heart was racing so fast that I'd only the briefest impression of the queen, but the king clearly remembered me and his smile was full of warmth.

"Mrs. Hart," he said. "I trust now that you've found your way to the Palace, we shall see a great deal more of you."

Being singled out like this was a great sign of favor, and I blushed.

"Thank you, Your Majesty," I murmured, praying he wouldn't say anything of Savage. "I'm honored to be here."

But all he did was nod and look up expectantly for the next lady, and I was spared. Pages appeared again to help with my train, and I curtseyed backwards (for no one could turn her back on royalty) the long way out of the room without mishap. As I was guided to yet another antechamber an eager young man hurried up to me.

"Please, Mrs. Hart, this way to the photographers," he said. "They are waiting to take your picture, as a memento of the day for you."

I knew better than to agree to that. Every ball in New York had photographers happy to take a stage picture for a sizable fee and then sell the images to the press. The less I had to remind me of this day, the better.

"Thank you, no," I said briskly, walking faster to pass him.

But he didn't give up, following me. "The New York papers have asked specifically for pictures of you, ma'am."

"Then the New York papers must be disappointed," I said. I glanced around me, looking for one of Savage's bodyguards, but saw none. I had my answer about them, then; my protective escorts must have ended with Savage's attentions, or perhaps he'd simply felt I wouldn't require them while I was in the Palace. "Now leave me at once, sir, else I'll call for assistance."

That was enough to make the man melt away from me. I'd planned to leave now, but not knowing my way out of the Palace and feeling safer in the hordes than alone, I fell in with the others. Lady Tremayne had vanished, her duty done, and I entered the reception room pointedly alone.

The large room was already filling with people, for here the ladies who'd survived the presentation ordeal were being noisily reunited with their fathers and husbands. A small musical ensemble played in one corner, and long tables were set with a light supper buffet. I was interested in nothing beyond finding my way out and summoning a cab, and I made my way through the crowded room as best I could. I nodded at the few faces I recognized, but didn't stop. I was in no mood for small talk, and the sooner I could retreat to my hotel rooms, the better.

I felt someone catch me around the arm. I scowled, determined to be as discouraging as possible as I turned around to face whoever had dared to grab me.

"Evelyn," Savage said. "I kept my word, didn't I?"

I gasped, shocked to see him and yet overjoyed, too. Unlike most of the other men, who wore bright uniforms or Court dress with medals and sashes, he'd chosen his usual black and white evening clothes for the reception alone, standing out from the rest in a devastatingly handsome way. I'd been so convinced I'd never see him again that having him here now was almost too much to bear. Only the fact that we were in such a public place kept me from throwing my arms around him and kissing him the way I wanted to.

He smiled crookedly. "Are you that surprised to see me?"

"I thought our—The Game was over," I blurted out in a rush. "I thought I'd never see you again."

He slid his hand higher along my upper arm to touch the bare skin above my long gloves, the slightest touch, but enough to make me shiver with longing.

"It could have been that, yes," he admitted. "It might have been. But I would have been an ass to let you go now, and I would've always regretted it."

"So would I," I confessed breathlessly, the purest truth. It wasn't a promise for eternity, not from either one of us. I knew that. But for now, it was enough.

"I'm not ready to let you go, Evelyn," he said. His voice rumbled rough with urgency. "Not when there is too much left unfinished between us."

I nodded, my emotions running wild as the very air

crackled with desire between us. All around us people were pausing curiously to watch, sensing that something dramatic, something scandalous, was about to happen between us.

I wasn't convinced it wouldn't.

"Beneath my dress, Master, I am still wearing your gifts," I said, my voice soft so that no one else could overhear. "They've squeezed my nipples tight exactly as you wanted, even as I bowed before the queen."

His eyes gleamed. "Then you earned your reward, Eve," he said. "Do you see that gallery, there, overlooking us?"

I followed his glance up. An open passageway with thick pillars ran along one upper wall. The space was dark, unlit, and appeared unused, with a screen of pierced stone to shield whoever walked along it.

"They say the old queen used to sit there when she wished to observe, but not be seen herself," Savage said. "His Majesty has told me how he'd put the space to better use with adventurous ladies when he was younger. There was the sense of being completely exposed to those below even if no one thought to look up—or at least they wouldn't as long as the lady kept quiet. That, he said, was the real challenge."

"Oh, Master," I said, my imagination racing ahead. "Is this another challenge, or a reward?"

He smiled. "For us, Eve, I believe it shall be both," he said. "I know how the possibility of interruption, of being seen, always inspires you."

I blushed, knowing how right he was, and lightly bit my lower lip. With him I'd always found the chance of being caught wildly exciting.

"Walk with me," he said, offering me his arm. "I know the way to the back stairs."

I tucked my fingers into the crook of his arm, perfectly

decorous, and we began walking together slowly through the crowd. We nodded at those we knew, but didn't stop, and even as Savage smiled benignly at this lord or lady he continued to describe what he intended to do to me as soon as we were alone. The small ensemble continued, to play in one corner, and their music masked his words—except to me.

"I want you to bend over by the balustrade, with your face before the screen," he said, his voice deep and seductive. "Will you do that for me, Eve?"

"For you, Master, I will," I said breathlessly.

He nodded, his sidelong glance knowing and tempting at the same time.

"As soon as we are upstairs, I want you to keep your hands on the balustrade and your legs wide apart and ass in the air, the way I like it," he continued. "Then I'll push aside your train and your skirts, and I'll fuck you hard. That's how you like it best, isn't it? Hard and fast and hot. All you must do is keep quiet. Not a sound. Because if you cry out, everyone will look up, and see you with my cock in your cunt, and know how you couldn't wait another minute for it."

I was already shamelessly wet from his words alone, and my sex was so swollen and ripe that each step was a kind of torment as the tension built within me. My nipples ached, and arousal made the rings tighten so much that I longed to rub them now, here, in the hallway outside the reception room. There were fewer other people here, and desire made me bold.

"Hurry, Master," I said, curling my fingers into his well-muscled arm. "You know I'm not good at waiting."

"Mrs. Hart, my lord, good evening to you both," said Baron Blackledge, suddenly looming to my left. "How lovely you are in your Court dress, my dear."

Instantly Savage stepped between us, shielding me from the other man with his body. Beneath his elegant evening clothes, he was coiled and ready to strike, his hatred for Blackledge barely contained.

"I warned you to keep away from Mrs. Hart," he said, each word edged like a knife. "She wants nothing to do with you, and neither do I."

But Blackledge only smiled, his bright blue eyes sinking in the fat of his cheeks. "You assume that I would force you to accompany me, Mrs. Hart, when nothing could be farther from the truth."

"I don't assume it, my lord," I said, unable to keep silent. "I don't because I know it to be true."

"Perhaps, perhaps," he said, his gaze roaming so freely over my bodice that I flushed, feeling that he surely must be somehow seeing through my dress to the jewels on my nipples. "But you see, I believe there are other ways to persuade you that we belong together. If you came to me of your free will, then—"

"That will never happen," I said vehemently. "Never. Good evening, my lord."

I turned away, but he caught my arm again, leaning so close into me that I felt the heat of his breath on my bare shoulders.

"'Never' is a word with little meaning to me, Mrs. Hart," he said easily. "I do not accept it. When I see something I want, I do not rest until it is mine, and you—"

"That's enough," Savage said curtly. "We are leaving."

But Blackledge laughed, slipping his hands casually into the pockets of his trousers, a gesture meant to show he'd no interest in answering Savage's obvious threat.

"Another moment or two, Savage, and I think the lady will be persuaded," he said, chuckling still. "As I said, I have no intention of forcing her to do anything against her will. Rather, I wish her to come to me of her own accord."

"She will never do that," Savage said curtly, distrusting Blackledge's show of bonhomie.

"Yes, yes, never this, never that," Blackledge continued easily. "How certain you both are of the future! But I still say Mrs. Hart will agree to join me for supper this very night, and do so, oh, within the next quarter hour."

"You're mad, Blackledge," Savage said. "And if we were not here in the Palace, I would show you exactly how I'd—"

"Forgive me, Savage, but it appears my estimation wasn't quite right," Blackledge said as a Palace footman bowed before us, bearing a silver salver with a sealed letter. "She'll be abandoning you for me within five minutes. I believe that's for you. I didn't think I'd have the pleasure of watching you receive it."

Savage glowered at Blackledge, then at the footman. "What is this?"

"It is for you, my lord," the man said, holding the salver up to him.

Savage stared at the letter with distrust for another minute before he snatched it up and broke the seal. He read the message swiftly, his face flushing.

"What kind of damned joke is this, Blackledge?" he demanded, crumpling the sheet in his fingers. "If you do anything to my son—"

"Not Lawton," I said quickly, already fearing the worst. "Oh, please, you cannot hurt that boy!"

Savage thrust the paper towards me; not only had he crumpled the edges of the paper, but his hand was shaking. As soon as I read the single sentence I understood why.

I HAVE YOUR SON.
  Blackledge

"Why should I believe you, Blackledge?" Savage said. His voice was sharp with anger, but I could also hear the fear. "My son was sent away from London earlier this morning in the care of a tutor."

"I thought you might say that," the baron said. "It was easy enough to pluck the boy when they stopped at an inn. The old fellow accompanying him hardly put up any fuss at all."

Relishing his advantage, he reached into the inner pocket of his coat and withdrew a single button, holding it out in his palm. I didn't have to look closer to recognize it as one from Lawton's jacket, engraved with the family's crest.

Savage snatched the button from the other man's hand and closed his fingers protectively around it. "Where is my son now?"

"In a cab not far from here," Blackledge said. "For now, he's safe."

"Take me to him," Savage demanded. "I want to see for myself that he's unharmed."

"What, and have you summon the police?" Blackledge chuckled. "I'm not such a fool as that. No, my people have orders to keep him safe for the next hour, unless I send word otherwise. But only an hour, just to make certain you attempt nothing foolishly heroic."

Savage let his head fall forward, swearing with frustration under his breath. I drew closer to him, placing my hand on his arm in wordless sympathy. To my surprise, he took my hand and linked his fingers into mine, as if I were his single lifeline in the middle of Blackledge's calculated cruelty.

"What do you want from me in return for the boy's safety, Blackledge?" he asked heavily. "Money, influence, whatever it is that a bastard like you craves. Name it, and give me back my son."

Blackledge chuckled again. "What I want is simple enough," he said. "I want your woman."

"No," Savage said, stunned. "That is not possible."

"Wait, Savage, please," I begged as my head spun with shock and guilt. I should have guessed that this was what Blackledge had meant by my willingness, but I'd never dreamed he'd resort to kidnapping and blackmail to get it. I truly had become his obsession, and it sickened me. The obvious solution would be to summon the police and have the baron arrested, but I knew that Savage would refuse to do that. I guessed that Blackledge himself must know that, too, or had simply been willing to gamble.

"Anything else, Blackledge," Savage was saying. "Anything else."

Blackledge only smiled. "I'm afraid not," he said. "Mrs. Hart is the only thing of yours that I desire, and the one I mean to have."

"You must take us to the boy first," I said, my voice shaking a bit with fear. I wasn't sure what would happen next, but Lawton had saved me once before and I meant to do my best to save him in return now. "We must see that he is as unharmed as you say before I agree to anything."

Savage looked at me sharply. "Evelyn, no," he said. "Do not even consider this, not for a moment."

I squeezed his hand to reassure him, hoping he would understand. But if I'd ever wanted proof that he cared for me then the look in his eyes—fear, love, and possessiveness, all rolled together—was more proof than I ever could want.

"I'm not considering anything yet," I said, choosing my

words carefully as I tried to both calm Savage and not antagonize Blackledge. "Lawton must come first."

Finally Savage nodded curtly. "Very well, Blackledge," he said. "Lead us—both of us—to where you're keeping my son."

The baron's eyes narrowed. "This will be done by my rules, Savage, not yours."

"Both of us together," Savage insisted. "I'm not letting you have her alone."

"Not yet," corrected Blackledge as he smiled at me. "Not yet."

I couldn't help but shiver and drew closer to Savage. Yet we'd no choice but to follow the baron from the Palace to his waiting motorcar. Savage and I sat facing Blackledge, and none of us spoke, the silence weighed with menace. Night had fallen, and clouds hid the moon and the stars. In their place the streetlamps offered their garish light, turning my white Court dress a sickly pale green and making all the costly embroidery glitter like a cheap theatre costume.

Mercifully, the ride was as brief as Blackledge had promised, and the driver stopped along one of the narrow, shadowy roads in Hyde Park. The road was deserted except for a nondescript hackney—much like the one of the men who had tried to kidnap me—parked on the opposite curb with its lanterns shaded.

The car hadn't even stopped before Savage's hand was on the door's latch.

"Don't," Blackledge ordered. "Any sudden moves and the boy will suffer. I told you, Savage, by my rules."

Savage froze, but his gaze remained riveted to the dark hackney. "Then where the hell is he, Blackledge? You promised you'd show him."

Blackledge leaned close to the motorcar's window,

drew his handkerchief, and waved it. The driver raised his whip in acknowledgement, and Lawton's pale face suddenly appeared at the window, his eyes round with fear.

"I must go to him," Savage said, again beginning to open the door, and I grabbed his arm to pull him back.

"Wait," I begged. "Don't rush."

"She's right, Savage," said Blackledge. "Though if you wish to see the boy suffer while I am left here with Mrs. Hart, then go ahead."

"Then let me go to him," I said. "I'll bring the boy into the street, where His Lordship may see him."

"Very well," Blackledge said. "I trust you shall be as obliging when we are at last alone together, Mrs. Hart. But no sudden moves from you, either."

Savage swore with frustration. "I cannot let you put yourself at risk, Evelyn."

"I will be fine," I said, impulsively kissing him on the cheek before I slid across the seat. I didn't wait for the driver to open the door for me but did it myself. Gathering my ridiculous train over my arm, I hurried around the car and crossed the street to the cab. Blackledge must have made another motion to the driver and whoever was holding the boy within, because as soon as I approached, the door opened. Lawton himself climbed out: alone, disheveled, and a little unsteady, but still unharmed.

He ran towards me. "I knew you'd rescue me," he said, his words in a rush of excitement. "Is Father here, too? Did you have to pay a ransom? The men hit poor Mr. Turner on the head and they wanted to do the same to me, but I kicked and fought, so they showed me respect, and I—"

"Hush, Lawton, and listen." I took his hand, pulling him close. "We're not out of the woods yet. You and I must walk slowly back towards that motorcar, where your father is waiting for you. No running, and no shouting. Do you understand?"

He nodded quickly. "I'll keep you safe, ma'am," he said. "That's what Father would want."

"Well, yes," I said. "Now let's walk together."

I straightened, and turned back towards the motorcar, and began to walk slowly with Lawton beside me. My heart was racing and my mouth dry. I'd no idea what would happen next, and I made a small, silent prayer that everything would work out as it should.

It didn't.

The motorcar's door flew open, and Savage came charging from it towards us, his expression fiercely determined. Automatically I smiled, and then noticed that Blackledge's bulky figure had filled the doorway behind Savage. By the carriage light I caught the metallic glint of the pistol in Blackledge's hand, now aimed squarely at Savage's back.

"Savage, no, behind you!" I shouted with terror, and pulled Lawton close to me, instinctively pressing his face against the bulky satin of my train so he wouldn't see what might—what could—happen next. I didn't want to see it, either, but I couldn't look away.

At my warning, Savage instantly wheeled back towards the car and lunged at Blackledge. Savage knocked the gun from his hand, sending it sliding across the pavement. Flailing, Blackledge struggled to recover, but Savage's fists had already found their mark. With all the rage that he'd had to suppress he pounded so methodically at the other man that he'd no chance of fighting back. I was surprised that neither the driver nor the men in the hackney came to Blackledge's assistance, but then, he wasn't a man who'd inspire loyalty and likely none of them wished to confront Savage now. I'd seen him like this before, and I knew where it could lead.

"Stop, Savage, please!" I cried. As much as I hated and feared Blackledge, I didn't want to see Savage kill him. "Stop now!"

Savage's head jerked up as he heard me, and that was enough for Blackledge. Those few seconds were enough for Blackledge to feebly bark an order to the driver. The motorcar accelerated, forcing Savage to stagger back from the path of the swinging door. Behind me, I heard the hackney drive away, too, the horse's hooves clattering on the pavement.

And then we were alone.

"What has *happened*?" demanded Lawton as he fought free of my train. "What did I miss?"

"Nothing," his father said, breathing hard. He bent to retrieve Blackledge's pistol from the street, uncocked it, and tucked it into his pocket for safekeeping. Then he looked towards me and held his arms open.

I ran to him and the safety of those arms, the warmth and security of that embrace. I was crying, though I couldn't say how or when I'd begun, yet I didn't want to part with him.

"You're safe," he said close to my ear. "He'll never have you, Evelyn. You're mine, and you're safe."

I could've stayed there forever, pressed against the strength of his body, but I belatedly remembered Lawton and began to push away. But Savage had already stepped free and bent to take his son in his arms. He closed his eyes, holding Lawton with fierce devotion, and I smiled, the tears starting up in my eyes again. How could I ever be jealous of that?

"Shouldn't we go to Scotland Yard, or at least the police?" I asked when at last they'd separated, though

Savage's hand remained on his son's shoulder. "Surely there's a case against Blackledge now."

But Savage shook his head. "I'm not going to give the papers a fresh scandal with my name attached," he said firmly. "None of us need that."

I sighed uncertainly. "But you've said yourself he's obsessed with me. What if he tries again?"

"He won't if you're no longer in London," Savage said. "Go abroad, away from his reach."

I sighed sadly. How could he have guessed my plans to go to Italy?

But I was the one who'd guessed wrong. He held his hand out to me, his smile warm and seductive, his black hair tossing lightly across his brow.

"Come with me to Paris, Eve," he said. "You cannot refuse, can you?"

I smiled as joy swept over me, and I slipped my hand into his.

"I can only obey, Master," I said softly. "I can only obey."